"You amaze me, Miss Glyn. Every female in my acquaintance seeks the pleasure of my company, but you continually toss it aside like so much lemon meringue."

"Indeed? I confess a growing lack of confidence in the females of your acquaintance."

Lord Blake gave a shout of laughter. "You are absurd, Miss Glyn."

"I am renowned throughout the ton," Miss Glyn said with a look of deep reproach, "for my propriety of thought."

"I am not such a gaby as to purchase such a declaration. You are too lightheaded to be convincing."

"But not too light to cross swords with you," Miss Glyn retorted.

"We shall see," Lord Blake said with a smile. . . .

THE HAMPSHIRE HOYDEN

Michelle Martin

FAWCETT CREST • NEW YORK

A Fawcett Crest Book
Published by Ballantine Books
Copyright © 1993 by Michelle Martin

All rights reserved under International and Pan-American Copyright Conventions. Published in the United States by Ballantine Books, a division of Random House, Inc., New York, and simultaneously in Canada by Random House of Canada Limited, Toronto.

Library of Congress Catalog Card Number: 93-90083

ISBN 0-449-22202-0

Manufactured in the United States of America

First Edition: June 1993

Chapter 1

Miss Katharine Glyn watched in amusement as Mr. Thomas Carrington struggled to pour her a glass of lemonade without—as was his habit—pouring the ladled liquid down his purple-striped evening coat, spilling it upon his shoes, or sloshing it over his dancing partner, the aforementioned Miss Glyn.

This particular endeavor, however, proved successful.

"Bravo, Tommy!" Miss Glyn cheered as the cup was safely transferred into her hands. "That was masterfully done."

"I've been practicing," young Mr. Carrington said with a blushing grin.

"And it shows," Miss Glyn warmly replied. "You shall be a paragon of the social graces before the season is out."

"Now, now, Katy, doing it too brown, don't you think? Don't forget the Bennett rout last week."

"Your arm was jostled, Tommy. I am convinced that your arm was jostled," Miss Glyn stoutly maintained.

Her attention was caught by Lady Huntington. Her bulk strapped into a gown that seemed to audibly groan from the intolerable strain imposed upon its seams, Lady Huntington, mother of five unmarried girls, was speaking earnestly to an elegantly dressed gentleman whom Miss Glyn had not

seen before. His hair was light brown and closely cropped, his eyes were gray and hooded as he assented without enthusiasm to whatever Lady Huntington had said. His triangular face was marked by a pair of high cheekbones and a square—almost jutting—chin. He was, Miss Glyn decided, amazingly handsome.

"Tommy, who is the exquisite trapped at the side of Lady Huntington?" Miss Glyn inquired.

Mr. Carrington obligingly followed her gaze, squinting at the fellow as he tried to make him out.

"Oh," he said without interest, "I believe that's Lord Blake. Follower of Braxton, you can tell by the coat. How can men dress so plainly?"

"Not everyone takes your delight in pushing forward the bounds of fashion, Tommy dear. What do you know of the plainly dressed Lord Blake?"

"Not much. He doesn't come to town often, I think. Oh, there is one thing: I've heard tell he treats his mistresses with a lavish hand. The muslin set stampedes him whenever he comes to town."

"Ah ha! 'He capers nimbly in a lady's chamber to the lascivious pleasing of a lute.' "

Mr. Carrington regarded her blankly.

"*King Richard the Third*, Act One, scene one."

Mr. Carrington regarded her blankly.

Miss Glyn smiled. "It is Shakespeare, Tommy, to the effect that I am delighted to discover a rake in our midst."

Mr. Carrington frowned in concentration. "Not a rake, precisely. He only gives carte blanche to acknowledged cyprians. Doesn't go in for corrupting innocents."

"Oh dear, he's merely a knowing one, then, like so many others."

Mr. Carrington grinned at Miss Glyn. "Sorry to disappoint you, Kate."

"Well, at least he has the good sense to be bored

2

tonight," Miss Glyn said, studying Lord Blake as he tried without success to disengage himself from Lady Huntington's conversation. "Have the Montclairs ever given an entertaining ball?"

"Not that I know of. Should we send for the embalmers?"

Miss Glyn wrinkled her nose at her glass of punch. "I think our hosts have already seen to it."

At this caustic juncture, Lady Danforth—overdressed and overpowdered—swept up to Mr. Carrington and Miss Glyn, and then swept Mr. Carrington away with her . . . to what sad fate, Miss Glyn knew not.

Left to her own resources, Miss Glyn wandered over to the pair of French doors nearest her, and then leaned against the chilled panes in an effort to escape the stifling heat of the overcrowded ballroom. Free from distractions, she was able to indulge in one of her favorite pastimes: surveying the vastly amusing foibles of society as they paraded themselves unabashedly before her laughing eyes.

She turned back to the non-rake, but further observation was blocked as Lady Huntington and he were joined by two other matrons of the *ton*, each of whom, Miss Glyn knew for a fact, were trying to unload their unmarried daughters on any worthy and unsuspecting fellow they could find. So the exquisite was another eligible entry on the marriage mart, was he? How tedious. He became less interesting by the minute.

Miss Glyn turned to search out something more enlivening and was happy to discover Lord Freddie Bingsley, the greatest dandy of their decade, conversing with their host. Hero to many young men of the *ton*—including Tommy Carrington—Lord Bingsley was ever scrupulous in surpassing his staggering sartorial efforts at each and every party and ball he attended.

Tonight, Lord Bingsley stood resplendent in an evening coat of pink and silver stripes, a waistcoat of baby blue flecked with gold, and an enchanting pair of pale yellow pantaloons. His thick blond locks were carefully curled *a la* Lord Byron; his cravat was tied in the newly fashionable (Lord Bingsley had created it only last week) Ganymede; and his collar points were so stiff and so high that his head was raised a good two inches above its normal position. He was, Miss Glyn thought in silent awe, magnificent.

Before Miss Glyn could begin to feel the dowd in his presence, her hostess, a plump matron of thirty years, six children, and an atrocious headdress of peacock feathers, approached her with an Adonis and a Satyr in tow. The Adonis was a blond young gentleman of very attractive countenance, a shy smile, and an adequate attire. The Satyr was the handsome exquisite Miss Glyn had seen conversing with Lady Huntington. He seemed to be arguing with Adonis, indeed, he tried to exit their march on Miss Glyn, but Adonis pulled him back with an appeal that made the Satyr groan audibly.

"My dear Miss Glyn," said Lady Montclair, drawing before her, "I wish to present to you Sir William Atherton and Lord Blake. Sir William has expressed a desire to meet Miss Fairfax and, as you are her chaperone, I thought it only appropriate that you should do the honors."

"Thank you, no," said Miss Glyn indifferently. "I am sure that you can perform the introduction with far greater elan than I."

"But . . . but Miss Glyn," said the golden Sir William, "if you are indeed Miss Fairfax's chaperone, it is only appropriate that I am made known to you first."

"Very well," said Miss Glyn, reluctantly turning

from the sleepy gray eyes of Lord Blake, "are you married, Sir William?"

Sir William flushed. "Good heavens, Miss Glyn, of course not! I have never even been engaged."

"I see. And how old are you?"

"Six-and-twenty."

Miss Glyn lethargically made use of her fan. "That is in itself suspicious. Any young man of six-and-twenty who has not been involved in at least two fruitless betrothals should be regarded with a wary eye."

"M-M-Miss Glyn, I beg your pardon! I-I-I've had no opportunity for fruitless betrothals. You see, I have been on the Continent."

"To what purpose?" Miss Glyn inquired.

Sir William stared at her.

Lord Blake nudged him and whispered in his ear.

Sir William flushed and replied, "Why, I have been engaged in the war, Miss Glyn."

"Ah," said Miss Glyn. "With any success?"

"I-I-I believe that I did my duty."

"No one can ask more than that, Sir William. From whence does your family hale?"

"Suffolk, Miss Glyn. We are an old family with a comfortable income. My mother is my only living near relation."

"And have you partaken of any scandal?"

"Good God, ma'am, no!"

" 'Tis a pity. Ah well, I suppose you will do." Miss Glyn decided. "Very well, Lady Montclair, you may present him to Georgina."

"Come, come, Miss Glyn, you must do the honors," Lady Montclair remonstrated. "Miss Fairfax is so inundated with eager young gentlemen that she would in all certainty pay no attention should I bring Sir William into her presence. But if you should do so, she would at least be encouraged to gaze upon him."

5

Miss Glyn smiled. "I fail to understand how she could do anything but gaze upon him. Very well, I shall do as you say. And you, Lord Blake, do you wish to be presented to Miss Fairfax?"

"Thank you, no," said Lord Blake with every aspect of ennui. "I find I am too overwhelmed by her beauty to do myself any credit in conversation."

Miss Glyn cast an amused eye at Lord Blake, and then began to search the ballroom for her dear friend and companion, Miss Georgina Fairfax, a twenty-year-old distributor of severe masculine palpitations by virtue of her glossy black hair, deep blue eyes, heart-shaped face, attractive figure, and sweet temperament. Additional palpitations were also created by her large fortune.

Miss Glyn spied her friend at last. She stood several yards to Miss Glyn's left, surrounded by six young sprigs of fashion.

"Come, Sir William," she said, pulling him toward Miss Fairfax's masculine throng.

She weaved her way through the gentlemen, using her elbow and her "Do excuse me, my lord," to good effect. Miss Fairfax's admirers parted, reluctantly, to admit her, and thus Miss Glyn was able to bring Sir William to stand before Miss Fairfax. She performed the introduction with becoming brevity.

But a grin began to insinuate itself upon her lips, and then burst into broad glory as she observed Miss Fairfax go suddenly weak-kneed, draining of all color before the overpowering aura of the blond god's smile. Never had she seen Miss Fairfax so dazzled. As for the young Olympian, he, too, seemed to have lost all sense of himself, retaining just enough presence of mind to lead Miss Fairfax out onto the dance floor.

Left to her own devices, Miss Glyn found herself

tackled in the next moment by Miss Elizabeth Carrington, sister to Tommy.

"Who is the young god on the dance floor with Georgina, and why didn't you give me a shot at him first?" Miss Carrington demanded.

Miss Glyn gave a summary of Sir William's life and expectations. "And perhaps you can tell me," she continued, "who is this Lord Blake who supported him during my interrogation? Do you know him?"

"No," Miss Carrington replied. "Just snippets of him. Apparently this is the first season he has been in town for years."

"Sounds a sensible fellow."

"And he has cartloads of money."

"Poor fellow. No wonder Huntington was hounding him. A fortune and a title. How common. He grows less interesting by the moment. Pity, he had the potential to amuse me."

"Kate," Miss Carrington said with a laugh, "everyone amuses you."

"That is true. But I suspect Lord Blake could do so intentionally. Tommy says he is beloved of the petticoat set. Did he bring a paphian with him tonight, do you think?"

"Kate, don't be absurd!"

"I am not absurd, merely desperate. If I don't find something to interest me soon, I shall fall asleep standing up."

She scanned the ballroom and quickly found her prey dancing with the second most beautiful woman in the room.

"Oh good God!" she exclaimed.

"What is it?"

"He knows Priscilla Inglewood. You see? He is actually smiling at her."

Miss Carrington followed Miss Glyn's gaze to observe the repugnant sight.

7

"That is how I know his name!" she said. "The Pomeroy sisters insist that Blake has returned to town on Priscilla's account."

"Do you tell me that he actually *chooses* to associate with Lady Perfection? Well, that sinks him beyond redemption in my regard. Pity, he looked . . . entertaining. Well, I shall seek another means of amusement. I have not yet spoken with the Duchess of Newberry."

"Be careful, Kate. Lady Mankin—a mere baroness—appeared tonight in almost an exact duplicate of her gown, and the duchess is furious."

"I don't wonder. Lady Mankin left, of course."

"Oh, of course! The poor thing was mortified. I doubt if she'll receive another invitation in the *haut ton,* and her application to Almack's is now quite, quite hopeless."

"Ah, the drama of the *ton.* Drury Lane can't touch it."

Miss Glyn wandered off a moment later to commiserate with the Duchess of Newberry. She then survived a quadrille with Mr. Tommy Carrington and fobbed off half a dozen gentlemen eager for her acquaintance . . . so that they might curry favor with Miss Fairfax.

Miss Glyn found it hard to keep her good humor in such situations for she detested toad-eating, particularly from gentlemen who cared only for a pretty face and a large fortune, rather than for the character that lay beneath. It was her task to keep such miscreants from Miss Fairfax's acquaintance, and she gave each gentleman a set-down that would haunt their dreams for decades to come.

That none of the eligible men in the *ton* were interested in Miss Glyn for her own sake she had learned many years earlier. She did not regret this state of affairs for she wanted no suitors, no badly written poetry, no husband. Her fortune, though not large, would keep her comfortable all her days, and she looked for no more than that.

Having deemed it time to depart, Miss Glyn began a rather prolonged search for Miss Fairfax, who was finally discovered in an intense tête-à-tête with Miss Carrington.

"Oh, Katharine!" cried the bewitching Miss Fairfax as she turned and beheld the amused face of her dearest friend. "This has been the most wonderful night of my life! I have just been telling Beth all of my thoughts and feelings. They cannot be stopped. They are like some great and powerful waterfall. They—"

"That is all well and good, Georgina," Miss Glyn interrupted firmly, "but before you drip all over the Montclairs' floor, I should like to point out to you that it is just past two, and I think we should be getting home. Beth, I suggest you attend your brother. I saw Tommy conversing with that Morwena Devon creature."

"What? That overpainted mantrap again?" Miss Carrington cried. "You would think Tommy would have more sense . . ." she said as she stormed off in search of her errant brother.

"Come along, Georgina," Miss Glyn said as she took her friend's arm and began to lead her from the room. "You have a full schedule tomorrow, and you need your beauty sleep."

"Tomorrow, tomorrow!" Miss Fairfax rhapsodized. "I shall see him tomorrow. Oh Katharine, so much has occurred in these last few hours!"

"That much is obvious from your feverish expression and glazed eyes. But you had better wait to tell me of it until we are in our carriage. An excess of emotion in the middle of a ballroom leaves one open to the charge of giddiness, a label that strips one of any claim to sophistication; and sophistication, my dear Georgina, is vital if one

9

wishes to maintain the proper countenance in the *ton*."

"Oh Kate," Miss Fairfax said, giggling, "you are so *absurd!*"

Miss Glyn, who had never heard Miss Fairfax giggle prior to this moment, was understandably alarmed. She whisked her young friend out of the ballroom and into their waiting coach. Having settled themselves and given their coachman the order to drive on, Miss Glyn leaned back grimly in her seat, cast a wary eye at Miss Fairfax, and said:

"Very well. You may begin."

"Now don't make such hobgoblin faces at me, Kate," Miss Fairfax said, laughing, "for I feel wonderful beyond all measure. I feel intoxicated and full of music and so very light-headed. I feel as if I could float up to the stars themselves, waltz around the Big Dipper, sing to the Archer, and ride upon the Great Bear."

"No mean trick, for you know your seat is lamentable, Georgina."

"Oh Katharine!" cried Miss Fairfax. "I am so happy! I have met the most wonderful, wonderful man! He is so beautiful it takes my breath away. I swear I could not utter a word the first five minutes of our acquaintance. He is so kind, so gentle, so intelligent, so very understanding of matters concerning the heart. He is grace incarnate, and yet so strong that I am certain he could carry me in his arms to the ends of the earth."

Miss Glyn could restrain herself no longer, and burst into a hoot of laughter. "Oh Georgie, if you could only hear yourself. I have never been so vastly entertained."

"But I am in earnest!"

"I know, my dearest, I know. That is what makes it all the more delightful. Forsooth, 'tis love at first sight! I never thought to see you succumb so completely. And to think I had a hand in the affair. I couldn't be more pleased."

"Katharine, I will not have you ridicule my feelings for Will . . . for Sir William."

"I *am* sorry," Miss Glyn said with great sincerity. "I shall do better, I promise. It is just that if you insist on offering me such provocation . . . but be that as it may," she said, hastily clearing her throat. "I am pleased you have fallen to a William. A man's Christian name is so vital to his character and to his wife's happiness. Take Basil, for instance. It is a name that reminds me forcefully of a weasel. It denotes a man that can be trusted with neither the ladies nor their purse. Then there is Percy. Avoid a Percy at all costs, Georgina, for he is inevitably wrapped within his good mother's arms with no desire to flee. Waldos tend toward the gout. Brians are overly devoted to the hunt, while Rogers are blatantly improper."

"Katharine, *really!*" Miss Fairfax exclaimed with another giggle.

"As for William," Miss Glyn said severely—two giggles in one night from Miss Fairfax were more than she was prepared to tolerate—"it is an admirable name on the whole. Full of strength and antiquity. Mind you, there is a tendency toward aggression—remember William the Conqueror—and a Willie could not be endured. Still, if you are very strong with him and refuse to be caught in such mawkish endearments as 'My Sweet Willie,' I think Sir William might do very well. My initial interrogation of Sir William was of necessity brief, and I will, of course, need further information before I give you my final opinion. He mentioned he has only a mother living?"

"Yes. His poor father died four years ago, leaving Sir William an only child."

"Excellent. How very commonsensical of him. You will be spared the necessity of finding hus-

11

bands for plain sisters, and free from paying off a wayward brother's debts. What are his views on children?"

"*Children?*" Miss Fairfax gasped. "Katharine, we only just met!"

"But my dear Georgina, from the way you were going into raptures about his strong arms, I just naturally assumed—"

"Katharine, really!" Miss Fairfax sniffed. "Sir William is merely a kind, intelligent, amusing, well-spoken young man with a generous heart and gentle eyes and—"

"And you are going to see him tomorrow," Miss Glyn said with a smile.

"Oh yes!" Miss Fairfax sighed luxuriously. "The Wildings have invited him to their rout tomorrow afternoon. Could anything be more wonderful?"

Their chaise drew up before the Fairfax home in Russell Court where the two women were greeted by Wainwright, the Fairfax butler for nearly twenty years.

"Good evening, Wainwright," Miss Glyn said, removing her cloak. "Dreadfully sorry about the abysmal hour. I tried to pull Miss Fairfax away at a decent time, but she was having one of her horrid successes and could not be pried away."

"That is quite all right, Miss Glyn," the elegantly balding Wainwright replied. "Ross and I were enjoying a cup of tea together in the kitchen just before you returned."

"Well, you mustn't let your tea get cold," declared Miss Fairfax. "Just lock up and go finish your cup. Katharine and I are going to bed immediately."

"Very good, miss." Wainwright bowed as Miss Fairfax and Miss Glyn began to mount the stairs to their rooms.

"Bed, indeed," said Miss Glyn. "Not until you

12

have told me all about Sir William Atherton, my girl."

"I have told you all that I know, Kate," Miss Fairfax replied. "You forget that we only met this evening."

"No, no, my dear. It is *you* who are forgetting."

"And what do you mean by that?"

"Nothing, Georgina, nothing!" Miss Glyn said. "Go to bed and dream of your ... new acquaintance."

"Oh, but he *is* wonderful, Kate!" Miss Fairfax cried as she impulsively hugged her friend. "I am sure that you two will get along famously tomorrow."

"Tomorrow? But I shall not be seeing him tomorrow, Georgina."

"But the Wildings' rout—"

"I am not going."

"Kate!"

"I told you a week ago that I had refused the invitation," Miss Glyn calmly stated. "Your popularity, Georgina, has forced me up into a level of society I cannot enjoy. To regularly consort with people filled with their own self-importance would drive a saint to homicide ... and we both know I am no saint. I eschew the Wildings' rout. I long to embrace Dante, Swift, Jonson! I'll not be denied."

"Yes, but now that I have met Sir William—"

"That is no reason for me to give up a day in the library, a day that I have been looking forward to for over a month. The pace you have set for us this season, Georgina, is ruining my intellectual life. Sir William has passed my initial inspection, and yours it seems. Let us see if he can rise to our expectations. You do have expectations, don't you, Georgie?"

"Oh yes!" Miss Fairfax breathed, caught herself, and blushed furiously.

"Excellent," Miss Glyn said with a smile. "We shall have Sir William riding through the streets of London proclaiming his undying love for you before the week is out."

※

Chapter 2

MISS GLYN AND Miss Fairfax had shared the Fairfax home in Russell Court for the last year and a half, since the death of Miss Fairfax's parents. With Miss Fairfax's elder brother, Jeremy, cavorting about in the cavalry (as Miss Glyn termed it), her guardians, Lord and Lady Egerton, had asked her to live with them. But Miss Fairfax had had the sense to see that their offer was halfhearted at best. With four daughters to marry off—three of whom were remarkably plain—and two sons with a decided predilection for pretty young women, the addition of Miss Fairfax to the Egerton household could have well been disastrous. It was then that Miss Glyn had proposed the Russell Court chaperone scheme.

Miss Glyn, having lost her mother when she was five, had gone to live with the Fairfaxes, her appointed guardians, upon the death of her father when she was sixteen, and she and Miss Fairfax had become bosom friends, despite the five years' difference in their ages. The deaths of Mr. and Mrs. Fairfax on the eve of Miss Fairfax's debut had drawn the two young women even closer together.

Ever one for concocting schemes of dubious propriety, Miss Glyn had proposed that, having passed her majority with no inclination to marry, she should act as Miss Fairfax's chaperone and diligently maintain her young friend's credit in the *ton* until Mr. Jeremy Fairfax, who was all of three-and-

15

twenty, tired of putting untold numbers of the French to the sword, returned to his London home and the proper supervision of his sister. Since Miss Glyn was noted in the *ton* for her intelligence and knowledge of the world (a reputation Miss Glyn had worked hard to achieve), the Egertons at last, and with becoming reluctance, accepted the plan.

For a year, then, Miss Fairfax and Miss Glyn lived alone in Russell Court in perfect harmony with one another, seldom going out, and seeing only the closest of their friends. At the end of the proper mourning period, however, Miss Glyn had insisted that her friend reenter society. Within a fortnight of her debut, Miss Fairfax was proclaimed the belle of the season, a veritable hit in fact, an accolade which left her rather bemused and Miss Glyn in paroxysms of laughter. With the Prince Regent taking particular notice of Miss Fairfax at her presentation, her success was assured and her time could no longer be called her own.

Miss Glyn, however, refused to surrender all of her own time to Miss Fairfax's success. Thus, rather than attending her friend to a rout she was quite certain would bore her to tears, Miss Glyn had dressed in a plain green housedress, instructed Wainwright that she was at home to no one, shut herself up in the library, sat in her favorite leather wing chair, curled her shoeless feet beneath her, and allowed her hungry eyes and mind to devour the first volume of Goethe's *Faust*. Her concentration, which had been absolute through Montesquieu, Swift, Wollstonecraft, and Dante, was destroyed at this juncture by the sudden appearance of Miss Fairfax, who burst into the library crying "Kate!" before she vigorously hugged her startled friend, and then threw herself down at the foot of Miss Glyn's chair.

"Good afternoon, Georgina," Miss Glyn said with great composure. "Did you have a pleasant day?"

"Oh Katharine," Miss Fairfax said as she rapturously hugged her friend's knees, "it was marvelous, fantastic, earth-shattering!"

"I gather you saw Sir William Atherton," Miss Glyn said with a wry smile.

"Saw him, spoke to him, danced with him!"

"I am so glad you stopped there."

"Oh Katharine, our views of the world are as one," declared Miss Fairfax as she turned her head up to face her friend. "Our hearts and minds share the same thoughts, the same hopes, the same dreams. And truly, he is everything I have looked for in a man. My impressions of him last night were not wrong. He . . . he is a gentle man, Kate, and yet so sure of himself. Calm and intelligent, and yet impulsive at times. Do you know, he stood up with me *three* times today!"

"Oh, now I must comment on that."

"Katharine!" Miss Fairfax cried in consternation, for she valued her friend's good opinion above all others.

"To stand up with you once is politeness. Twice bespeaks affection and respect. But *thrice* bespeaks a violence of emotion that you would do well . . . to encourage, Georgina."

"Oh Katharine," Miss Fairfax cried as she hugged her friend once more. "You dear, sweet, wonderful woman. How you do carry on!"

"I was about to say the same of you."

"If only you were in love with some worthy man, my happiness would be complete."

"I beg you, Georgina, spare me your worthy man. You know I shun both love and marriage. I am happy as I am. Why would you wish such misery on me?"

"Love is not misery, Kate."

17

"Of course it is. If it does not deceive you as to the intentions of the gentleman in question, leaving you open to ridicule, it swamps you with anguish as you await the gentleman's call, his request that his name be placed on your dance card, or a summary inspection by the gentleman's good mother. Every female I have known who has fallen in love loses her wit and humor, and I ask you, Georgina, how could I be anything but miserable if I were in love and no longer able to ply my silliness in London's drawing rooms?"

Miss Fairfax suddenly gasped with horror, her face draining of all color. "Katharine, Sir William is calling on me tomorrow. I asked him to join our other morning callers. He has said that he will do so!"

"Excellent. I shall be able to interrogate him within an inch of his life. It is my duty, after all."

"Yes, but you . . . he . . . I . . ."

"We. Yes, dear, pray continue."

"Katharine, your tongue—"

"My tongue? That will make a foursome. What could be more pleasant?"

"Restraint," Miss Fairfax said firmly. "Restraint would be much more pleasant."

"Georgina—"

"Oh Katharine," cried Miss Fairfax as she turned her imploring blue eyes upon Miss Glyn with full force, "I do not mean to criticize, and you know I love you very much, but . . . well . . . you have a tendency to say rather barbed or bizarre things when you think no one is attending, and Sir William might construe them in quite the wrong way, not knowing you and loving you as I do and . . . well . . . I am afraid you might frighten him off."

"Georgina," Miss Glyn replied as she gripped her friend's shoulders, "any man that is scared off because of my absurd antics would not be worth having."

"But he is! That is . . . I mean . . ." Miss Fairfax said as she colored. "He is so very worthy a gentleman, and rather quiet, and I *do* so want to make a good impression on him in my home. It is only for a little while, Kate, until he knows you better. Then you may banter with him to your heart's content. But until then, could you practice a little restraint and curb your tongue? For me? Please?"

"For you, Georgina, I would cut my tongue out with a rusty dagger," Miss Glyn declared.

"I do not think that will be quite necessary," Miss Fairfax said with a smile, and then she leapt to her feet. "I must go tell Cook what to prepare for tomorrow's callers. Oh, if only I knew what he likes! *Why* didn't I think to ask him?"

"I daresay you had other things on your mind."

But Miss Fairfax had hurried distractedly from the room and so missed this last comment.

Miss Glyn's finger twirled a loose tendril of brown hair.

So Georgina had fallen at last, had she? Miss Glyn had long expected this event, for her friend had a large heart eager to embrace love when it was proffered. Still, it was a pity. She had enjoyed the last year and a half of her friend's company. Trust a man to turn her comfortable world upside down. She could not understand why women fell in love with men, for they were invariably hurt and disappointed by their *object d'amour*. Either the courtship went well and the marriage was a disaster, or the courtship crashed on the rocks of masculine indifference or cruelty. Thank God, thought Miss Glyn, that she was too experienced to allow such stupidity to besiege her.

Miss Fairfax, however, was eagerly leaping into love and must be protected from any potential hurts or follies. Miss Glyn had spoken lightly of interrogating Sir William within an inch of his life, but there had been some meaning in her words. It was her duty to insure that Miss Fairfax would be safe in Sir William's arms; that her dear friend would suffer no disappointment, no heartache, no disaster.

And if Sir William passed muster and if Miss Fairfax still wanted the fellow, Miss Glyn would insure that he posted the banns with all due haste.

☀

Chapter 3

THE FOLLOWING AFTERNOON, Miss Glyn was entertaining Mr. Thomas and Miss Elizabeth Carrington, Lord Falkhurst, Lord Mowbry, and Lady Mary and Lady Elvira Pomeroy in the large blue drawing room. Miss Fairfax was also present, but her heart was pounding with such violence that she was able to hear but very little over the roar in her ears and was thus of little use in furthering the conversation. The situation was made all the more difficult by the fact that the gentlemen—with the exception of Mr. Carrington—had come expressly to call on Miss Fairfax.

Miss Carrington did what she could to help and was of some use for she was a pretty and charming blonde with a large dowry behind her. She had also been informed of the case in which Miss Fairfax and William Atherton stood, and so doubled her efforts to distract these morning callers. Nonetheless, Miss Glyn was beginning to feel the strain of amusing such single-minded gentlemen when Wainwright stepped into the room and announced:

"Sir William Atherton and Lord Blake."

Miss Glyn turned and beheld the young Adonis of the Montclair Ball and his striking companion, boredom intact. Ah well. She could take the good with the bad. She could survive a morning visit with a friend of Priscilla Inglewood. She would simply ignore him, there were others here who could entertain Lord Blake . . . if any friend of Lady Inglewood's could be entertained.

Observing Miss Fairfax walking with dazed determination toward the two gentlemen, Miss Glyn moved swiftly to her side. They were thus able to provide a united and proper front to their two newest morning callers.

"Sir William," Miss Fairfax said in her softest voice, "I am so glad you could come."

"It is a great pleasure to see you again, Miss Fairfax," Sir William replied with equal softness, his face pale from the strain of withstanding Miss Fairfax's beauty. "I . . . have taken the liberty of bringing one of my oldest friends with me. May I present Lord Blake?"

Lord Blake bowed, raised Miss Fairfax's hand to his lips, and declared in a low and, to Miss Glyn, oddly evocative voice that stopped the breath in her throat: "I have heard of you often, Miss Fairfax, but never have I dared to enter your radiant presence until this moment."

Miss Glyn blinked. Her breath and good sense returned. "He only talks flummery," she told herself, "and that is more telling than his voice."

"How kind of you," Miss Fairfax said, ". . . to say so, that is, Lord Blake. Any friend of Sir William's is assured of welcome in my home. Sir William, you know Miss Glyn, I believe. Lord Blake, allow me to present you to *my* oldest and dearest friend, Miss Katharine Glyn."

"I am delighted to see you again, Miss Glyn," Sir William said with a bow. "Your name is seldom from Miss Fairfax's lips."

"How singularly foolish of her," Miss Glyn murmured, missing Lord Blake's sudden smile. "I, too, am delighted, Sir William, for I continue to hear nothing but good of you and am always glad to admit a paragon into my home. I have not, however, heard much of you, Lord Blake."

"No?" said Lord Blake, raising one dark brow.

A quick dig of Miss Fairfax's elbow into her ribs recalled Miss Glyn to her vow of sobriety, and she quickly added: "And it does you credit, I am sure. It seems to me that nowadays the only people one hears of are those who are draped in scandal. Would you like tea?"

Lord Blake gravely agreed that tea seemed like a capital idea.

Miss Glyn nodded to Harriet, their parlor maid, and two cups of tea were produced instantaneously. The foursome moved to a settee where Miss Fairfax and Miss Glyn seated themselves while the two gentlemen stood before them.

"I recall, Sir William," said Miss Glyn, "that you have recently foresaken the military for civilian life."

"Yes. I returned to England four months ago. I have been in London only a fortnight."

"Providence must have smiled upon you for you appear in remarkably good health," Miss Glyn observed.

"I have been fortunate, yes, despite all of the carnage," Sir William replied. "My arm was grazed last year. That has been the only injury I received."

"Your mother must be so relieved to have you safely home once again," Miss Glyn said.

"Indeed, yes. It was for her sake, really, that I took the discharge," Sir William said. "She was dreadfully worried about me and was finding the estate too much of a burden. I shouldn't really have stayed away for so long."

"Very commendable." A sidelong glance informed Miss Glyn that Miss Fairfax was staring at Sir William with a beatific smile on her lovely face and would be of little use in the conversation. Sir

William was equally dumbstruck. Miss Glyn steeled herself and turned to Lord Blake. "And you, my lord? Have you also taken part in the conflict?"

"Good heavens, no!" said Lord Blake with a shudder. "War is simply ruinous for one's wardrobe. I've also heard that the French delight in charging at one with a bayonet. All in all, it seems a very poor means of spending one's time."

"How very astute," Miss Glyn murmured. "Um, Georgina? Georgina?" she said, nudging her friend from her daze.

"Hm? Oh . . . oh, what is it, Kate?"

"Lord Blake and I were discussing gardening, and he has just mentioned that Sir William has a decided fondness for greenhouses, which is most fortunate, Sir William," Miss Glyn said, turning to the equally dazed knight, "for we have a splendid one in the back garden. Perhaps Miss Fairfax could be prevailed upon to give you a tour?"

Miss Fairfax blinked rapidly several times, gasped "Oh!" twice and said: "Oh yes, what a wonderful idea, Kate. That is . . . if you would enjoy such a tour, Sir William?"

"I would enjoy touring the Egyptian sands if you were there, Miss Fairfax," Sir William fervently avowed.

With these two so easily dispatched, Miss Glyn rose to stand before Lord Blake.

"We were *not* discussing gardening, Miss Glyn," he said.

"No?" Miss Glyn said, crinkling her brow.

"Most assuredly not."

"How silly of me," Miss Glyn murmured as she began to move away. "I thought we were."

Lord Blake gazed after her, amusement lightening his soul.

Miss Glyn, meanwhile, was brought up short by Lord Mowbry—a portly gentleman of pink complex-

24

ion—who roundly declared: "I say, Miss Glyn. That Atherton fellow just absconded with Miss Fairfax!"

"No, no, Lord Mowbry, you have it quite backward. It is Miss Fairfax who has absconded with Sir William," Miss Glyn said.

"Eh?"

"Well, Georgina implored me not to breathe a word of this," Miss Glyn said confidingly as she took Lord Mowbry's arm, "but I know I can trust to your discretion. Poor Miss Fairfax is suffering from a nearly fatal case of Sweet Willie's Disease."

Lord Blake turned to hide his grin.

"Never heard of it," Lord Mowbry stated.

"Oh, it is very rare and nearly incurable," Miss Glyn assured him.

"But what's this got to do with Atherton hauling her off into the garden?"

"Why *everything*, dear Lord Mowbry. You know, of course, that Sir William has just returned from the war?"

"Yes, yes, yes, but—"

"Well, it is a closely guarded secret, but I am certain I can tell you *all*," Miss Glyn said with the greatest excitement. "Sir William saw a good deal of action in the Egyptian desert, and it was there that he came upon a sunburned Gypsy who taught him many wondrous skills including," Miss Glyn concluded triumphantly, "the cure to Sweet Willie's Disease. Even now he is struggling to bring our dear Miss Fairfax back from the very brink!"

Lord Mowbry eyed Miss Glyn, decided he did not like what he saw, declared that he really must leave, and stomped from the room.

Lord Falkhurst—a handsome man of one-and-thirty—accosted Miss Glyn a moment later. "Katharine, did you see Miss Fairfax go out with that Atherton creature?"

"I believe I did see something of that sort. Of course, my eyes are not what they once were."

"Why aren't you with them as is your duty? You could hardly call the two of *them* out there *alone* proper, could you?"

"Far more proper than the thoughts rattling around in that dark mind of yours, Falkhurst," was Miss Glyn's quelling reply.

Lord Falkhurst paled, a muscle twitched in his clenched jaw. He was a cold-blooded young earl possessed of a handsome shock of dark brown hair, a pair of grim black eyes, a fine figure, and a commendable fortune. He had also, in their youth, been betrothed to Miss Glyn.

"Now Bertie," Miss Glyn continued with a radiant smile (for she knew that Lord Falkhurst detested that childhood nickname), "you mustn't pout. It makes you look like a sulking schoolboy . . . even at your advanced age. Come, clear that dark mien and let us converse in a civil manner. I'm sure we can do it at least once. I shall start. How is your Uncle Archibald? I believe he is suffering from kidney stones?"

"He is quite recovered, thank you," Lord Falkhurst said with a total lack of interest.

With an outraged gasp, Miss Glyn leapt to her feet, struck Lord Falkhurst's handsome face as hard as she could, and cried out: "How dare you, sir?! How *dare* you insult me in my own home? Leave! Leave at once!"

Seven startled pairs of eyes surveyed this amazing tableau.

"Katharine," Lord Falkhurst hissed, "have you lost your mind? What the devil do you think you're doing?"

"*No* apology can ever atone for your conduct, Lord Falkhurst," Miss Glyn declared in ringing accents, bright patches of red staining her cheeks. "Leave this house and never darken our doorway again!"

Glancing around at the now noticeably hostile occupants in the drawing room, the confused and rather shaken Lord Falkhurst could but bow stiffly and do as he was bid.

Miss Glyn turned from observing this welcome departure to see that Lord Blake was leaning against the fireplace mantel watching her speculatively. Well, she had only promised sobriety in Sir William's company, after all. She ignored his lordship.

"Oh, you poor dear!" the Ladies Pomeroy cried as one as they fluttered around Miss Glyn.

"How dreadful for you, how truly dreadful," Lady Elvira Pomeroy breathed.

"The man is a cad," Lady Mary Pomeroy proclaimed. "Mama has always said that Lord Falkhurst is a cad."

"The way you stood up to him, your eyes shining, your head so high!" Lady Elvira cried. "Goose pimples ran all up and down my spine!"

"You were magnificent, my dear," Lady Mary said. "Simply magnificent."

Tears in her brown eyes (for she always immersed herself completely in whatever role she was playing), Miss Glyn took a hand from both of the Pomeroys in hers, clasped them fervently to her breast, and said: "Such dear, good friends! So obliging. So considerate." But here all words failed her.

"But my dear, you must lie down. You must lie down at once!" Lady Mary said.

"Indeed, yes," Lady Elvira agreed. "You require a cold compress and some dandelion tea to help you recover from this wretched business."

Walking them out of the room, Miss Glyn replied: "You both are so kind. I cannot thank you enough for your consideration. How should I survive without friends such as you?" Wainwright, seeing his cue, held the front door open for the Ladies Pomeroy. "I can only hope you will forgive this inexcusable disruption of your morning. Your next call in our home will be far more pleasant, I assure you."

The two sisters assured Miss Glyn that they were not in the least put out, advised her to remember the dandelion tea, and stepped out the door, their heads instantly locked together in excited conversation.

"We will receive no more callers this morning, Wainwright," Miss Glyn informed the grave butler. She made her way back to the drawing room. The Carringtons peered at her from around the door.

"That is the end of this morning's entertainment," she said cheerfully, moving between brother and sister and slipping an arm through each of theirs. She began to lead them to the front door, talking gaily as she went. "It was such a pleasure seeing you again. Give my regards to whoever you think it best, remember me in your prayers, and now, adieu."

"B-B-Beg pardon?" Mr. Carrington stammered, halfway into the hall.

"I am throwing you out," Miss Glyn informed him.

"But whatever for?" the befuddled Mr. Carrington demanded.

"Because you are here."

"But . . . but . . ."

"Come *along*, Tommy," Miss Carrington said firmly as she pulled her poor brother toward the front door. "Sister Beth will explain everything. Good-bye, Kate," she called over her shoulder. "I had a marvelous time."

"Why thank you," Miss Glyn called in reply. "We really must do this again sometime."

Gay female laughter was her only answer as Wainwright bowed the two Carringtons out the door.

With a hearty sigh for a job well-done, Miss Glyn returned to the drawing room, closed the door behind her, turned, and beheld the handsome figure of Lord Blake leaning against the fireplace mantel.

"What," Miss Glyn demanded, "are you still here?"

"Oughtn't I to be?" Lord Blake said imperturbably as he advanced upon Miss Glyn. "I am, on my oath, positively quaking in my shoes at the thought of what you might do to throw *me* out of the house."

"You are wearing boots," Miss Glyn observed.

Lord Blake carefully scrutinized himself through his quizzing glass. "With these breeches? I should hope so!"

"I shall, nevertheless, endeavor to make your exit as painless as possible," Miss Glyn continued in a stifled voice.

"I *am* grateful. But must I go?"

"As the bard so astutely observed, 'Unbidden guests are often welcomest when they are gone.' But wait," Miss Glyn said, holding up a hand. Her brown eyes closed for a moment in thought and then reopened. "You are, as I recall, a friend of Sir William Atherton, are you not?"

"I believe that I can lay some claim to friendly ties, yes."

"Drat," said Miss Glyn with a sigh. "Since *you* are a friend of Sir William Atherton and Sir William is a friend of Miss *Fairfax*, I should insult Sir William by throwing you out, mortify Miss Fairfax, and bring a thousand unhappy curses down upon my innocent head. You shall stay," Miss Glyn reluctantly declared.

"You are too kind."

"No, merely boxed in. Have you been a lord very long?"

"All of my life."

"Ah."

Lord Blake surveyed her through his quizzing glass. "From your tone, I gather I have lived in error. Are you, like the French, not fond of the aristocracy?"

"Fond? In a sense I am, I suppose, for you are all frightfully amusing. But outside of that . . ."

"Nothing much to say for us, eh?"

Miss Glyn found Lord Blake's smile particularly charming.

"I'm sorry, no. There's small choice in rotten apples."

"Said someone in a play about another Kate," Lord Blake drawled. "But we're not a bad lot on the whole, you know. And it's rather pleasant being in the *haut ton*. Good food, marvelous clothes . . . I quite enjoy the elegancies of life. To live in rags cannot be pleasant. If you saw the Moroccan bed jacket I was being fitted for earlier this morning, you would not view us so harshly, I assure you."

"I would not change my opinion for a bed jacket. An evening coat, perhaps, but never a bed jacket. I saw you dancing with Lady Priscilla Inglewood at the Montclair ball. Have you known her long?"

"From the cradle."

"Ah."

"Dear me, have I committed another indiscretion?"

"Rather, you have startled me, my lord, for I cannot conceive why, being a friend of Lady Inglewood's, you have chosen to enter the lion's den."

Lord Blake twirled his quizzing glass on its chain. "You amaze me, Miss Glyn. You apparently dislike Lady Inglewood, a paragon of maidenly virtues, and you deride the noble classes. What is the source of such freakish attitudes?"

"There is nothing to titillate you, my lord. I was used badly by many of the *ton* in my youth and made to feel quite low. I do not choose to court such unpleasantness again."

"And Lady Inglewood?"

"The same answer holds. 'She speaks poiniards, and every word stabs: if her breath were as terrible as her terminations, there would be no living near her; she would infect to the north star.' "

"*Much Ado About Nothing*, Act Two, scene one, and not very apt, I think."

"Let us agree to disagree. Lady Inglewood will not thank you for coming here today. She will think you the freak and undoubtedly demand satisfaction. Perhaps you should leave the country for a lengthy period of time."

"No, no, there is no other country as amusing as England."

"I would not know, having never traveled beyond our shores, but I am glad to hear you say it, for I have long suspected that England has not been given the credit it deserves in world opinion. Do you read, Lord Blake?"

The corner of his mouth quirked up. "On occasion."

"We have an excellent library. Perhaps you would like to make use of it until Sir William returns."

"You dislike my company?" Lord Blake woefully inquired.

" 'I do desire we may be better strangers.' "

"*As You Like It*, Act Three, scene two."

"I commend your knowledge of Shakespeare, but not your friends. Our acquaintance is too short to give me any understanding of your company, but I cannot like your circumstances. I am well past my majority, sir, and make it a point to live my life according to my desires. I choose not to associate with any friend of Lady Inglewood's, and I believe she is adamant that no friend of hers associate with me. I suggest you not return to Russell Court."

"You wrong an honorable woman with these aspersions. Lady Inglewood is no martinet to bend her friends to her wishes."

"Oh come now, sir, talk no such nonsense. You said you have known her from the cradle."

"And as such I know her for a charming, intelligent woman, well respected in the *ton*."

"Indeed. Could anything be more objectionable?"

"You speak in riddles, Miss Glyn."

"This is my home, Lord Blake. I speak as I choose."

Lord Blake leaned back against the mantel, negligently crossed his ankles, and regarded her with his sleepy gray eyes. "We are at loggerheads, I see. Let us, then, agree to disagree about Lady Inglewood. Do not, I pray you, deliver me into the library. Let me stay and hear you speak as you choose . . . and have another cup of tea. You serve very good tea, Miss Glyn."

Resigned to her fate, Miss Glyn sighed heavily and refilled his lordship's cup.

She took this lull in the conversation to study this friend of a friend of a friend in more depth. Lord Blake was dressed at first sight in the very height of fashion. His coat of silver with red roses patterned throughout was molded across his broad shoulders with the obvious skill of a Scott or Weston; his waistcoat was of a dark maroon that revealed the quizzing glass hanging upon a silver chain; his breeches expertly delineated a pair of long, well-muscled legs; his Hessians were nearly blinding.

On closer inspection, however, Miss Glyn observed that Lord Blake's shirt points were not at all de rigueur. They were, in fact, appallingly low to the point that Lord Blake was actually able to turn his head freely in both directions! While he had been able to effect a perfect Ganymede for his cravat, this was, in part, offset by a head of light brown hair that effected no *style* whatsoever. It was simply cut short and brushed with its own natural wave. His long, slender fingers bore but one ring, a family signet. It appeared, therefore, after so severe a scrutiny, that the Corinthian was not quite what he seemed.

The object of her blatant survey was openly surveying Miss Glyn in turn, which amused her no end. Seldom had anyone, let alone a man, thought her of sufficient interest to pay her more than half a glance, let alone the toe to head study she was currently undergoing.

Her head tilting, a smile dancing on her lips, Miss Glyn demanded: "Are you quite through?"

Taken by surprise, Lord Blake smiled and shook his head a little.

"I beg your pardon. I was lost in speculation. Do you never let anyone see behind the arch mask you wear?"

"But 'tis not a mask! It is the heart and soul of my character, Lord Blake. You would not have me go naked into the world? Only think of the impropriety!"

" 'Tempt not a desperate man.' "

Miss Glyn pressed her hand to her mouth to keep from laughing at this quotation.

Satisfaction dwelled in Lord Blake's gray eyes. "I find that I am still awash in confusion. Would you be terribly offended, Miss Glyn, if I asked you a rather personal question?"

"On the contrary," Miss Glyn replied, determinedly regaining her composure. "I find personal questions from perfect strangers totally diverting, for one can make any reply that comes into one's head and how could a stranger determine if one is speaking the truth or not? And since we shall not be meeting again, I may let my imagination hold full sway. Ask away, my lord."

Lord Blake stared at Miss Glyn a moment, cleared his throat, and said faintly: "I am merely curious as to the reason behind your striking Lord Falkhurst with such force upon his informing you that his Uncle Archibald had recovered from an attack of kidney stones."

"Why, because I have longed to slap Lord Falkhurst for years!" Miss Glyn declared as if that were the most obvious reason imaginable.

"Do you often have these violent urges?"

"Only around Lord Falkhurst."

"You dislike the gentleman?"

"You praise him too highly. Shakespeare had him right: 'When he is best, he is a little worse than a man, and when he is worst, he is little better than a beast.' "

"I take it you do not enjoy his company?"

" 'I dote on his very absence.' "

"That is two from *Merchant of Venice*. Can you contrive a third?"

" 'God made him, and therefore let him pass for a man.' "

"Brava, Miss Glyn!" said Lord Blake, clapping, albeit laconically. "I see I shall have to brush up on my Shakespeare to converse with you measure for measure. But why choose today to strike Lord Falkhurst when you have waited years for the opportunity?"

"Oh, I doubt if I should have had the temerity to do so had I not been able to discern three positive effects from such a praiseworthy deed."

"And they were?"

"First, I would fulfill a long-cherished dream, as I have already explained. Second, I would be assured of effecting his hasty retreat from my home. And third, I could feel fairly certain of stirring up a whirlwind of unpleasant gossip that will hound the blackguard for weeks to come for, by what I consider a masterful stroke of luck, Lady Elvira and Lady Mary Pomeroy were witness to the entire shocking episode and will have spread the tale throughout London by sunset. They are the most incorrigible gossips, you know."

"I *have* heard rumors."

"I really am very fond of them," Miss Glyn continued, valiantly suppressing an insistent chuckle. "I think them the most diverting women in the *ton*. They know every scrap of gossip that floats about London, and they always get it muddled up. Rumors are wont to change with the wind, as you are undoubtedly aware, Lord Blake. But what Mary and Elvira do to gossip is an unparalleled art. I have often started a rumor about myself that I might discover to what great heights it had been raised a se'ennight later by the awesome imaginations of the Pomeroy sisters. It is most entertaining."

"You lead me astray, Miss Glyn. I quite dote on your nonsense."

"Fear not. 'Tis but an aberration. Men are notoriously fickle."

"Nay, madam, you wrong me! 'My affection hath an unknown bottom, like the Bay of Portugal.'"

Miss Glyn was surprised into a giggle, which, supported by the terrible temptations she had already endured in this conversation, quickly became helpless laughter.

Sir William Atherton and Miss Fairfax chose this moment to return to the drawing room. Sir William seemed perplexed by the surprising sight of Miss

Glyn laughing at his laconic friend. Miss Fairfax's expression, however, was one of mingled horror and fury.

"Kate!" she cried (and would have stamped her foot had Sir William not been there). "What *are* you going on about?"

Lord Blake hid his smile.

"I do beg your pardon, Georgina," Miss Glyn gasped. This seemed to steady her, for she regained her innocent expression of a moment earlier as she advanced upon Sir William and Miss Fairfax. "Lord Blake was recounting the most delightful tale concerning camels in the Himalayas that is much too shocking to bear repetition."

Lord Blake stared at Miss Glyn, but she paid him no heed.

"I am *so* glad you have both returned," she continued. "I was prepared to send out the Bow Street Runners to look for you. *Dear* Sir William," she said in the same breath as she looped an arm through one of his, "do come sit and chat with me a moment. Miss Fairfax has monopolized your company, and I have so looked forward to having a word with you."

"But Miss Glyn," Sir William stammered, "where are your other guests?"

"They . . . recalled a previous engagement," Miss Glyn replied vaguely. "Georgina," she called over her shoulder as she led Sir William to a dark green settee, "endeavor, if you can, to entertain Lord Blake."

For the next half hour, Miss Glyn engaged Sir William in the most decorous of conversations, holding true to her vow of sobriety, while still questioning Sir William on every aspect of his life, as was her duty. She quickly ascertained that Miss Fairfax was not mistaken in her regard. Sir William's character was on his face and a charming

36

character it was, too. She could further their romance with no fear of harm coming to her friend.

Recalled to a sense of the time, Sir William rose and declared that he and Lord Blake really must take their leave.

"Oh, I am distraught," said Miss Glyn as she rose with Sir William. "My dear sir, you must promise me faithfully that you will call again upon us tomorrow. I have taken great pleasure in your company."

"It would be an honor, Miss Glyn," Sir William replied with a grateful smile and a bow.

Skillfully maneuvering Miss Fairfax and Sir William together so that they might have one last word before saying adieu, Miss Glyn stepped back a few feet to find herself at Lord Blake's side.

"That was masterfully done," Lord Blake said approvingly.

She considered him a moment. "I thank you, my lord. Overseeing a flowering romance can be so very challenging and quite, quite exhausting. If one did not receive enough compliments for one's labors, one might begin to wonder if all of the tedious effort was in any way worthwhile."

"Do you disapprove of romance, then, Miss Glyn?"

"Of course I do, as any sensible person should. Romance renders the most intelligent person a blithering idiot. Georgina is already giddy with rapture. I doubt if I can bear up under the strain."

"Be strong, Miss Glyn," Lord Blake counseled. "You have but to recall the words of Ralph Bottsway, a noted Lancastrian dung salesman, and all your difficulties will seem but the beating of moth wings in a hurricane: 'Trouble may beset you from all sides, your lordship,' said he to me. 'Your crops may fail, your well run dry. Your sheep kidnapped, your children sheared . . . but at least we ain't got locusts.' "

A gurgle of laughter was startled from Miss Glyn.

"Go away," she demanded, "and don't return. I'll not be bested in my own home by a mere aristocrat, let alone a cradle friend of Priscilla Inglewood."

Lord Blake bowed and finally succeeded in prying his comrade free from the aura of Miss Fairfax's charms. Good-byes were said with pleasant melancholy all around as Wainwright bowed the two gentlemen out of the house.

"Oh Kate!" Miss Fairfax cried as she ecstatically threw herself into Miss Glyn's arms. "I am so happy! I cannot tell you of the glory raging within me. It is as if a golden light had suddenly shot itself into my very being!"

"Yes, yes dear," Miss Glyn said soothingly as she began to lead Miss Fairfax up the stairs to their rooms.

"Oh Kate," Miss Fairfax reiterated with a happy sigh as she entered her room and threw herself down upon her back on her bed, "he is everything that is charming and amiable. Do you know," she said, suddenly sitting up, "he has a springer spaniel named Minx that adores cornish pastries just as much as my dear little Scotty used to?"

"The mind boggles," Miss Glyn murmured before returning to her own room.

*
Chapter 4

EQUALLY BOGGLED WAS the mind of the most honorable Marquess of Blake Park, Baron of Willoughby-on-the-Marsh, and gartered knight of the realm, Lord Theodore Francis Beauregard Quentin Blake. He had not expected a morning call on two fashionable ladies of the *ton* to have passed so quickly and so entertainingly. His experience with such morning visits had led him to shudder on his drive to Russell Court. But William had importuned and who was he to say nay to a friend? To Russell Court he had gone and what had he found? No solicitous inquiries as to his health and his parents. No waxing poetic about the lovely weather. No minute discussion of the most recent social events. Instead, there had been beauty and charm and Miss Katharine Glyn. She had been wholly unexpected and continued to intrigue his lordship as he expertly maneuvered his team of grays through the London noontime traffic.

She was the most determined madcap he had ever met . . . nor had she made any push to set that cap for him. This in itself was extraordinary for he had been ardently pursued by every title-hunting female in England these last five years.

Lord Blake paused in his reflections. Had Oliver really died five years ago? The pain he felt whenever he thought of his brother, stabbed his heart once more. With a nod to the quotational Miss Glyn, his lordship still thought Hamlet to have had the right take on life: "How weary, stale, flat, and unprofitable seem to me all the uses of this world." London in springtime, William in love, had not changed this view. But Miss Glyn, while not calling this melancholy into question, had at least added amusement to the uses of the world. Perhaps his brief sojourn in town would not be a dead loss after all.

Clearly his companion felt the same, for Sir William Atherton, at his side atop the phaeton, had been ecstatically enumerating the virtues of Miss Fairfax since they had left Russell Court and, as they drew near White's, showed no inclination to modify his ecstasies.

"Be silent, I implore you, Will," said his lordship as he tossed the ribbons to his tiger, Scranton, and jumped from the phaeton. "We are about to enter hallowed halls where loud exclamations of adoration will be rightfully derided."

"What, are we at White's so soon?" Sir William said, looking around him in amazement.

"Yes, puppy, we are," Lord Blake said, amusement dancing in his gray eyes. "And we are late for lunch, judging by the atrocious uproar of my stomach. Come and dine, Will. Such exertions as you have undergone this morning require refortification. A leg of mutton comes to mind."

Sir William jumped from the phaeton and followed his friend into White's. "As it happens," he said as they nodded to their various acquaintances, "I find myself without appetite."

"I don't doubt it," Lord Blake said dryly. "At least come and have a glass of port and lend us your company, such as it is."

They entered the dining room. Lord Blake quickly spied Mr. Robbins and Lord Braxton at a table near the center of the room, and joined them with many hearty hale-fellow-well-mets. Although he had long ago chosen to be an island, it was good to find he was not completely adrift. It was so damnably lonely dealing only with servants, tenants, and charities every day of his life. It was even becoming ... misery. Pained longing when in company, lonely misery when alone. He knew no other existence now and was troubled by this discovery, for surely this was not how he had planned to live his life.

Ruthlessly pushing aside such unhappy reflections, Lord Blake determined to enjoy the oasis his friends offered. Lunch was ordered and consumed amid conversation veering wildly between horse races, the most recent presentations at court, and the fickle hearts of women.

Mr. Peter Robbins—attired in a brown riding coat, buckskins, and Hessians—was waxing particularly strong at the moment upon the topic of one Jamison Knox, a bounder of the lowest order, who had had the effrontery to steal Mr. Robbins's latest mistress from him two days earlier. The disconsolate lover—his height, coloring, and nose proclaiming him a relative of his host—they were, in fact, cousins—was seated in some agitation opposite Lord Blake.

The right honorable Earl of Braxton sat to Lord Blake's right and was clearly entertained by Mr. Robbins's sad tale, going so far as to delicately bury his laughter in an intricately wrought lace handkerchief. Lord Braxton, a languid gentleman of thirty years, was accounted the greatest pink of the *ton* next to Lord Freddie Bingsley. They were, in fact, arch rivals, with Lord Bingsley continually searching out the new, the daring, and the far-fetched, while Lord Braxton essayed the subtlety of a skillfully cut coat, the proper shade of stockings to highlight one's calves, and the delicate manners and interests that were a compendium of such a wardrobe.

To Lord Blake's left sat Sir William Atherton, apparently bearing the full brunt of Mr. Robbins's diatribe. Closer observation, however, revealed that Sir William was lost in the Elysian Fields conjured by his enraptured heart.

"Come, come, my dear boy," Lord Braxton said to Mr. Robbins, "you must expect such cruel desertions by the fairer sex when you insist upon cavorting about in those too hideous riding breeches of yours and talking of nothing but . . . but *farms*," said his lordship with a grimace, "and boxing matches, and such other boring and indelicate topics that must and *do* offend the feminine ear. Ah Peter, if you would only let me take you in hand, I could have you surrounded by a bevy of blushing beauties. Why, I might even procure you a virtuous and beauteous maiden for your bride."

"Bride?" cried Mr. Robbins, thoroughly aghast. "Good God, Braxton, women are all well and good as an occasional amusement, but . . . but *marriage* . . . ?" Here the poor Mr. Robbins shuddered violently. "I think I need another drink, and *no* help from *you*, my lord." .

Lord Blake summoned their waiter, and their glasses were promptly refilled.

"What say you, Will," Lord Braxton appealed to Sir William. "Do you not find it distressing to have to own Peter as one of your closest friends?"

"What?" Sir William said in a dazed fashion as he shook his fair head. "What were you saying, Nigel? I'm afraid I wasn't attending."

"Our William has attended nothing save a speaking pair of blue eyes these last three days," Lord Blake informed the company.

"Do tell," Mr. Robbins said with the greatest interest. He leaned toward Sir William with obvious relish. "Fallen at last, has he? Who's the bit of muslin that's got you all unglued, Willie boy? Tell Uncle Peter *everything*."

"I *won't* have you speak of Miss Fairfax in such a fashion!" Sir William hotly declared.

"Good God!" ejaculated Lord Braxton. "Fairfax? *Georgina Fairfax?* The greatest, sweetest beauty to trod London's golden streets in over a decade? I say, my boy, you *do* have excellent taste!"

"Theo, *tell* them it's not like that," Sir William implored.

A smile hovering on his lips, Lord Blake cleared his throat and gravely intoned: "William is under the rule of a pure and hallowed love untainted by mere physical or earthly considerations. He has been raised to another, higher, plane unsullied by the pettiness and woes of our uncouth world. Have I got that right, Will?"

"I'll not have you ridicule my regard for Miss Fairfax!" declared Sir William.

"It is nothing of the kind, Will," Lord Blake said soothingly. "I speak the truth and have described only what I myself have observed. Will and I," Lord Blake informed Mr. Robbins and Lord Braxton, "have just paid a call upon Miss Fairfax and her chaperone . . . a Miss Glyn, I believe. Even I must confess to a total lack of desire to leave their company."

"She *is* lovely, is she not, Theo?" Sir William cried eagerly.

"Hm? Oh yes, I found Miss Fairfax quite . . . charming."

"Charming?" Sir William ejaculated. "Why, she is breathtaking! A goddess in mortal form. Miss Fairfax," he declared, blue eyes glowing, "is the very epitome of true womanhood."

"I always thought Will would be the first to succumb to Cupid's arrows, for he's had a romantic bent from the age of ten," Mr. Robbins commented. "Certainly *I* have no turn in that direction; Braxton is already enamored of his looking glass and Theo is apparently immune."

"I prefer," said Lord Blake, "to think of myself as disinclined. Every eligible female cares only for two attributes: my title and my fortune. Why should I ruin a good night's sleep with such baggage?"

"Theo, you must resign yourself to the practicalities of your position," said Lord Braxton with a smile. "No sensible female could ignore *such* a title and *such* a fortune. He is a stubborn fellow," said the earl to the others at the table. "Eligible girls offered to him left and right, eager mammas parading their daughters' wares at the least provocation, Priscilla Inglewood eagerly entering the lists against all comers, and yet he refuses to post the banns."

"I pray you, Nigel, not to disparage Priscilla," said Lord Blake with some severity. "She is a noble, beautiful, intelligent young woman with strong ties of friendship to my family, and I won't hear a word against her."

"She is a harpy who will hound you to the altar unless you tell her plainly you won't have her," Mr. Robbins said.

"What rodomontade," said Lord Blake. "Why should I insult a childhood friend when I have never given her the least reason to believe I think of her in a matrimonial light?"

"You've inherited your brother's lands, titles, and expectations, why not his fiancée?" Lord Braxton said.

"Besides," said Mr. Robbins, "I'll wager her father has filled her head with matrimonial expectations in your stead. An avaricious old dog, the Earl of Inglewood."

"His daughter does him credit," said Lord Braxton.

"That is enough, both of you," Lord Blake declared. "You wrong both me and the Inglewoods with such talk."

"But Theo," said Mr. Robbins, "it is such fun planning your future bride. You must marry, and everyone knows it."

"Most particularly Priscilla," Lord Braxton wryly added.

"You've passed your thirtieth birthday without a bride in sight," Mr. Robbins continued. "Pretty soon you'll be old and crotchety, and unable to attach even the most determined fortune-hunting female."

"Except, perhaps, Priscilla," said Lord Braxton.

"That is enough, Nigel!" Lord Blake snapped. "I believe, gentlemen, that I understand my duty to marry and produce an heir better than any of you. When I am able to tolerate the thought of having some female ensconced at my side for the rest of my life, I shall send a notice into the *Gazette*. Until then, we were discussing Will's heart, not my own."

"Heart?" queried Lord Braxton. "We were not discussing your heart, Theo, for I believe we are all sensible enough to realize that you will flee any lures a woman casts toward that moribund organ. No, no, you will enter the marriage rolls sensibly, with all matters of practicality considered. I daresay, love and happiness will not even enter into it."

"You begin to bore me, Nigel," Lord Blake replied, and would have said more but for the footman who stepped to his side to announce that Lord Falkhurst wished to have a word with him in the library.

"Falkhurst?" said Mr. Robbins. "I didn't know you were on speaking terms with that great block of ice."

"We have had a nodding acquaintance for years," Lord Blake replied as he stood, "and shared the same drawing room this morning. Gentlemen, if you will excuse me for a moment?"

Lord Blake strolled from the dining room into the library, and found Lord Falkhurst brooding over a glass of port as he stared down into the library grate.

"Your servant, sir," said Theo with a slight bow.

"Ah, there you are, Blake," Lord Falkhurst said, setting down his glass and turning toward him.

"I trust you have recovered from that shocking breech of civility in Russel Court?" said Lord Blake.

"I pay no heed to that hellion Kate Glyn and nor should anyone else. The *ton* won't tolerate much more of her insolence. But I did not wish to discuss that country hoyden with you. I want to put a word in your ear regarding Miss Fairfax."

"Miss Fairfax? What have I to do with that delightful creature?"

"You can warn Atherton off of her."

"I?" said Lord Blake with one arched brow. "Why should I do anything so impertinent?"

"You are his sponsor and—"

"Sponsor? Not I. Will is well past his majority with a good family and sound fortune behind him. He has no need of sponsors. Indeed, Falkhurst, I think it is to him you should direct this warning."

"The boy is in the throes of calf love," said Lord Falkhurst with growing impatience, "as anyone here can tell you, for we've all heard his ravings today. He'll not listen to a rival. I can but hope he will listen to you."

"And why, pray tell, should I warn him off of Miss Fairfax?" Lord Blake inquired, removing an invisible speck of dust from his coat sleeve. "They make a very pretty couple."

"I speak only for the boy's benefit. He'll make a

public fool of himself if he doesn't stop dangling after Miss Fairfax. She has more sense than to give her hand to a callow, graceless youth."

"But enough sense to favor your attentions, hm?"

"I believe I stand first in the lady's regard, yes."

"Ah, what happiness to have a mind so little assailed by the doubts and fears that torment we lesser mortals. I can clearly see, Falkhurst, that Will is sadly mismatched with you in any competition . . . for Miss Fairfax's affections."

"Then make him know it, Blake. My patience won't tolerate his ardor much longer."

Lord Falkhurst strode off, Lord Blake's amused gaze following him. "Lord, what fools these mortals be," he murmured before strolling back to the dining room to rejoin his friends.

The cover had been removed from the table, fresh glasses and brandy provided.

"And what did the Black Earl want?" Lord Braxton inquired as Lord Blake dropped onto his chair.

"Far more than he had a right to expect" was his reply. "Our conversation had a rather Shakespearean tone, I thought. I am hounded by the bard today."

"Good God, the theater!" ejaculated Sir William.

"Careful men," Mr. Robbins cautioned. "This ordeal over Miss Fairfax has apparently unhinged the knight's mind."

"No, no, no!" the distraught Sir William cried. "You don't understand. Georgina . . . I mean, Miss Fairfax told me that she and Miss Glyn are attending the theater tonight. *We must go!*"

Lord Braxton shuddered. "Not with me," he said. "The emotional violence of the theater is disastrous for my digestion. I have foresworn all theatrical amusements."

"Peter?" Sir William implored.

"Do but *think*, Will," Mr. Robbins replied. "You

know I can't abide that effeminate raging up and down the boards in tights. I'm not surprised Braxton hasn't the stomach for it."

"Theo," said Sir William, turning despairingly toward Lord Blake, "you, at least, must accompany me tonight. Were I to go alone, I should never have the temerity to approach Miss Fairfax's box when she will undoubtedly be surrounded by so many more worthy suitors than me. My courage would drain from me like water through a sieve. You *must* support me tonight, Theo, you must!"

"Very well," said Lord Blake with a sigh. "It might be tolerable at that. And I have just recollected that my new evening coat was delivered this morning. Yes, I most certainly shall attend. The theater is the best of all possible places for displaying one's wardrobe. I am surprised, Nigel, that that consideration alone has not reconciled you to Drury Lane."

"The audience dresses in nothing but flash," Lord Braxton sniffed, "and I abhor flash."

"I quite agree. But someone must be on hand to set a good example, don't you think?"

"You, I suppose," Mr. Robbins said bitterly.

"Certainly," Lord Blake replied, "if Braxton will not heed the call to arms."

Mr. Robbins turned on the earl. "I blame you, Braxton, for turning a true out-and-outer into a fop of the lowest order."

"Fop?!" cried Lord Blake. "Fop? I shall call you out for denigrating me in such a manner, Peter. *Bingsley* is a fop. *I* am blessed with a well-developed sense of style."

"Bah!" said Mr. Robbins.

"Don't blame me," Braxton murmured in Mr. Robbins's private ear. "Blame the Frenchman's bullet that shot the mooring out from under our stylish brethren."

"You would like my new coat, Peter," Lord Blake continued. "The green is exactly like that of the wood at Insley, where you slaughtered that six-hundred-pound stag."

"Bah!" Mr. Robbins reiterated.

"Very well, Will," Lord Blake declared, undeterred by such censure, "you alone shall be favored tonight with the aura cast by my new coat."

*

Chapter 5

FOLLOWING A LENGTHY game of cards at White's, in which Lord Blake emerged with a far heavier pocketbook than when he had entered, he returned home to partake of a leisurely evening meal before surrendering himself to the tender mercies of his trusted valet, Maxwell, who spent his days in unceasing worry over the care and presentation of his lordship's wardrobe.

"I think," said Lord Blake as he studied himself in the full-length mirror in his dressing room, "that a simple ruffed ascot would be best."

"I quite agree, my lord," Maxwell replied. "Classic simplicity is always best when one is forced to partake of the more vulgar forms of public entertainment."

"Quite," Lord Blake said dryly.

Creating the ascot against his lordship's dull gold waistcoat, Maxwell inquired of his master's evening itinerary.

"Be of stout heart," Lord Blake said, "no disaster shall befall your efforts tonight. I plan only a quiet foray to the theater, a quick call upon the familial abode, and an early appointment with my pillow."

"No midnight fencing matches? No horse races at dawn, my lord?"

Lord Blake thought of Mr. Robbins's recent condemnation of his interests and smiled. "No. No, I have checked my calendar, and it is quite free of

any such delightful diversions ... for this evening."

"I am heartily glad to hear you say so, my lord,"
Maxwell said as he slipped a gold-chained quizzing
glass over his master's head and stepped back to
see what his skilled hands had wrought. He was
not displeased.

"I took the liberty," said he, "of sorting your
lordship's mail. It is on your desk in the study. I
noticed a letter from the Reverend Otherby."

"Ah, good. Hopefully he has news of our new
school."

"Another school, sir?"

"For girls this time. Near Danforth. You can
never have too many schools ... particularly for
the indigent, Max."

"No, my lord."

Lord Blake scrutinized himself in his mirror.
"Splendid, Max. What would I do without you?"

"I shudder to think, my lord."

"You've had Scranton bring 'round my phaeton?" Lord Blake inquired, his lips trembling.

"It is ready at the door, my lord."

The marquess collected Sir William, and they
drove to Drury Lane, purchased their tickets, and
moved into the theater. Lord Blake forced himself
to bow and smile at the many acquaintances who
greeted him. Lord, how he hated such a show! He
spied Priscilla Inglewood in a box and bowed to her.
She inclined her golden head to him and then returned her attention to the throng of male admirers
vying for her attention. All were noble and well
heeled. Why the devil couldn't she marry one of
them and leave his conscience alone? Was Braxton
right? Was she waiting for him to make her the
next Duchess of Insley?

Lord Blake had never considered Lady Inglewood
as anything more than a family friend, yet ... in

many ways she would make the perfect wife: beautiful, elegant, imperturbable, knowing what to say and when to say it at each and every occasion . . . and she would not tug at his heart. He could go through the day without loving her or needing her; at night he could share her bed without longing; in the morning kiss her cheek at the breakfast table without thought. There would be no chance of pain in such a marriage. Perhaps . . . perhaps he should seriously consider fulfilling her ladyship's expectations . . . and those of her father.

The thought made him suddenly uneasy for he could not but admit that he found it distasteful for Priscilla to have turned from Oliver to him less than six months after Oliver's funeral. She had been steadfast ever since. "For the dukedom, not me," Lord Blake muttered. Could he really be married to such a mercenary? But then, what was the difference between all the other females on the marriage mart so vigorously pursuing him? Lord Blake sighed. Clearly this was a matter that required more thought.

Stepping into their box, which granted them the greatest freedom to see and to be seen by the rest of the audience, Lord Blake and Sir William removed their cloaks and took their seats.

"Well?" Lord Blake demanded as he crossed one well-formed leg over the other.

"I haven't seen her yet."

"I was not referring to Miss Fairfax!"

"What?"

"My coat, Will," Lord Blake said with a sigh. "What do you think of my new coat?"

"Oh," Sir William said, torn between amusement and his concern for finding Miss Fairfax, "it is . . . very handsome, Theo."

"Handsome? It is *magnificent*! It is Raoul De-Bries and myself at our best! The color brings out my eyes. The cut is extraordinary—notice the cut, Will—so exquisitely does it shape my shoulders and torso. Handsome, indeed! You won't find a better coat in all of London. Even Braxton can't match it."

"There!" Sir William suddenly cried in a hoarse voice. "She is there!"

He was pointing toward a box to their left that was jammed to overflowing by a good dozen male members of the *ton*. Through the crowd, however, they could clearly discern the rather distracted Miss Fairfax and her amused friend, Miss Glyn.

"Popular, isn't she?" Lord Blake commented wryly.

Sir William sank back into his seat. "With such wealthy and titled attendants schooled in all the arts of flattery, how can I hope to win her?"

"Now, now, Will," said the marquess, patting his disconsolate friend's arm. "You have money enough and a respectable title. What is more, you have twice the looks and thrice the character of any man in that box . . . particularly Lord Falkhurst. Don't give up the hunt before it has even started. Go after her, Will, with every means at your command. If you don't, she just may come after you."

"Theo! Do you think—"

"I do not think, lad," Lord Blake intoned, "I know."

A horn sounded just then, and the audience began to make their way to their seats in anticipation of the opening curtain. This headlong flight afforded Lord Blake an excellent opportunity for observing both Miss Fairfax and Miss Glyn.

Having conversed with her for less than an hour, Lord Blake knew the beautiful Miss Fairfax to be an intelligent, charming, sweet young woman, and he had been able to form this opinion of her after but a few moment's study of her face. Everything was revealed there. She was straightforwardly open and honest, an unusual phenomenon in either sex. It was easy to understand how William had been caught.

Lord Blake's scrutiny turned next to Miss Glyn, and he found a whimsical smile flicker across his lips. She was ... a highly unusual young woman and, unlike Miss Fairfax, was not at all transparent. You would not know her character merely by observing her face. Dark brown hair and eyes, slender nose, full lips ... they were nothing out of the ordinary. Her face and figure, presently revealed by a gown of red and brown silk that fell well off her shoulders, created an attractive, but certainly not arresting, whole. Yet Lord Blake could not take his eyes from her.

Miss Glyn possessed a highly developed sense of the whimsical and the boldness to express it which he could not but admire. Her mind, which his lordship judged far shrewder than she would ever publicly reveal, had almost an overabundance of imagination that she apparently employed for no other purpose than her own amusement.

On second thought, Lord Blake checked himself as he recalled the absurd things she had said of him and to him, perhaps she used her wit as a means of discovering what sort of fish she found herself in company with on any given occasion. Then again ...

Lord Blake stopped and shook his head with a smile. The simple truth was that he did not know *what* to make of Miss Glyn. He was intrigued by her, a state of being that in itself intrigued him, for the marquess seldom felt such interest in another human being. He had worked hard to make this so. Clearly Miss Glyn bore further investigation, if only to excise her from his thoughts.

The lights dimmed at that moment, and Lord Blake was forced to turn his eyes to the stage where the curtain was rising upon the overwrought machinations of the Capulets and the Montagues. At several points before the first curtain, he caught himself slipping into the grip of Morpheus and was forced to exert the utmost willpower to stay awake. If only there were some kindred soul to support him in this adversity! But, alas, Shakespeare's one error in judgment had a strong following. To his immediate right, Sir William sat breathing in every word of the play as if his very life depended upon it. Ah, well. Not everyone was as discerning as himself. Sir William had other admirable qualities.

To their left, Miss Fairfax sat in her box, leaning forward as if straining to catch every word, every emotion, every thought that the players sought to wring from Mr. Shakespeare's script. Then Lord Blake's eyes were caught by a movement to Miss Fairfax's left. He struggled to focus his gaze in the murky depths of the theater and was finally able to discern the figure of Miss Glyn, supine in her chair as her left hand lethargically waved a fan. Her right hand struggled to rise to stifle a yawn of immense proportions . . . but was too late.

The curtain fell at last, and the lights arose—with Sir William Atherton—for the intermission. Lord Blake regarded his companion suspiciously.

"You cannot be thinking," said he, "of leaving our box?"

"But this is the perfect opportunity to visit Miss Fairfax. Do get up, Theo. Her box is relatively empty just now."

"My dear William," said Lord Blake, arranging himself to best effect in his chair, "you must *never* leave your box. You must wait with a regal, world-weary expression for admirers to come to *you.*"

"Theo, don't talk such fustian," Sir William said in a quelling voice. "You said you had come to support me in my pursuit of Miss Fairfax."

"I came to display my new coat, Will, I thought that I was quite clear on that point this afternoon. Had I known that you intended to desert our box like some impetuous *cit*, I—"

"Theo," Sir William said, "that is quite enough. You're frightfully amusing on the whole, but this isn't the time for it! You must learn some restraint, Theo. Really you must. As your friend, I implore you to accompany me to Miss Fairfax's box. My future happiness might well be at stake!"

"Oh, very well," Lord Blake replied, sighing heavily. "If you must hold your declining years over my head—"

"No speeches now, Theo," Sir William said hurriedly as he pulled Lord Blake to his feet. "Her box is already filling!"

Pulled reluctantly from his warm, cozy box by his determined friend, the marquess soon found himself hailed from all sides by a wide variety of acquaintances as he was jostled, bumped, and pushed by the theater patrons. Slowly he and Sir William made their way forward. It seemed, thought his lordship, that Will was right to hurry. Already, Lord Falkhurst had installed himself at Miss Fairfax's side and was successfully fending off the approaching horde of admirers whilst engaging her in conversation.

A determined man, the Black Earl, and a ruthless one by all accounts. No wonder Miss Fairfax preferred the honest adoration of William to, as Peter had described him, that great block of ice.

Miss Fairfax's clear, musical laughter wafted over the heads before them. Sir William stumbled forward, bumped into two equally eager young gentlemen, and then began to painfully wend his way through the throng, endeavoring to catch Miss Fairfax's eye.

Observing his progress with growing amusement, Lord Blake decided that his services were no longer required. Miss Fairfax's overburdened box reminded him of nothing so much as an overfull stockyard, his coat would surely not escape it unscathed. He would find other means of entertainment.

At that moment his ears caught the sound of far from decorous female laughter. Looking for the source, Lord Blake spied Miss Glyn standing at the far end of the Fairfax box, her back to the stage as she leaned against the box banister, holding her sides as she observed the determined struggles of the young men before her. Without hesitation, Lord Blake circled the box and entered it from the far end.

"Good evening, Miss Glyn," he said with a slight bow.

Startled at being addressed, Miss Glyn turned her head, her large brown eyes growing wide as she recognized Lord Blake.

"The friend of a friend of a friend," she said coolly.

Lord Blake smiled at his title and her unwelcome. "Do you direct the pilgrimage to Miss Fairfax's side?"

"She is frightfully popular, isn't she?" Miss Glyn said good-humoredly. "The animalistic behavior of the adoring hordes takes a bit of getting used to, but now I find it quite diverting. Did you know, Lord Blake, that the vulgarity of the crowd rises in direct proportion to the exalted titles contained therein? I have been making a study."

"Fascinating," Lord Blake murmured. "Why, it is enough to dampen one's enthusiasm for one's exalted birth. Is this lonely vigil that I have just interrupted the only means you have of reaping the benefits of Miss Fairfax's popularity?"

"I believe you are trying to ask if I am always

shunted aside in this manner and left to my own devices."

"Well . . . the question did flicker across my somnolent brain, yes," Lord Blake replied.

"Then I shall answer you with a resounding yes! Nor, in answer to your next garbled question, would I have it otherwise. Miss Fairfax is left with bruised toes, a torn gown, and a beastly headache each time she endures such crushing devotion as is presently being enacted before you. It is enough to suppress all moral scruples and drive one to the brink of rudeness. Indeed, on one or two occasions I believe I have actually seen a martial gleam light Miss Fairfax's eyes. She was, however, able to restrain her baser instincts, more's the pity."

Lord Blake expressed his sympathy. "But why remove yourself from the fray? Should you not exert yourself to latch onto one of Miss Fairfax's rejects for a profitable trip to the altar?"

Miss Glyn laughed. It was warm and bubbly and tickled Lord Blake's spine.

"Bluntness becomes you, my lord. As it happens, I have no desire to drag any one of that herd to the church, for I don't want to marry. I find men to be occasionally amusing, but often irksome and always disappointing. I don't wish to put you to the blush, sir, but it is my experience that men are universally shallow and care only for the beauty and dowry of the women on whom they dance attendance."

Lord Blake's eyes widened. "I begin to lose all liking for myself. I must guess that you speak from experience, Miss Glyn."

"And observation."

"And so you will live a barren sister all your life, chanting faint hymns to the cold fruitless moon."

Miss Glyn tsked at Lord Blake. " 'Would it not grieve a woman to be overmastered with a piece of valiant dust? To make an account of her life to a clod of wayward marl?' "

Lord Blake sighed and shook his head. "I really must find a chink in your Shakespearean armor, or I'll be out of all charity with myself."

"Search all you like, I enjoy trouncing the nobility. That is a *very* handsome coat you are wearing!"

"It *is* wonderful, isn't it?" Lord Blake said happily.

"Simply stunning. I have not seen a better styled coat this entire season. Braxton will be green with envy. You quite cast him in the shade."

"You are too kind."

"Not at all. I am glad to discover one spark of light in the midst of such theatrical mediocrity. Whither has the glory of the English stage fled?"

"The Cotswolds," Lord Blake replied, "if tonight's performance is any indication. The players have somehow managed to make an already tiresome play interminable."

"I am glad to hear you say it," declared Miss Glyn. "Do you know, Lord Blake, you are the first person I have ever come across who has the good sense to dislike *Romeo and Juliet*?"

"What, you, too?" Lord Blake stared at Miss Glyn with both surprise and a growing pleasure.

"Yes, I am a sister sufferer of Shakespeare's overwrought pen. I must tell you, Blake, that meeting you here has quite rescued my evening. Hope once again wells within my breast. To think that there is a kindred soul filled with ennui when forced to endure hours of Shakespearean rodomontade! I begin to feel quite giddy."

"I am happy to be of service to you, Miss Glyn," Lord Blake said with a bow that effectively hid his smile.

"You have the power to do me another service, if you would."

"Anything to aid a sister sufferer," Lord Blake gallantly replied.

"Reassure me that Sir William Atherton is not in the throes of some silly infatuation that will burn off in a day."

"He claims to have suffered a mortal wound from Cupid's bow."

"Yes, I've had to listen to the same sort of idiotish pronouncements, too. How can you stick it?"

"By being grateful I am not in the same case."

Amusement lifted the corners of Miss Glyn's mouth. "Come tell me more about the mortally wounded Sir William."

"Why?"

Miss Glyn faltered and then rallied to say with great heartiness: "Well, why not? It would be great fun! You could tell me about his affair with the village vicar's wife, his several duels, his profiteering in the war, his many gaming debts, and his poor eye for horseflesh. Then *I* could tell you all my foolishly idealistic first impressions that you could brutally cut to ribbons, thus filling me with disillusionment and shame. *Then* you could recall a rich and dying uncle of his who is planning to leave him two million pounds, a North Sea seal, and some stock in an Indian pheasant-feather farm; and then *I* could give my blessing to the match, and everything would be as right as rain!"

Lord Blake stared at her, awestruck.

"Is something wrong, Lord Blake?" Miss Glyn inquired.

"Why have I not met you before?" he demanded.

"Good heavens, why should you have wanted to?" Miss Glyn retorted. "I am not beautiful. I am not rich. I am not even, at times, civil. I have just recollected, however, that I *am* the gatekeeper to Miss Fairfax's company. I can take you to her if you wish."

"How very nonsensical of you, Miss Glyn," Lord Blake chastized.

"My point exactly, Lord Blake."

"And what point is that, Miss Glyn?"

"Why, that it is nonsensical to wish to meet me when there are so many worthier females in the *ton* desperate to meet a gentleman with so well-fashioned a coat."

"Did you not earlier express that self-same desire?"

"Not at all. I expressed an appreciation at observing the coat, not meeting it."

"You are hard, Miss Glyn," Lord Blake said in a stifled voice.

"Not at all, merely condescending."

Lord Blake gave a shout of laughter that startled not only him, but several of his acquaintances nearby. "Thus is all of my consequence turned to dust," said he.

"*Have* you any consequence?"

"A good deal, I fear."

"Hence your association with Priscilla Inglewood. I am amazed you had the temerity to enter this box, my lord. Lady Inglewood will not thank you for it."

"Pray, what has she to say to this or any conversation I hold?"

"A good deal by all accounts. She'll think you disloyal for doing the niceties in the enemy camp, you mark my words."

"Ah," said Lord Blake, studying her through his quizzing glass, "so you are at war, then?"

"What a bacon-brained thing to say! *Women* do not engage in warfare. We indulge, at most, in an occasional skirmish . . . but the more blood we can draw, the better."

"My understanding of the feminine mind grows

at a riotous pace. What, besides Shakespeare, have
you to say against Lady Inglewood?"

"Why nothing, sir . . . in public."

"What, then, does she dislike in you?"

"Why everything, sir. Is that not obvious?"

Lord Blake contemplated the fashionable Miss
Glyn. "How so?"

"But can you not see that I am everything the
good lady abhors?"

"There may be something in that."

"Indeed, a plethora, I fear . . . but not enough to
make me think of reformation. Why are you talking with me, Lord Blake? You are being shockingly
disloyal. Lady Inglewood has a prior claim upon
your company. Should you not be thrilling her ear
with clever *bons mots*?"

"Alas, the lady does not think them at all clever.
She is a sensible woman, as you know."

"I know no such thing. How can she dislike the
true wit of an educated man? She sinks lower in
my estimation by the minute. How can you be loyal
to that iceberg?"

Lord Blake's gray eyes narrowed. "I am not so
hard as to withdraw my friendship from a good
woman suffering the unfortunate absence of a sense
of humor. I daresay, she dislikes you for your
whimsy."

"I wish you would not justify her dislike for me,
Lord Blake. Lady Inglewood and I are happy in our
animosity. She turns vermilion at the sight of me,
and I grow claws whenever in her presence. I refuse
to like her, sir. If you insist upon defending her to
me, I shall throw you out of this box at once."

That the threat was serious, Lord Blake had not
a doubt. How had mere words from Lady Inglewood
raised such animosity in Miss Glyn's breast?

"You amaze me, Miss Glyn. Every female in my
acquaintance seeks the pleasure of my company,

but you continually toss it aside like so much lemon meringue."

"Indeed? I confess a growing lack of confidence in the females of your acquaintance."

"Are you one of those women who delights in disparaging her own sex?"

"Pray do not insult me, Blake. I disparage those deserving of disparagement, whatever the sex. Any cradle friend of Lady Inglewood's must expect to come in for my severest frowns. Speaking of which, do but observe Lady Inglewood looking daggers at us."

Lord Blake turned to discover that Lady Inglewood was, indeed, glaring at them. He bowed to her, which she refused to acknowledge, going so far as to sweep around to give her smile to some fresh-faced attendant. So Miss Glyn had not overstated their feud? It was an interesting point.

"Be careful, Lord Blake, or you'll be turned to stone by Lady Perfection Incarnate."

"Who?"

"Priscilla Inglewood, of course."

Lord Blake gave a shout of laughter. "You are absurd, Miss Glyn."

"I am renowned throughout the *ton*," Miss Glyn said with a look of deep reproach, "for my propriety of thought."

"I am not such a gaby as to purchase such a declaration. You are too light-headed to be convincing."

"But not too light to cross swords with you," Miss Glyn retorted.

"We shall see," Lord Blake said with a smile. "Your servant, Miss Glyn."

A swift glance as he left the box informed Lord Blake that Sir William had reached Miss Fairfax's side relatively unscathed and held the whole of her attention. Making his way through the milling audience, Lord Blake pondered his conversation with Miss Glyn. Through all the whimsy she had held to her guns: she disliked Priscilla and wanted nothing to do with him. To which should he be loyal: his love of whimsical conversation, or a lifelong friend?

"Theo? Theo! I pray you come dance attendance on me."

Lord Blake looked up and discovered Lady Inglewood summoning him. He chose to obey, studying her as he made his way to her box. The only child of an avaricious earl, Lady Inglewood was a tall, beautiful blonde with commanding hazel eyes and a dowry of thirty thousand pounds. At four-and-twenty she should have married long ago. But for the death of his brother, Oliver, five years earlier, she would now be his sister-in-law. Because of the death of his brother, she might become his wife.

"Ah, Priscilla," said Lord Blake, raising her outstretched hand to his lips, "you grow more beautiful each time I see you."

"What flummery!" Lady Inglewood said with a pretty laugh. "For you know full well, Theo, that I am practically on the shelf!"

"Judging by the crush of admirers in your box, you will never have to view the world from such an unhappy vantage point."

"Yes, I daresay, I could have any of them I choose. But none are to my liking," said Lady Inglewood with a speaking glance at Lord Blake.

Lord Blake forced a smile. "You are too particular."

"Perhaps. But tell me, Theo, how long have you been in town and why have you not called on me?"

"I've been back less than a fortnight and have called on no one, my dear Priscilla, save a bunch of loutish men who indulge in cards and wine with gay abandon."

"I trust you will find more appropriate entertainment during the rest of your stay?"

"I believe I am now ready to sample a wider array of London's pleasures."

"Such as dining with father and me tomorrow night?"

"I shall count the hours," Lord Blake said with a bow.

The horn sounded, signaling the end of intermission. Lord Blake began to make his adieus, but Lady Inglewood's hand on his arm held him back.

"Just one more word, if you please, Theo," she said quietly. "I saw you speaking with Kate Glyn earlier. I would warn you off her, if you'll heed my advice."

Lord Blake regarded his cradle friend. "Am I to understand that I stand in some danger from Miss Glyn?"

"Oh, no, only from associating with the creature. She is not good *ton*, Theo. Her father was a country nobody, her mother a vicar's spawn. She insists on flying in the teeth of all respectability and convention, delighting in the shock she accords the arbiters of the *haut ton*."

"Indeed?" Lord Blake said, studying the stitching on his coat cuff. "And what of her friend, Miss Fairfax?"

"Oh, Miss Fairfax is quite unexceptional! No one can say a word against her. It is a great pity that the Egertons saddled her with so inappropriate a chaperone as Kate Glyn, for her character only harms her charge. Miss Glyn seems to have pulled the wool over their eyes."

"But not yours, I take it, Priscilla?"

Lady Inglewood's smile was condescending. "I believe I understand a good deal that goes on below the surface of the *ton*."

"We have all noted your perspicacity," Lord

Blake agreed, made his adieus, and returned to his box with a sigh.

Well, that had done it; his back was up. The marquess would be the first to admit to stubbornness. He had now been warned off thrice from Kate Glyn's company: once by Priscilla Inglewood and twice by Miss Glyn. Loyalty to Lady Inglewood warred with his dislike of having his friendships ordered to suit others. Certainly, he should heed Miss Glyn's wishes and forbear from pushing their acquaintance further, but the stubbornness in him wanted to make her like him in spite of herself. He had little time to ponder why he should care whether Miss Glyn liked him or not, for he was joined a moment later by an ebullient Sir William Atherton, who, in greeting, sighed rapturously as he sank into his chair.

"A second view of my coat has left you with a higher opinion, I see," Lord Blake drawled.

"An angel, an absolute angel," Sir William said as he stretched happily in his chair.

"Raoul DeBries is a genius, I will grant him that. But an angel?"

"So sweet-tempered, so charming, so lovely."

"William," Lord Blake said severely, "do you know something of DeBries that I do not?"

"Who?" Sir William asked, startled from his reverie.

Lord Blake cheerfully consigned his friend to perdition and asked him what progress he had made with Miss Fairfax.

"Theo," Sir William declared, "I am in love!"

Chapter 6

HAVING RETURNED THE enraptured Sir William to his lodgings following the dismal conclusion of *Romeo and Juliet*, Lord Blake turned his grays toward Grosvenor Square and his ancestral home. He pulled his team to a stop before the front walk, handed the reins to his tiger, Scranton, and then jumped to the ground and strolled toward the front door.

He paused.

This was harder than he had thought. A conscience was a miserable possession. He had avoided his family for nearly a year, not because he disliked them, but because he loved them too well. He feared the happiness love brought. He feared the love waiting beyond this door, and wished he was a coward so he could avoid this meeting.

But, alas, he was not a coward.

One slight tug on the bell, and the door was opened by Hamilton, the Insley butler for the last seventeen years.

"Hello, Hamilton, old bean," Lord Blake said as he stepped into the entrance hall.

"Lord Blake!" Hamilton gasped. "Is it really you, sir?"

"Well put, Hamilton," Lord Blake replied as he handed his hat, many-caped greatcoat, and gloves to the butler. "I gather that is a subtle hint of the parental censure I am about to endure. A wayward son's lot is not a happy one, Hamilton."

"No, my lord."

"The duke and duchess in the front drawing room?"

"Yes, my lord."

"Well, I'll just go announce myself, then."

Lord Blake sauntered off to the drawing room. He stopped before the double doors, threw them open with a flourish, stepped into the room, and announced in ringing tones to the startled occupants: "Behold! The return of the prodigal son!"

Having glanced up, the Duchess of Insley returned to the letter she was writing from her place on a dark gold settee. "Who is it, Fitzgerald?" she asked her husband. "Anyone we know?"

Suitably chastised, Lord Blake strode to the duchess, took her hand in his, kissed it, and said: "*Maman*, you grow more adorable with each passing day."

"Nine months and three days, to be precise," said the duchess.

"Just so," Lord Blake replied with a smile at this chilly welcome from his devoted mother.

The Duke of Insley, a tall man of fifty-six years, was seated at the oak desk near the garden window. "Well, Theo, have you no greeting for your father?"

"Your pardon, *Pater*," Lord Blake said with a grin. "Beauty before duty and all that." He advanced to the duke and raised his quizzing glass to one eye. "A new coat, I see. And very handsome it is, too. Have you finally taken my advice and left that club-fisted Wilmington for someone of more refined tastes?"

"I'll have you know that Wilmington made this for me only last week!"

"Really?" Lord Blake raised one brow. "Well, one

must always make allowances for an occasional gaffe."

The duke chuckled. "It's good to see you, son."

Lord Blake bowed.

"If you must insist on reminding us of your existence, do not stand there in idle chit chat, Theodore," the duchess intoned. "Come and tell me about yourself."

"Theo, Mother," Lord Blake said with a pained expression on his handsome face as he sat on the sofa opposite her. "Theo, I implore you. I had no voice in your atrocious selection of my Christian name, but I do have some say in what I am called in my adulthood."

"Theodore was your grandfather's name," said the duchess with some severity.

"And he hated it just as much as I do. Told me once it reminded him of a squirrel."

The duke's chuckle was hurriedly followed by a cough.

"As we have not heard from you in nearly a year," the duchess said, with a quelling glance at her errant husband, "may we assume that you have been idle?"

"Mother, I protest!" Lord Blake said, rising from the sofa. "How can you think such a thing after viewing my newest coat? Mark my words, *this* will be the model against which all others shall be compared and found lacking."

His lordship struck several dramatic poses to show the coat to its full advantage, before returning to his seat.

"It is a very handsome coat," the duchess conceded, struggling against the smile that lurked at the corner of her lips. "But enough of this foolishness. We have gone nine months without your company or any word of your continued existence. What news have you for us, Theo? What news?"

69

Lord Blake adjusted the lace at his wrist. "The Ganymede has become *de rigueur* among the London tulips after but a week and a half of existence. Bingsley has a decided hit, there can be no doubt. The Prince Regent lost a wager with the Duke of Richmond and was forced to subsist on nothing but cucumbers and water for a week. Lady Lacson is propounding pineapple and cherry puree for age spots, while—"

"Theo," the duke interrupted, "we do not wish to hear the latest *on-dits*. We wish to hear real and concrete news of you and your activities. Kindly drop the mask for a few moments and give your parents a little pleasure in their declining years."

"I had hoped this madness would have left you by now," said the duchess. "I should have known by your absence that it had not. If you continue this charade much longer, Theo, you may lose forever the man you once were."

"It would be a blessing," said her son.

"I liked that man," the duke said, "and I'd like to hear what he's been doing with himself since his last brief visit."

"Yes," said the duchess with some impatience, "have you been happy? Have you been lonely? Have you been well?"

Lord Blake sighed, leaned back against the sofa, and stretched his long legs out before him. "I toured Rosebriar and Danforth these last few months," he replied instead. "Fredericks has done an excellent restoration job on Rosebriar Manor. Best shape its been in in years. He's gone ahead with some of the experiments we discussed last year, and we should have a bumper crop."

The duke joined his wife, his hand clasping hers and giving it a reassuring squeeze.

"With the war," Lord Blake continued, "that means an excellent profit despite the heavy outlay for new equipment and the greenhouses we used to test the new seed. Llewellyn took me all over Danforth. The flocks are in excellent shape. We lost very few lambs. I am looking into a copper mine in Cornwall and a dairy in Hertfordshire; I have been experiencing the need of late to expand my interests."

"Do you think it wise to invest in a copper mine, Theo?" the duchess inquired. "The market has been depressed these last two years. You could easily lose your shirt."

"I have many shirts, Mother. I doubt if I should mind losing one. Unless it should be the blue silk, of course. Life would be devoid of all meaning if I lost the blue silk."

"And what of your friends, Theo?" the duke inquired.

"I think they could withstand the blow, although Braxton would undoubtedly be most distraught for at least a se'ennight. He is quite partial to blue silk."

"I *meant*, what has happened to them recently?"

"Ah! There I have you," Lord Blake replied, sitting up with an air of excitement, "for I bring you gossip of the ripest variety. William Atherton has proclaimed himself this very day to be madly in love. You would not know him. He has become a model of moonstruck manhood, a veritable fool."

"Theo, stop being so cynical," the duchess commanded, "and tell us with whom Sir William is in love!"

"But of course. She is one Miss Georgina Fairfax: beautiful, intelligent, charming, and possessed of some wit."

"Georgina Fairfax?" the duchess exclaimed. "Good God, he *is* sunk!"

"That *was* my impression," Lord Blake said with a smile.

"Has he any hope of success, do you think, Theo?" the duke asked.

"Some, I believe," Lord Blake replied. "Certainly that is the impression formed by her chaperone, a quizzling named Glyn."

"Katharine Glyn?" the duchess demanded.

"Yes. Do you know her?"

"No," the duchess said, "only of her. She is a favorite with Lady Jersey and Lady Montclair, although Priscilla Inglewood has little good to say of her."

"Miss Glyn is under a similar handicap with regards to Priscilla," Lord Blake commented. "Miss Glyn is an odd creature, very different from Miss Fairfax. Will and I called on them only this morning. It was Will who called on Miss Fairfax, actually. I was brought along for moral support and then left to the tender mercies of Miss Glyn. You know, I quite began to fear for my life. She violently struck Lord Falkhurst with a most resounding lack of conscience."

"Good heavens," said the duke. "Why would she do such a thing?"

"She said that she had always wanted to do so."

"Brava!" the duchess trumpeted. "It was long overdue."

"You speak in riddles, Mother," said Lord Blake, "and have me quite agog. Explain yourself. I hang on your lips."

"Falkhurst and Katharine Glyn were betrothed when she was but fifteen," the duchess said. "It was all arranged by their families. The old earl was keen on bringing the Glyn lands, which were substantial, into the Falkhurst fold. Cartloads of money were involved, of course. However, Miss Glyn's father died the following year and one week to the day after the funeral, young Falkhurst broke the engagement and went off on a hunting trip to Wales."

"Now that you mention it, I do recall that little

drama," the duke said. "There was a good deal of ill-feeling against Falkhurst at the time. The club gave him a cold shoulder whenever he came through the door."

"But why end the engagement?" Lord Blake asked, curiosity supplanting the mask for the moment. "With the father out of the way, Falkhurst had only to marry Miss Glyn to immediately claim all the Glyn lands."

"On the contrary," the duchess replied, "Falkhurst learned that the bulk of Glyn's estate went to a first cousin in York or some such heathenish place, should Miss Glyn be unmarried at the time of her father's death. A betrothal of long-standing was not considered a mitigating circumstance. She was left a comfortable income but no lands and certainly no title to bring to her fiancé. There was nothing to lure the pride of a Falkhurst."

"Very bad *ton*," the duke harrumphed. "I never liked the fellow. I'm glad to hear Miss Glyn struck back."

"And so there *is* reason to her madness," Lord Blake murmured as he studied the tip of one gleaming boot.

"Well, my dear," said the duchess to her son, "now that you have returned to town, may we hope to see something of you? Will you come to dinner tomorrow night?"

"I must cry off, fair *Maman*. Priscilla Inglewood has a prior claim on my stomach."

"What, have you called on her before seeing your own parents?" the duchess said.

"No, no, 'twas sheer chance that we met. I've just come from Drury Lane, you see. Priscilla is quite as beautiful as ever . . . and still unmarried. Shall I remedy that faux pas, do you think?"

His parents stared with growing consternation at their son.

"Are you serious, Theo?" said the duke. "Do you mean to marry Priscilla?"

"The thought has occurred to me." Lord Blake leaned back against the sofa and studied the gold work of his quizzing glass. "It has recently been pointed out to me that I am getting on in years. It is time to marry and have children. I know my duty."

"You have always known your duty, Theo," the duchess said quietly, "but is Priscilla the right wife for you?"

Startled, Lord Blake dropped his quizzing glass and sat up. "But, Mother, she is exemplary, all the world knows it! Oliver meant to marry her, and you know his taste was always excellent. Besides, she will do as well as any other, and she is certainly more deserving than most. She might already be contemplating her happy succession into duchessdom had it not been for my stupidity."

"Misplaced guilt and obligation are no reasons to marry, Theo," the duke said.

"I know the Insleys always marry well, but your father and I are not so severe," said the duchess. "You might marry for love, my dear."

"I think not," Lord Blake said dryly.

"Well do not, I pray you, rush into a marriage you might soon regret," the duke said. "Think on it a while longer, Theo."

"Don't you want me to marry and produce the requisite heir and a spare?" Lord Blake asked.

"We want you to be happy, Theo," the duchess said.

"That," her son retorted, "is not possible."

*

Chapter 7

HAVING CAJOLED THE Egertons, Miss Fairfax's aunt and uncle, into issuing an invitation to Sir William for their forthcoming ball, Miss Glyn then drove Miss Fairfax in her phaeton to visit the Pomeroy sisters. Her father had placed her on a horse soon after she learned to walk. She demanded that he teach her to drive a few years later and, amused by her precocity, he had obliged. There had been an uproar when she had first driven through Hyde Park at the tender age of eighteen, but the scandal had quickly evolved into fashion as several young ladies of the *ton* (refusing to be cast in the shade by a country drab) began to imitate her startling accomplishment. A few could manage a gig or curricle, none, however, could drive a team of horses, for none had Miss Glyn's skill, and so they returned to the comfort and safety of their coachman's services. Miss Glyn, however, continued to make her calls driving her own phaeton, continued to elicit several shocked stares every day she did so, and was contentedly aware of them all.

It was a fine, temperate March afternoon. The winter had been mild, and, while the first blossoms of spring had yet to appear, there was a tinge of warmth to the air that promised rain showers rather than snow showers in the coming weeks.

"Look at Chaucer's and Cervantes' ears," Miss

Glyn said, indicating the painfully alert ears of her team. "They are just dying for a mad romp."

"I pray you will convince them of the impropriety of such an action," Miss Fairfax nervously replied.

"Why, where's your sense of adventure, Georgie?"

"It flees whenever confronted by hairy, four-legged monsters."

"I think it very magnanimous of me to like you despite your aversion to horses," Miss Glyn commented as she skillfully maneuvered between a London to Bath day coach and a fat barouche. "I had not realized I had so noble a character."

They turned onto the Promenade and made their way down that fashionable thoroughfare at a leisurely trot, stopping occasionally to chat with an acquaintance before pressing on.

Suddenly Miss Fairfax gripped her friend's arm and shouted in her ear: "Kate, *stop*!"

Miss Glyn was so shocked by this attack that she jerked violently upon the ribbons, which set Chaucer and Cervantes to rearing up in their traces. This left Miss Fairfax quaking with terror despite the fact that Miss Glyn had made a quick recover and had the team under control but a moment after the furor had begun.

"Would you be so kind, Georgina," said Miss Glyn through gritted teeth, "as to tell me just *what* you are going on about? There, there, Chaucer," she said to the quivering bay. "It's all right, Cervantes. Steady on, old thing."

"I am so dreadfully sorry, Kate," Miss Fairfax said with great sincerity, her heartbeat returning to a calmer pace. "It is just that I observed Sir William approaching and wished to have a word with him."

"Atherton?" ejaculated Miss Glyn. Looking up for the first time since their *petite aventure* began, Miss

Glyn spied Sir William—horror stamped upon his handsome brow—mounted on a chestnut and accompanied by Lord Blake, who sat astride a magnificent dappled Thoroughbred. His lordship quickly went up several notches in Miss Glyn's estimation for having so good an eye for horseflesh. As for Sir William, however: "He is quickly becoming far more trouble than he is worth," she muttered.

The two gentlemen advanced to Miss Fairfax's side of the phaeton and pulled to a stop.

"Miss Fairfax, are you all right?" the ashen Sir William demanded.

"Oh, of course," Miss Fairfax said quickly, but with a most becoming smile of welcome. "There was no danger, and it was really all my own fault. It was so foolish of me. I startled Chaucer and Cervantes without thinking."

"Who?" Lord Blake inquired.

"Katharine's bays," Miss Fairfax explained.

"Miss Glyn's?" Lord Blake said, startled, for the animals were prime specimens of flesh and blood.

"Raised them from pups," Miss Glyn said with a grin. It came to her that she always felt like smiling in Lord Blake's presence, and that this was a dangerous weakness on her part. There were too many damning facts lodged at Blake's door for her to be happy in his presence. She removed the smile from her face.

"But how can you say there was no danger?" Sir William demanded. "Those great beasts could have easily gotten their heads and gone careening down the street to God knows what horrible end!"

"Steady on, Will, steady on," Lord Blake murmured.

"But there was no danger, Sir William," Miss Fairfax reiterated. "Katharine is an excellent

77

driver. She was in control the entire time. It was a magnificent piece of work."

"Thank you, Georgina," Miss Glyn said gravely.

"Your pardon, Miss Glyn," Sir William said stiffly, "but I cannot think it wise for two young women to go driving about London by themselves. The occasions for trouble or injury are too many."

Observing the color rise in Miss Glyn's cheeks while a dangerous gleam lit her brown eyes, Lord Blake broke in quickly with as soothing a voice as possible.

"I think my overbold young friend does have a point," he said. "I know it is the fashion in recent years for young women to drive themselves about, but simply because it is the fashion does not necessitate conformance. Wasp-waisted corsets are currently the fashion for some gentlemen of the *ton*, yet you would never see me effect such a mad-brained style."

"Theo, I don't think—" Sir William began.

"Now," Lord Blake blithely continued, "if you had the acknowledged skill of the Hampshire Hoyden, I would feel no qualms in the matter, but since you are not she and since you *are* driving about the most idolized young woman in London, I think it best that—"

"But Lord Blake," Miss Glyn interrupted with wide eyes and a guileless expression, "I *am* the Hampshire Hoyden."

There was a moment of stunned silence.

"What?" demanded Lord Blake while Sir William stared at Miss Glyn in utter disbelief.

"Tell them, Georgie," Miss Glyn said, nudging her friend.

"Kate, you know how I detest that nickname," Miss Fairfax said.

"Oh, but it is so very colorful," Miss Glyn pouted, "and I spent so many hours thinking it up and then convincing the Pomeroys to tell everyone of it. How can you say you detest it?"

Lord Blake, recalling all the outrageous stories he had heard about Hampshire's most famous export to London ... and all the outrageous things Miss Glyn had said and done in their brief acquaintance, felt the scales fall from his eyes.

"Of *course* you are the Hampshire Hoyden," he breathed. "I should have known it from the beginning. This is a story to tell my grandchildren. To actually have met the Hampshire Hoyden ... !"

A red-faced Sir William stammered his apologies to Miss Glyn, which she calmly accepted.

"Now that we are all in each other's good graces once again," said Miss Glyn, "I must inform you, Sir William, that you are to expect an invitation to the Egerton ball."

"You will come, won't you?" Miss Fairfax asked.

"Only if you promise to attend as well, Miss Fairfax," Sir William replied.

"I think," Miss Glyn dryly commented as Miss Fairfax became suffused in a pretty blush, "that you can be fairly certain of Georgina's attendance."

"May I hope you had a hand in issuing my invitation, Miss Fairfax?" Sir William inquired with what that young lady considered an overwhelmingly charming smile.

"I may have made the request," she replied, "but it was Katharine's argument that swayed my aunt and uncle."

"Then I am deeply in your debt, Miss Glyn," Sir William said with a bow.

"Can it be," Lord Blake said in wonder to Miss Glyn, "that you not only got someone to listen to your nonsensical notions, but to agree to them as well? I would not have thought such a thing possible."

"Had you any respectable connections in the *ton*,

Lord Blake—aside from Sir William, of course—you would undoubtedly have heard me praised for an intelligent and well-ordered mind that far exceeds the limitations of my sex."

"I really must get around more," Lord Blake laconically replied, "for I only hear such praise from you."

Miss Glyn's brown eyes narrowed. Shakespeare rose in her defense. " 'There's neither honesty, manhood, nor good fellowship in thee.' "

Knowing the onset of a quotational duel when he heard one, Lord Blake retorted, " 'Thou art the Mars of malcontents.' "

" 'I am nothing if not critical.' "

" 'Tis not my speeches that you do mislike, but 'tis my presence that doth trouble ye. Rancor will out.' "

Miss Glyn's stunning retort was frozen on her lips by an imperious female voice.

"Theo! How fortunate to come on you like this."

An ornate barouche pulled beside and a little forward of Miss Glyn's phaeton. Lady Priscilla Inglewood, in a fetching pink pelisse, leaned out the window.

"Your servant, Priscilla," Lord Blake said with a bow and a smile.

"You have not forgotten your pledge to dine with us tonight?"

"I am counting the minutes."

"Father is most looking forward to your company, for you know he prizes your skill at piquet above all others. He adjured me not to be a rattle-pate at dinner and chase you off before he had had a chance to take your measure over a deck of cards."

"Now Priscilla," said Lord Blake, holding back a sigh. He detested the Inglewood card table, for it carried with it the earl's open hints of future matrimonial bliss betwixt their two houses, "All the world knows you are the furthest thing from a rattlepate. And how should I be chased away from such charming company as yours? I am not such a ninnyhammer. You know Miss Glyn and Miss Fairfax, I believe?"

"Yes, of course," Lady Inglewood replied. "How are you, Miss Fairfax?"

"Horrendously late to an appointment," Miss Glyn broke in. "You will excuse us? It was wonderful running into you, Sir William. We really must press on, however. I am sure I speak for Miss Fairfax when I say that we look forward to seeing you on Tuesday night."

"It will be a distinct pleasure," Sir William replied as Miss Glyn set her bays to a trot.

Lord Blake's cheerfully doffed hat was passed by with only the slightest of nods by Miss Glyn, her air decidedly frosty. Oh dear. Had he deprived himself forever of her amusing company by publicly speaking with the enemy camp?"

"Poor Miss Fairfax," said Lady Inglewood with a sigh, "to be forced into company with so rude a duenna. You will remember what I said last night, Theo, and not cultivate an acquaintance with Miss Glyn?"

"I remember well what you said, Priscilla. 'Twas a very apt description of the Hampshire Hoyden."

"An atrocious nickname, isn't it, and yet it suits Miss Glyn very well, I think. I shall see you tonight, Theo," she said, and then ordered the coachman to drive on.

Lord Blake stared after her.

Miss Fairfax, meanwhile, was taking her friend to task.

"Kate, how could you be so rude as to drive off like that?"

"We said our good-byes with great formality, I thought."

"You slighted Lady Inglewood, however you care to phrase it."

"Good."

Miss Fairfax sighed. "I don't know why you dislike each other so."

"I have told you before, Georgie, I dislike anyone who is perfect, and Priscilla is—"

"Perfection Incarnate. Yes, I know. But why cannot you laugh her off as you do everyone else?"

"It is an old story, best forgotten."

"Tell me anyway."

"Georgina—"

"*Kate.*"

Miss Glyn sighed heavily. "When I was sixteen, and had the great misfortune to be betrothed to Bertie Falkhurst, I attended a summer ball as his family's guest. Priscilla was there. As she had lived most of her life in London, and I all of my life in Hampshire, she was far more sophisticated than I, though a year younger in age, and for some reason took a perverse pleasure in repeatedly humiliating me before the entire company. I was quite green, you know, and forever saying and doing the wrong things in such distinguished company, so she had a great deal of opportunity for sport. She continued in the same manner during my first London Season. It is hard to forgive such ... unkindness, harder still to give up engaging her in battle, for there is such satisfaction in besting her. And now, of course, the battle is quite fierce, for I am your closest friend."

Miss Fairfax goggled. "What?" she gasped, her hand seizing Miss Glyn's arm and pulling her to a stop. "Katharine, what can you mean?"

Regretting her words the moment they had been spoken, Miss Glyn tried to pass off the comment, but Miss Fairfax was determined to understand her.

"It is quite simple, Georgina," Miss Glyn said

quietly, "Lady Perfection was the shining light of the *ton* from her debut, but this season has seen her supplanted by your much more charming self, and she resents the demotion. She simply reeks of jealousy."

"Yes, I know. But what has that to do with you?"

"Georgina," Miss Glyn said with a fond smile, "everyone knows that it is impossible to dislike you. Priscilla would find herself in instant disfavor if she let her hostility toward you show openly, so she attempts to attack you through me. As I am the nearest to you, I am the easiest means of doing you harm."

"How awful!" the tenderhearted Miss Fairfax cried. "How abominable that you should be used in such a fashion."

"My dear Georgina," Miss Glyn replied with real amusement, "I do not mind it in the least. In fact, I relish our animosity. It is so tiring being sweet and patient and kind to everyone. It does me a world of good to vent my spleen on such a deserving creature. She cannot hurt me, for I care naught for what she values, and I get a bit of fun in now and then for my own entertainment, so rest easy."

"Oh Kate, I feel wretched over this business."

"There is no need," Miss Glyn replied warmly. "Just you mind your step around dear Lady Perfection. She has the ability to do you a good deal of harm if given the opportunity."

"Kate, you cannot be serious."

"I am in deadly earnest, Georgina. She is a dangerous woman, despite the lovely facade. 'You had best beware her sting.'"

"Shakespeare again," Miss Fairfax said with a rueful smile. "Oh, you bluestockings."

"As it happens, the paraphrase was most apt. Lady Perfection's sting lies in her adder's tongue, which can spread the most malicious of tales at will. Mark me in this, Georgina."

"I will, Katharine, I will," Miss Fairfax replied, laughing.

Miss Glyn was not reassured.

Chapter 8

LORD BLAKE WISHED that he had thought to include
a fan in his wardrobe for the Egerton ball. His jaws
were aching with the need to yawn in the face of
the tedious attentions of a strident mamma and her
two vapid daughters who were, on their oath, simply overwhelmed to be making his lordship's acquaintance. They trusted the duke and duchess
were well? They tittered at whatever he said. The
strident mamma was astonished to learn his lordship was not to attend the Wraxton ball later that
week, for the Wraxtons were frightfully good *ton*
and were particularly fond of her two vapid daughters.

With a limp excuse, Lord Blake escaped, only to
be captured by one of his father's oldest friends and
regaled with an ardent recitation of a day of hunting. His lordship was unsure, as Sir William Atherton hurried up to him, if he should be grateful for
this potential rescue from fondly recalled muck and
mire, for Sir William's eyes were glazed with unbridled infatuation.

Deciding that he had heard his fill of romantic
twaddle from Sir William, Lord Blake quickly cut
short the hunting story and absconded, immersing
himself in the crowd so that no one who sought him
could find him. Although grateful to be swallowed
whole by the titular masses, his lordship found,
upon looking around him, only tedium at best, ir-

ritation at worst. He could discuss the most recent bouts at Jackson's with the pack of Corinthians before him, the latest court *on-dits* with Lady Jersey's followers on his right. He might partake of an endless game of cards in the Egerton salons reserved for that purpose, or cast his fate to the winds and give himself over to the matchmaking mammas.

He wanted to tilt back his head and roar with frustration, bitterness, and loneliness. Nearly four hundred people were crammed into the Egerton home, and the ache in his soul only grew stronger. Seeking relief, Lord Blake turned to the devoted couple near the large potted palm on his left.

"Greetings charming parents," his lordship called as he strolled up to the elegant duo. "Evening Your Grace," he said with a bow to his father. "You're looking well, despite all of Wilmington's efforts at sabotage."

"I'll have you know, Theo," the duke retorted, "that I am in the very pink of fashion."

"Just so," Lord Blake murmured with a smile. "Dearest Mother," he cried, turning to the duchess, "you are simply magnificent. You should always wear that shade of midnight blue. It brings out the color of your eyes to perfection."

"My dear son," the duchess replied, allowing Lord Blake to kiss her cheek, "to see you twice in one week has quite thrilled my aging heart."

"Fustian, *Maman*, your heart is as young as springtime. Sprites and elves caper at your heels. Speaking of which, I have astounding news: I have met the Hampshire Hoyden."

"No!" said the duke. "How marvelous for you! I've heard she's the best pair of hands in London. She could even give you a run for your money, Theo, if you ever engaged her in a carriage race to Brighton."

"I'll have to propose it," Lord Blake said with a

smile. "Miss Glyn has already displayed a remarkable ability with the ribbons. I think I had best wager carefully."

"Miss Glyn?" said the duchess. "The Fairfax chaperone?"

"She and the Hampshire Hoyden are one and the same."

"Indeed?" said the duchess. "Then she is undoubtedly here tonight. You will introduce us, Theo."

"That may be difficult. She insists on severing the connection."

"Why is that?" asked the duke.

"She dislikes my title and my friendship with Priscilla Inglewood."

"Indeed?" said the duchess. "My interest in the Hampshire Hoyden grows by leaps and bounds. You may sever the connection, Theo, *after* you have introduced us."

"Yes, Mother," Lord Blake said with a bow. "I will do all in my power to present her in the most amusing light." He began his search for the unsuspecting Miss Glyn.

She had enjoyed two country dances, one waltz, and three very boring conversations at the Egerton ball when she found herself standing beside Miss Fairfax, who was, for the moment, unaccountably bereft of male companionship. They spoke quietly together, Miss Fairfax complaining of the excessive flattery she had recently suffered in the company of four different suitors.

"What, jaded so soon?" a cool voice inquired from behind the two women. They turned to behold a beautiful young woman in dampened green muslin. Her head was a mass of blond curls that skillfully set off her oval face and long, slender neck.

"Lady Perfection!" Miss Glyn exclaimed with

87

every aspect of pleasure. "Now I understand the chill in the air."

Miss Fairfax quickly intervened. "What a lovely gown, Priscilla!" she exclaimed. "I've not seen another like it. How flattering it is to you, and what a superb design. I quite envy you. I feel cast into the shade by comparsion."

Lady Inglewood, who agreed with this assessment, replied: "It is, based upon one of my original designs. Mrs. Foote was good enough to make it up for me."

"How fortunate you are. I have longed to have Mrs. Foote make me a dress, but she is in such demand that I have had to be put on a waiting list."

"How very unfortunate," Lady Inglewood said with a smile, for it was she who had threatened Mrs. Foote with utter ruin if she so much as executed a handkerchief, let alone a gown, for Georgina Fairfax. "You have heard, I suppose, that last night at Lady Jersey's rout the Viscount Chamberlin proposed to me in front of the prince, the Duke of Insley, and Lady Jersey. My father, unfortunately, opposed the match, and so I gave my regrets to the viscount. He was quite crushed. I felt so sorry for the poor boy."

"What a sad thing to have to spurn so romantic and worthy an offer," said Miss Fairfax.

"And what a lucky thing for Chamberlin," murmured Miss Glyn.

"Indeed, Georgina," said Lady Inglewood, "it was sad to refuse so flattering a proposal, but I have had at least a dozen like offers. And, of course, Insley's heir is interested in offering for me. My father tells me he anticipates receiving Lord Blake's addresses before the month is out (Miss Glyn stared at this). The Insleys are old family friends, so I cannot believe that my father waits in vain. I can only hope that you will somehow contrive to receive half so flattering an offer, Georgina."

Even Miss Fairfax's eyes widened at such a cut, but it was Miss Glyn, fury already shrieking within her, who entered the lists on her friend's behalf.

"There is little to support such a hope, Lady Perfection, for Georgina will marry for love, not a title and a cold, ornate crypt to house her on her death. Mind you, I quite see the suitability of placing *you* there. Will it take long, I wonder, for the marquess to find someone to warm the sheets you will chill? He has a reputation, does he not, for acquiring lightskirts the way some men buy shoes."

Lady Inglewood's fan snapped closed in her hands. "Eight seasons in town have failed to improve you, I see. You are still the rough country hoyden with more poison than wit. You may deceive others in the *ton* with your insolent ways, but not me. I'll not stand here and be insulted by the common offspring of a country drunkard!"

She stormed off.

"Kate, how could you?" Miss Fairfax gasped.

"Odious, monstrous man!" Miss Glyn stormed. "How dare he make me like him when he is on the point of taking Priscilla to his marriage bed!"

"Kate, what are you talking of?"

"*Blake!* He is heir to the Duke of Insley—good God, *Insley*—and he is Priscilla's expectation. The blackguard should be shot!"

"But why does this upset you? What do you care who Lord Blake weds?"

Miss Glyn stopped and then smiled at her friend. "Bless your sensible nature, Georgina. You are quite right. The minute Lady Perfection is married off, we shall enjoy peace once again. Let her have her marquess, it will serve him right."

Sir William chose this moment to approach his Aphrodite and claim her for the next dance. Miss

Fairfax tripped gaily away, leaving her friend to glower in peace.

She was not left alone for long. Lord Blake signaled his parents to follow him, strode quickly up to Miss Glyn, and was halfway into his bow when she burst forth.

"You!" she hissed. "You ... you monster!" and here she stamped her foot.

"I?" said Lord Blake, taking a step back in the face of so much fury.

"Heir to Insley, pet to Inglewood! *How* could I have wasted an entire week of my time on you?"

Lord Blake regarded her from under hooded eyes. "My curiosity grows by leaps and bounds at every conversation with you. Have you something against the ancient and noble house of Insley?"

Miss Glyn snorted. "I deride your ancient house you ... you *reprobate*. I have fallen into stupidity of the lowest order, thinking some simpering heir to Insley could be anything more than ... than a disagreeable *annoyance*."

"As I think on it," said Lord Blake, studying his gleaming fingernails, "I don't believe I have ever simpered in my life."

Miss Glyn was startled into a laugh.

Lord Blake smiled down at her. "There, that is much better. I like your laugh, Miss Glyn, for there is honesty in it and good humor, when you aren't glowering at me."

"I pray you, Blake, do not make me laugh when I abominate you."

Thinking Miss Glyn needed little help in amusing his eavesdropping parents, he retorted: "You cannot be so cruel as to abominate a fate I did not choose."

"Nonsense. You choose Lady Inglewood quite freely."

"I meant," said Lord Blake with some severity, "my father's estate."

"You needn't worry about *that*. Lady Inglewood means to have it."

"There! That is exactly why I insist on talking to you. Oblige me by answering a riddle."

"I have no desire to become Queen of England, stab my eyes out, and wander about the country in rags, thank you."

Lord Blake paused. "There are some," he observed, "who would be quite shocked by your knowledge of *Oedipus Rex* for I believe it to be the height of impropriety for a lady's delicate mind to be sullied by such antique literature."

"Flummery!" Miss Glyn paused. "Actually, I don't believe I have ever had a delicate mind to be sullied. Have I thereby missed a choice piece of entertainment?"

Lord Blake smiled. "I don't believe you would ever miss a chance for ... entertainment, Miss Glyn."

"But I have the whole of this last se'ennight! Oh, the fun I have missed. Well, I shall just have to abuse you with a good deal more warmth from now on."

"But I do not quite understand," Lord Blake said, manfully controlling his laughter. "Why must you abuse me simply because I am a marquess?"

"My treatment of people descends in direct proportion to their elevation in society, for you may be sure that the higher one sits in the *ton*, the more useless one becomes—your excellent wardrobe not withstanding. I would not give a ha'penny for the entire English peerage even if you wrapped it up in a red bow and got it to sing 'The Naughty Lady From Arabia.'"

Lord Blake choked.

"Why did you not tell me you are heir to a duke's crypt?" demanded Miss Glyn.

"In all honesty, I thought you knew. This is the severest blow to my consequence. I shall have to resort to brandy presently."

"Before you become castaway or even shot in the neck, tell me why I have never seen you nor heard of you before this."

"I have been touring my father's estates for most of the last five years," Lord Blake replied between his chuckles, "and only settled back in town three weeks ago. As for hearing of me, I daresay the difficulty lies in my advancing in succession to my father's estate. The family titles underwent a most horrendous scrambling. Even I have difficulty recalling my proper name. Mind you, I'd as lief not be a marquess—'I'll give my jewels for a set of beads, my gorgeous palace for a hermitage, my gay apparel for an almsman's gown'—but the family simply won't oblige."

"A marquess," Miss Glyn said. "Heir to Insley." She shook her head. "How could I have been so blind? Priscilla Inglewood is a fitting revenge. And yet, I think I must pity you. How dreadful to be made into a duke! How any parent can be so unkind as to thrust upon an unsuspecting child a centuries-old encumbrance reeking with dust and obligations I do not know. It is most unfeeling of them! You should speak to your parents, Lord Blake, indeed you should."

"I have tried," his lordship replied with a melancholy sigh, "on several occasions, but they are recalcitrant."

"You poor dear. I do feel for you. You need uplifting, and I know just the thing: a petticoat. You are fond of them, I believe."

Lord Blake choked. "I beg your pardon?"

"You are not fond of petticoats?"

"Yes . . . No! . . . I mean . . ."

"Oh dear, you mean my terminology was wrong?" Miss Glyn anxiously inquired. "Not having any brothers, I often get the better cant terms quite muddled. Is it garters? Corsets? I have it, *shifts!*"

"No, no," Lord Blake said in a stifled voice, "petticoat was the correct term."

"I am so glad. It is so mortifying to be thought a Mrs. Malaprop, for all that she was so very amusing, for you must agree, Lord Blake, that good humor on certain occasions can overset even the most appalling blunders."

"Bearing that in mind," Lord Blake said with a mischievous grin that charmed Miss Glyn rather than warned her, "I should like to introduce you to my parents."

At his lordship's urging, Miss Glyn turned to their left and beheld the amused and elegantly attired figure of the Duke of Insley, the more reserved Duchess of Insley at his side. Miss Glyn did not doubt that they had heard the whole of her conversation with Lord Blake.

The color drained from her face. Desperation drove her to speech.

"How delightful to meet you at last! Your son," she said with a murderous look at the sorely amused Lord Blake, "has told me so much about you, I feel as if I have known you for years. But is that not often the way of things?" she said with a brilliant smile. "My father was a hunting companion of our good king in their salad days, and he used to tell me the most diverting tales of our monarch. But then, when we were finally introduced, I was dreadfully disappointed in the king, for he was not at all as Papa had described him. Of course, the king *was* mad at the time, so I suppose that might have had something to do with it, but my illusions were quite shattered and I was forced to seek solace in bowls of berries and cream for the next week. But you, I see, shall not drive me to the berry patch, for you are quite wonderful. Lord Blake," she said with a chastising frown, "you have *not* done your family justice in our conversations. They are not at all low-browed frumps. Are you enjoying the ball, Your Grace?" she asked the duke.

"I cannot recall when I last spent a more entertaining evening."

"I am so glad," Miss Glyn said faintly.

In truth, Miss Glyn was rattled beyond all bearing. She had not felt this cast down since her first season in London when she had discussed with one of England's greatest rakes the difficulties she and her father had endured mounting their prize bull on his harem of brown-eyed cows, mentioned George the Third's growing madness to the prince at her presentation, and laughed outright at one of Lady Jersey's newest hats. The town, in turn, had laughed at her, at length. The humiliation she had suffered then was equal to what she suffered now, and she felt no compunction at blaming Lord Blake for this present misery. Not only had he egged her on in their antic conversation, he had not bothered to warn her of the consequences.

Miss Glyn had one or two shreds of decency within her. She knew how to behave properly and when to do so. However much she may have castigated Lord Blake, she had heard naught but good of the Insleys and would have hoped to make a good impression, if only to soothe her own ego and maintain her hard-won reputation in the *ton*. What might come of this night's work she knew not, but Miss Glyn, her fury mounting, would insure that Lord Blake felt the full repercussions.

As the Duke of Insley concluded the tale of a Scottish ball he had attended in his youth, the duchess broke in.

"You have been in town some time, I believe, Miss Glyn?" said she. (Miss Glyn bowed.) "And you are yet unmarried?" (Miss Glyn bowed again.) "Do you not fear becoming an antidote?"

"On the contrary," Miss Glyn said with a surprised smile. "I'm not such a ninny as to inflict myself with a groom. All about me are marrying, Duchess. Allow me, if you will, to enjoy the good fortune of not being wed."

"You are adverse to the marriage mart?"

"I am adverse to counting myself as low as the market sets me. In my dim distant youth, I had the misfortune to be an heiress and was thus taken to the *ton's* ample bosom as one of its own, despite my lack of beauty and social graces. When I was no longer an heiress, I was kicked out of the purple, either castigated or ignored. It dealt a death blow to my romantic naïveté that I have been grateful for ever since. When I was an heiress, I was a commodity fit only for the marriage mart. Now that my income has been reduced, I am fit for the world. Let it tremble at my feet!"

The duchess laughed. "There is sense in the midst of your absurdity. Until recently, my son, too, has been averse to the marriage mart."

"It is just as well. It would not be kind to saddle any female with his rule."

"Do you imply that marriage with me would be anything less than bliss?" Lord Blake demanded, arms akimbo.

Miss Glyn regarded him calmly.

"Will no one defend me?" Lord Blake cried.

The Insleys regarded their son calmly.

Lady Inglewood came up to the party at this uncomplimentary juncture.

"Good evening, Your Grace," she said. "Duchess, how lovely to see you tonight."

"Priscilla, you are looking beautiful as always," said the duke.

"Your father is well, I trust?" said the duchess.

"He is in the card room," Lady Inglewood said with a condescending smile. "He may not be well, but he is happy. Theo, pray give me your support as I dance attendance on the Duchess of Newberry. I did not pay her the requisite morning call this week, and I'm sure she wants my head. Perhaps you can distract her, for you know how she dotes on attractive men."

Lord Blake knew a trap when he met one, and knew, too, that he could not with any civility escape the one Lady Inglewood had presented. He therefore bowed to Miss Glyn and gave his arm to Lady Inglewood.

"I am always happy to play St. George for you, Priscilla. Lead me to your dragon."

"Dear Theo, I do not know what I would do without you," Lady Inglewood said with a triumphant smile to Miss Glyn before leading Lord Blake away. But when they were out of hearing, Lady Inglewood's tone changed. "How could you, Theo. How *could* you give your countenance to that Glyn woman by introducing her to the duke and duchess, particularly when I had charged you with not furthering the acquaintance?"

"Mother asked to meet her," Lord Blake replied mildly.

"Could you not have advised her against so foolhardy a notion? You know what Miss Glyn is. Her incivility could only affront someone of your parents' stature."

His lordship's gray eyes narrowed. "As it happens, Priscilla, I do know what Miss Glyn is, and for that reason alone would have wished to make her known to my parents. They were well entertained by her, and she by them. It is a pity they were not acquainted before this."

Lady Inglewood snapped her fan shut against her open hand. "Are you blind, Theo, bewitched, or drunk? Kate Glyn fully lives up to her title. A hoyden she was born and a hoyden she continues. Had you suffered at her hands as I have suffered, you would not speak in this . . . *insulting* manner."

Lord Blake paused. "And how has she wronged you, Priscilla?"

"Only this evening she accosted me. Words cannot describe the indignities I suffered. She is monstrous, Theo, and I mean to make you see it. She is a jealous, exacting, vituperative woman, never happy unless her odious tongue causes another human being pain."

Lord Blake observed the angry flush in Lady Inglewood's cheeks. "Those are strong words, Priscilla."

"They are mild compared to those she has publicly hurled at me. This is why I ask you not to dance attendance on the hoyden."

"In point of fact, Miss Glyn has thus far not even stood up with me for a cotillion."

"Theo," Lady Inglewood said with an exasperated sigh, "I wish you would not continually apply your wit to serious matters. This is very important to me."

"I do see that, Priscilla. Indeed, I see a great deal."

Miss Glyn, meanwhile, watched the pair walk off, their heads together in conversation. "I thought she wrestled him away with becoming determination," she observed. "I can but applaud her skill, for they do look well together. Lord Blake moves with some grace. I suppose he fences?"

"At the least provocation," the duchess replied.

"Excellent. Perhaps I can persuade him to accept my challenge."

"You *fence*?" the duke and duchess said as one.

"Certainly. When I was thirteen I made a wager with my father that, if I could drive his newest phaeton and his best team of horses through the dairy gateposts thrice in succession at a gallop without scratching the paint, he would allow me to study fencing; and if I lost, I would give up pestering him about it again and pay for any necessary repairs I incurred. Needless to say, I won. Of course, the fact that I had got up at two in the morning to dig up the posts and move them another foot and a half apart might have had something to do with my success, but I prefer to recall my driving skill on the day in question."

"Ah, yes," the duchess said with a smile, "you are the Hampshire Hoyden."

"The terror of three counties and all of London," Miss Glyn said with a grin. "Papa wanted a son, and I always tried to oblige him."

"Hence your familiarity with petticoats?" the duchess inquired.

"The Hampshire Hoyden rides to ruin again," Miss Glyn said with a sigh.

"My dear Fitzgerald," cried the duchess, "she is blushing!"

"I am not!" Miss Glyn hotly protested. "I would never do anything so missish. I . . . am merely experiencing a sudden elevation in temperature . . . or coming down with some rare tropical disease. I have not yet decided which. Do you think you could contrive to have Lord Blake spend the night with you?"

The Insleys stared at her.

"I cannot blame you for not wanting him," Miss Glyn continued, "for he is trying beyond measure. How odd that Lord Blake should claim such delightful people as his parents. Are you sure he was not a foundling left on your doorstep?"

"Quite sure," the duke said, chuckling.

"Pity. His ruin will bring you some pain, I fear."

"Ruin?" the duchess exclaimed. "What *are* you planning?"

"My revenge, of course. He has used me badly, you must own it."

"Oh we do. How exciting," the duke said gleefully. "Regina, we are to see the Hampshire Hoyden in action. What will you do, Miss Glyn?"

"I have . . . a friend, Phoebe Lovejoy. I think she will serve my purpose very well . . . if you can contrive to have Lord Blake spend the night with you and take breakfast in the morning."

Chapter 9

LORD BLAKE AND the Duke and Duchess of Insley had been at breakfast a mere fifteen minutes on the morning after the Egerton ball when a footman entered the dining room bearing a gaily wrapped box.

"What on earth is that?" the duke exclaimed, his cup of coffee arrested in midair.

"This was just delivered, Your Grace," the footman replied. "I was told to place it at once in Lord Blake's hands. The carrier was most insistent upon this point. There is a letter, as well, addressed to the duchess."

The box was deposited on the table in front of Lord Blake as the duchess opened the letter.

She stopped.

She stared.

"What on earth . . . ?" she murmured.

"What is it, Regina?" the duke asked.

"I don't quite . . ." the duchess said in a stunned voice.

"Read it aloud, Mother," Lord Blake said. "You've got us thoroughly agog. Read it aloud."

"I think perhaps I had better," the duchess said. "It begins: 'Dear Duchess, here is hoping this letter finds you and your husband, the duke, well. From what Teddy has told me, though, you and the duke are never poorly.' "

"Teddy?" said the duke, an amused smile directed at his son. "Whoever can that be?"

"Our correspondent cannot mean me," Lord Blake retorted, a forkful of trout halfway to his mouth. "No one has ever dared to call me Teddy in my entire life."

"May I continue?" the duchess inquired to great chilling effect. She returned to the letter. " 'You may be wondering how a girl in my station comes to know your son—' "

"*What?*" Lord Blake exclaimed, choking on his trout.

" 'We met,' " the duchess continued reading, " 'when one of my gentleman callers turned nasty on me in the middle of the Berry Patch Tavern. Teddy was a real hero, like Robin Hood or Guy Falkes, and we became fast friends afterward. But I want to assure you, Duchess, that I never accepted a farthing from him, not even when little Joey was born—' "

"Now wait just a minute!" Lord Blake exploded. "Mother, I swear I *never—*"

But the duchess read on relentlessly. " '. . . when little Joey was born, nor no presents neither except what I'm returning to Teddy today. Not that he didn't try to give me a quid or two, but like I told him from the start, you can't put no price on love, nor your kids neither.' "

" 'Yes, I loved your son, Duchess, and he loved me, but I knew we could never stick it, despite all of Teddy's promises. Then, when I learned little Nellie was on the way—' "

"*Two?*" the duke exclaimed. "Why Theo, you *are* prolific!"

Laughter danced in his son's gray eyes.

" '. . . Nellie was on the way, I knew we'd have to end it so I could get spliced to a man who'd look after me and the kids. There's just so much a girl can do on her own and with the seventy percent Mother Brown takes off the top, there's hardly enough left to keep body and soul together. So I married Percy and told Teddy we would have to part . . .' This next part is blurred," the duchess said, "as if the poor girl had been crying.

"Let me see," she said, squinting at the page, "is that an *A*? No, no, an *M*. It goes on: 'My heart was breaking when we said good-bye, but I knew it was for the best, and Percy's been good to me and my little ones, so I've got no complaints. The only trouble we've had is when Percy found the only present I let Teddy give me last year and how he did shout! But I calmed him down soon enough and promised to send it back, and so I have, and now everything is right as rain.' "

His rampant curiosity demanding satisfaction, Lord Blake began to rip the pink paper from the box, not noticing his father stifling his laughter in his napkin.

" 'Tell Teddy,' " the duchess continued reading, her voice growing more steely with each succeeding sentence, " 'that Joey and Nellie send their love and are learning their letters as fast as anything. Your obedient servant, Phoebe Lovejoy.' "

Lord Blake drew from the box a brilliant red satin nightshift with a bodice that was cut distressingly low, its side seams made from black lace. The front and back of the shift were embroidered with ribbons and thread depicting, as near as could be made out, the *Rape of the Sabine Women*. The Duke of Insley turned away from this indelicate sight to hide his laughter.

Lord Blake's shoulders were trembling, as were his hands. He was forced to set the garish garment down on the table. The duke was hooting into his napkin but the duchess, apparently, was not amused.

"Theodore," she intoned, "*what* is the meaning of this letter and that . . . that . . ." she said, waving a finger at the brilliant shift, ". . . that horrific garment, and *who* is this poor Phoebe Lovejoy creature?"

"Who else?" Lord Blake crowed. "The Hampshire Hoyden!"

His lordship erupted into laughter, burying his head in his arms on the table, while his parents smiled at each other in surprise and growing satisfaction.

Chapter 10

ON THE SECOND morning following the Egerton Ball, Miss Glyn and Miss Fairfax sat in two blue chairs opposite each other, a tea tray resting upon a small table between them, as they lazily sorted through the morning mail.

"Oh *no!*" Miss Fairfax ejaculated.

"What is it?" demanded Miss Glyn.

"This," said Miss Fairfax as she waved a newly opened envelope and its contents in the air. "*this* is a letter from the Duchess of Insley."

"Really? How very nice."

"Nice? *Nice?* I warned you this would happen. I warned you! And now see what has come of your inattention. *This* is an invitation to a small, informal garden party that the Duke and Duchess of Insley are giving tomorrow."

"Indeed? That sounds very pleasant."

"Pleasant?" the horrified Miss Fairfax cried, unable to credit what she had heard. "*Pleasant?* After you sent them that *dreadful* shift and that absurd letter, in spite of all of my entreaties not to, you now consider public humiliation *pleasant?!*"

"Perhaps I did not hear you properly. I thought we were invited to a garden party."

"That is only a pretext, you must realize that. The Insleys will get us in front of the *haut ton* and then wreak their revenge! You should never have sent that dreadful shift. Never, never, never. I don't care *what* Lord Blake did to you. Oh, what the Insleys must think of us," cried the distraught Miss Fairfax, and she shuddered.

"Georgina," replied Miss Glyn with admirable calm, "I do not think you can be in your right mind."

"Oh! You . . . you—"

"Have you ever noticed that you repeat yourself whenever you are upset?"

"I do *not* repeat myself," Miss Fairfax furiously declared.

"Yes, you do."

"I don't, I don't, I *don't!*"

"There, you see?" Miss Glyn said happily.

"You are *so* infuriating," seethed Miss Fairfax.

"Yes, I know," Miss Glyn replied with a smile. "What are you planning to wear to the Insley garden party?"

"Wear?" gasped Miss Fairfax. "Nothing!"

"Georgina!"

"I meant," Miss Fairfax said grimly, "that I would rather place myself in pillory than attend that party."

"Don't be ridiculous. Of course you will go. Who will chaperone me?"

"You cannot think to attend?!"

"Where is your head today, Georgina? Of course I will attend. It should be great fun."

"After sending that shift? Have you no shame?"

"None whatsoever," replied Miss Glyn. "Now do reconsider, Georgina. To refuse an Insley invitation is tantamount to social suicide, you must see that."

"I don't care."

"Have your own way then," Miss Glyn said with a sigh. "I will make your regrets and create some sort of an excuse for you: malaria, the pox, an elopement, something on that order."

"Very well, very *well*, I shall go and rue the day

105

I was ever born, I have no doubt," Miss Fairfax said bitterly.

"Good girl."

There was a moment of grim silence as Miss Fairfax stared at her friend. "How do you manage it?" she demanded.

"Manage what?"

"How do you manage to get me to do things I have no desire to do?"

"But Georgina, you will have a marvelous time tomorrow," Miss Glyn said soothingly. "Trust me."

Miss Fairfax had several rejoinders to make, none of them civil. Fortunately for Miss Glyn's blushes, Wainwright entered the parlor to announce with no trace of emotion that Sir William Atherton had come to call.

"So early?" drawled Miss Glyn. "My, he *is* eager."

Miss Fairfax's darkling glance silenced any further comments Miss Glyn might have made. She shrugged her shoulders with good humor and began to gather the debris of that morning's post.

Miss Fairfax sent Wainwright off to fetch Sir William and then began a flurry of activity to make herself presentable. She even attempted several poses in her chair, decided the sofa might show her to better effect, quickly crossed the room and at first reclined, then sat upright, then lounged against its soft blue and green striped cushions.

Miss Glyn, it must be noted, restrained herself admirably during this agitated activity, only allowing herself to murmur, "Careful, Georgina. You will exhaust yourself before he ever appears."

Sir William burst into the room. His blond locks were in wild disarray, his cravat tied simply (at best), his handsome figure attired in riding breeches and a dark brown riding coat, his blue eyes seeing only Miss Fairfax.

Without pausing to catch his breath, Sir William strode across the room, dropped to both knees before his heart's desire and, taking one of her hands in both of his, declared: "Dearest Georgina, I have just come from the Pomeroys, and they have told me what I cannot believe: that you are betrothed to Lord Falkhurst. That you leave tonight for Gretna Green!"

"What?!" squeaked Miss Fairfax.

"They said that all of London knew that he meant to pay you his addresses, but I—fool that I am—did not know. I should not be here, I know I should not. You have given your word and your hand to another, and yet I must and shall reach for my own happiness."

Sir William thereupon covered Miss Fairfax's hand with fervent kisses.

Deeming this a scene unfit for her calloused eyes, and trusting Miss Fairfax to set Sir William aright regarding Lord Falkhurst, Miss Glyn discreetly withdrew from the parlor and then retreated into the library.

With a heavy sigh, she began to wander aimlessly around the large, darkened room. There could be no more doubt. Miss Fairfax had found her Adam, her Romeo, her prince. Drat the man for being so perfect for her. The time had come to find another domicile. To stay under the same roof with the soon-to-be newlyweds—as she knew her friend would suggest—would be untenable. She would feel like a St. Bernard amongst turtledoves. No, it would not do.

Miss Glyn sighed again. She had spent the last year and a half preparing herself for this eviction, but now that the moment had come, she felt pained beyond bearing. To know that soon she and Miss Fairfax would never again share a morning such as this one; that she would never again have such easy access to her friend's time and heart, swept Miss Glyn with sorrow. No longer would Georgina be at her side to join in her jokes, to cajole her out of her doldrums, to speak sensibly in the midst of all her silliness, to hear her darker thoughts. The magnitude of such a loss was numbing.

Marriage was all well and good, Miss Glyn supposed, but it was terribly hard on female friendships. A married woman suddenly found her time occupied by home, servants, husband, children, with little time left for herself, and less still for her friends.

The imminent marriage of Miss Fairfax to Sir William was but one more loss to add to Miss Glyn's private tally: her mother, her father, the home in which she had lived all her life, the future Falkhurst had led her to rely upon in her naïve girlhood, Mr. and Mrs. Fairfax, and now Miss Fairfax. This was another instance of proof, as if she needed any more, that she should not let herself love others, for they always left or disappointed her. And the pain was always unbearable, as it was now.

Miss Glyn took a deep breath, punched a sofa pillow, and began to pace the floor, hurling several uncomplimentary names at herself for indulging in such melancholy. The Hampshire Hoyden should not repine, she should act! When all was said and done, there was much to be said for marrying off Miss Fairfax. London had long ago palled for Miss Glyn. She had had to work harder and harder to enjoy town life, and now it was not even fun sparring with Lady Perfection. Miss Glyn stopped in mid-stride. It had not been fun sparring with Lady Perfection since she had met Lord Blake.

She blinked. There were dangers in town life . . . and . . . and of course great tedium. Clearly the time had come to make a change. She was a country girl born and bred, and to the peace and beauty of the country she would return. Her income was sufficient to purchase a house with perhaps fifty acres. Her father had insured that she could not return to the home of her childhood. Would the pain of that loss never ease? Her father's lack of respect for her abilities, which she had been able to deny when he was alive, had been ruthlessly borne in on her at his death and the reading of his will. "No female is fit to manage Tryon Hall, particularly my daughter." Hard to bear the grief of a father's loss, harder still to suffer his disregard and tyranny. And then there had been Falkhurst to deliver the *coup de grace* a week later. And Miss Fairfax could not understand why she disdained marriage!

Miss Glyn shook herself. Well, there was ample opportunity now to build a new home, a new life. She would rusticate in earnest: raise horses and cows, sheep and chickens; grow corn and wheat; keep a vegetable garden; attend to her dairy; and bless her good fortune that she had escaped London when she had.

Oppression swamped Miss Glyn, and she tried to sort it out. For a moment her breath caught: what loneliness she was planning for herself, and what loneliness she already endured! Miss Fairfax, though a dear friend, could not share in the quirks of madness which lightened Miss Glyn's days; did not enjoy the same authors, plays, or activities which enlivened Miss Glyn's life. And soon there would not even be her sweet companionship to unite them.

Miss Glyn violently shrugged off her unhappiness. What could not be helped would be managed as well as possible. She had lived with loneliness all her life. She would continue to do so.

Unable to keep her curiosity at bay any longer Miss Glyn stole up to the door adjoining the parlor, silently opened it a crack, and peered inside. Sir

William had apparently said something to the moment, for Miss Fairfax was on her feet and locked in what could only be termed a passionate embrace. Clearly Sir William knew what he was about, and Miss Glyn shrewdly suspected that Miss Fairfax did as well. Summoning all the moral and social discretion at her command, Miss Glyn closed the door on this torrid scene and went to find an absorbing book.

※

Chapter 11

"AND THEN I declared three queens!" Lady Inglewood said triumphantly. "The color drained from Bingsley's face, the cards slipped from his hand. 'I have been led to rack and ruin by the fair Helen of Piquet!' he cried. It was most amusing."

Lord Blake managed a smile.

"His taste in clothes is atrocious, of course," Lady Inglewood continued, "but the Bingsleys are frightfully good *ton*, and Freddie can be quite the charmer when he has a mind to it."

Lord Blake roused himself to civility. "Lord Bingsley could not help but be eloquent when faced with so lovely a foe."

Lady Inglewood continued happily in monologue while Lord Blake tried to appear interested. His parents had promised him entertainment if he attended their garden party; thus far entertainment had not been forthcoming.

Then Miss Glyn and Miss Fairfax were announced. Startled, Lord Blake looked up to find both young women greeting the duke and duchess, Miss Glyn saying something that set his father laughing. It was all Lord Blake could do not to laugh as well, and he did not even know the joke.

"Oh, this is monstrous!" Lady Inglewood exclaimed. "How dare Kate Glyn flaunt herself in such noble company? I daresay she was not even invited."

111

"On the contrary, I suspect she headed the guest list."

"I trust the duchess has more sense," Lady Inglewood replied with great superiority. "Miss Glyn is clearly here to find an exalted husband for Miss Fairfax. She undoubtedly stole the invitations!"

"Let us test your theory, Priscilla," said Lord Blake, looping her arm through his and pulling her toward Miss Glyn with unbridled enthusiasm.

Lady Inglewood smiled triumphantly at her foe. The marquess would soon put the Hampshire Hoyden in her place.

Miss Glyn, having observed his lordship's determined advance, summoned all of the bluff courage she possessed, and smiled up at him, speaking before he could say a word.

"Lord Blake, I am surprised to see you here. I heard that you had fled the country, an angry blacksmith at your heels."

His levity, which had been poorly restrained since receiving Phoebe Lovejoy's package, burst forth without warning. Lord Blake erupted into laughter that he had no hope of suppressing and so fled without a word.

Impotent fury flooded Lady Inglewood's breast. Blake had insulted her . . . and in front of Miss Glyn!

"How typical of you to abuse your host not five minutes after entering his home," she hissed.

"Getting married any time soon, Prissie?" Miss Glyn retorted with a smile.

Lady Inglewood gasped in outrage. "Hoyden!" she snapped and then stalked off.

This was indeed marvelous, to rout both Lord Blake and Lady Inglewood so easily within a minute of each other! Miss Glyn directed her steps to the food tables. Victory in battle required sustenance. She had not known what to expect from the

Insley invitation. She could not guess why she had been raised into such august company. But come what may, she was content to have vanquished Theo Blake so well.

Lord Blake, who had fled to the gardens and had there taken himself most severely to task for so weak a defense and so complete a lack of an offense against Miss Glyn, determined that his manly pride would not permit him to be so easily routed. He reversed his steps and marched back into the salon, drawing before the provocateur just as Miss Glyn was about to sample a pear tart.

She raised her dark brows questioningly, which sent a tremor through his lordship, but he managed nonetheless to say with some composure: "Good day, Miss Glyn. Warm weather we're h-h-having, isn't it?"

He could restrain himself no longer and once again burst out laughing, which once again sent him into headlong flight.

Miss Glyn bit happily into the tart, consuming both it and a glass of lemonade.

The marquess, meanwhile, finally had the sense to fortify himself with a straight shot of very strong whiskey secreted in the library for just such emergencies. Squaring his shoulders, he marched back into the salon and drew before the Hampshire Hoyden once again.

"Back so soon?" inquired Miss Glyn.

"I cannot stay away," Lord Blake gravely replied. "Something draws me to this spot."

"It was my impression that something continually propelled you *from* this spot. I thought it might be due to a sudden financial collapse. Bow Street Runners? Shifts?"

"Petticoats," Lord Blake grimly corrected.

"Sorry. Petticoats. You really are in a most emotional state today. I wonder if I am safe with you."

"Far safer than I with you."

"Why, whatever can you mean, Lord Blake?"

"Phoebe Lovejoy."

"You are changing your name? Or is she an acquaintance of yours?"

The marquess manfully suppressed a chuckle. "I am not changing my name, and I have come to know Miss Lovejoy and her lurid imagination quite well recently."

"How am I to understand such cryptic comments?"

"Oh, come now, Miss Glyn, you have an excellent mind, put it to use. Allow me to jog your memory: a pink-wrapped box, a tearstained letter, little Joey and Nellie, the *Rape of the Sabine Women*?"

"Please, my lord, you are putting me to the blush."

"Impossible! The duchess, on the other hand—"

This almost undid Miss Glyn, but she kept a firm grip on her laughter and managed to say with seeming innocence: "Your nerves appear disordered. Let me make you a gift of our supply of James's Powders."

"For shame, Miss Glyn," his lordship replied severely. "It is not at all proper for an unattached woman of the *ton* to offer a gift to an unattached gentleman of the *ton*."

"No?" Miss Glyn said meekly.

"Most emphatically not. Tongues, and other bodily parts, will wag, Miss Glyn, be assured."

Miss Glyn was startled into a ripple of laughter.

"Virtue is its own reward," said his lordship with a smile. "You should laugh more often, Miss Glyn, it becomes you."

" 'I am undone by thy quips and thy quiddities,' " quoth she.

Lord Blake preened himself. " 'I am not in the roll of common men.' "

Miss Glyn guffawed. " 'The trumpet of his own virtues.' "

" 'Greatness knows itself.' "

" 'He doth nothing but talk of his horse,' " marveled Miss Glyn.

Lord Blake gave it up and enjoyed his laughter.

Miss Glyn smiled at him. "Do you aspire to nothing more than besting me in a Shakespearean quotational duel?"

"My only ambition is to modernize the ruinous farming techniques on the Insley estates and fend off my inheritance until I am an antique."

Miss Glyn was so stunned by this declaration that she stared up at Lord Blake. "I am seldom surprised by another human being, but now I find myself stunned by the prospect of seeing you in an agricultural light. Are you quite serious?"

"Quite," Lord Blake replied with a smile.

"You will make a most interesting chapter in my autobiography," Miss Glyn said, shaking her head. "I am convinced of it."

"You honor me," said Lord Blake with a bow.

"Indeed, I do. Originally you were just to be a footnote."

Lord Blake burst into laughter once more.

Lady Inglewood, on the far side of the room, watched this charming tête-a-tête with mounting anger. All of Lord Blake's protestations of friendship and respect meant nothing when he flaunted his interest in the hoyden like this! That he enjoyed Miss Glyn's company had been clear even to Lady Inglewood. But she had assumed, as she had with his other interests, that her own long friendship and family connection to the Insleys would sway him irrevocably toward choosing her as his bride. After all, everyone knew that an heir to Insley must marry well, and how better than to the daughter of the Earl of Inglewood?

Her father had already set about entrapping him, telling anyone who would hear him that she would soon be Blake's bride.

"Don't you worry, my dear," the earl had said with a loving pat on her hand. "I'll bring that young whelp up to snuff and in pretty short order. The boy knows his duty to you. I'll make it impossible for him to escape doing the right thing. When all the *ton* openly expects him to pay you his addresses, he'll have no choice but to propose."

But was Kate Glyn deliberately broadening his matrimonial horizon? For all that the she-wolf publicly disdained marriage, Lady Inglewood would not put it past her to lust for the weighty title of duchess.

And Lord Blake sought out her company. The whole of the *ton* had remarked it. Was her father wrong? Would Theo escape their snare for the net Kate Glyn had cast?

Oh, that would be humiliation! The covert glances directed toward her every minute of the day. The cool civility of Regina Insley to withstand whenever they met. The open acknowledgment that she was almost an antidote: four-and-twenty and unmarried, without a prospect in view, without a dukedom in her future. It was too horrific, too frightening to bear.

If only Oliver had lived, Lady Inglewood said over and over to herself. If Oliver had lived, she would not have had to set her cap for Theo and would not now be withering from mortification. She had been sure of Oliver when she was only sixteen. Betrothed to him at eighteen, to be married at nineteen and the Duchess of Insley by ... thirty? Why not? Fitzgerald and Regina could not live forever.

But Oliver was dead. There was only Theo Blake left. And now, was there even he?

After all of her planning, all of her work, all of her dreams.

Nothing?

No, it was impossible! Lady Inglewood had not a doubt that Lord Blake keenly felt his obligation to her. He would bow to public opinion and propose. It would not be a love match, but what of that? She had not loved Oliver, either. But it would be a match. If Kate Glyn did not interfere.

The subject of these dark thoughts had parted from Lord Blake to wander from glittering group to glittering group of guests, impressed at moving in the highest echelons of society, but not, it must be confessed, wholly entertained. She had found in her childhood that the titular nobility was, on the whole, a crashing bore, and some fifteen years later she found that this precocious judgment still held true. This was why she appreciated the Insleys so much. They were completely unexpected, open, honest, and always entertaining. Very rare birds, indeed.

"Lost in the clouds of the Muses, Miss Glyn?" a friendly voice inquired.

"Your Grace!" exclaimed Miss Glyn as she turned to discover the Duke of Insley smiling at her. "I was just thinking of you."

"For a man of my years to dwell in the thoughts of such a lovely and delightful young woman is a very great compliment indeed."

"You *are* marvelous," Miss Glyn said with open admiration. "If you were not already so well married, I think I would set my cap for you."

"And I, Miss Glyn, if I were but twenty years younger, would most assuredly set my cap for you," the duke replied, chuckling.

"But it wouldn't do, you know."

"No?"

"The truth of the matter is that I have no desire

to be a duchess, indeed, I cannot imagine a worse fate. And I would make such a wretched duchess, Your Grace, for I continually find myself doing the most bizarre things, which show a lamentable lack of sensible thinking on my part. Certainly I would have a rough go of it when confronted by the awesome reputation of the current duchess. There are few, if any, who could fill her shoes. I would feel foolish even trying."

"You know," said the duke, an odd expression on his face, "I believe Theo has the same problem."

"Filling his mother's shoes?"

"No, no," the duke said with a smile, "his brother's, Lord Wycomb. Oliver." The duke's sigh was wistful. "He was a wonderful boy in every sense. One of those paragons, you know, who manages to do everything well, yet friendly and affectionate. We all assumed he would inherit the title, the lands, everything. Theo most of all. He was sincerely grateful he didn't have that weight on his shoulders. Used to joke with Oliver about it all the time, but we knew how . . . impressed he was with Oliver's ability to manage it all. Then suddenly . . . the burden fell on Theo's shoulders. It has been five years and still . . . . at least Theo was there. Oliver did not die alone."

"There?" Miss Glyn said, perplexed. "But I understood your son to have died in the Peninsula Campaign, and Lord Blake told me once that he had not fought in the war."

"Fought? No, that is quite right. But he had taken part in a quiet way on behalf of the government. Oliver, as heir, could not fight, of course, but he was mad to take part, and envied Theo all his patriotic activities. He insisted on following Theo to the Peninsula, to celebrate the cawker's birthday is how he justified it. Theo has always blamed himself . . . Oliver should not have gone to the front

118

lines, you see. He persuaded Theo to take him for a quick tour. Fighting suddenly broke out and ... Oliver's death ended any patriotic ideals Theo might have had. He hardly mentions the war anymore. He has devoted himself instead to the Insley estates, blaming himself unrelentingly for Oliver's death, and hiding behind the thick veneer of a dilettante."

"There is a reason for every mask, Your Grace. But why are you telling me all this?"

The duke took her hand between both of his and smiled warmly at her. "The duchess and I wished to extend our deep gratitude for all you have done on Theo's behalf."

"I?!"

"You have taught him to laugh again, Miss Glyn. Yours is a rare gift that can never be properly repaid."

"Please, Your Grace, I beg you," said Miss Glyn with a blush, "your praise is unwarranted. I have done nothing to ... Oh, good God, what is *he* doing here?" she suddenly demanded.

The gentleman to whom Miss Glyn referred was Lord Falkhurst, handsome in a rust-colored coat, dusty gold waistcoat, and tan breeches.

"He sits too high in the *ton*, my dear," the duke replied. "We could not slight him, in spite of the fact that Falkhurst is an abominably cold fish."

"A very apt description," Miss Glyn said with a smile.

"Come," the duke said, offering his arm, "allow me to remove you from his obnoxious presence. The garden is just coming into bloom and is really quite lovely."

While Miss Glyn enjoyed the gracious company of the duke, Miss Fairfax floated in the aura of happiness that she and Sir William Atherton had woven around themselves on the loveseat they had

119

claimed but five minutes after Miss Fairfax had entered the room. To say that they were oblivious to all about them would be to state the obvious. One eager gentleman after another approached the couple only to be met by Miss Fairfax's vacant gaze and civil smile, which said far more clearly than any words might have done that they would have a better chance of maintaining a snowball in purgatory than furthering their suit with Miss Fairfax.

Among the many guests to observe this intense tête-à-tête was an increasingly incensed Lord Falkhurst. In December, he had convinced himself that after months of determined courtship, his suit not only prospered but had all the earmarks of succeeding with Miss Fairfax. The thought of acquiring Meadowbrook and Pennington, the estates that made up the bulk of Miss Fairfax's dowry, had put Lord Falkhurst in the best frame of mind he had enjoyed in years. That she had shown him no more favor than she had to any of her other suitors occurred to him not at all. To those of Lord Falkhurst's stamp, any friendly feminine smile or pleasant conversation grew into the realm of abject adoration in very short order.

To have this worldview so rudely shaken by the sight of the clearly enamored Georgina Fairfax blushing at every word Sir William uttered filled Lord Falkhurst with a rage that left him pale and trembling. It took every ounce of self-restraint on his part to keep from storming up to Atherton and breaking his pretty neck.

"Careful, Bertram," Lady Inglewood advised as she reached his side, "your petulance is showing."

"I will thank you, Priscilla," Lord Falkhurst seethed, his hands clenched, "to keep your observations to yourself."

"I advise you to keep a rein on your temper."

"I am in perfect control."

"Not with that murderous gleam in your eyes, you're not. You cannot have seriously hoped to win Georgina Fairfax's hand?"

Lord Falkhurst's burning glare indicated that he had.

"Oh Bertram, how foolish of you," Lady Inglewood exclaimed on a trill of laughter, "when she claims Katharine Glyn as her best friend!"

"If I was foolish, you are equally so," Lord Falkhurst bitterly retorted.

"I don't know what you mean," Lady Inglewood said, blushing furiously.

"Why dear, sweet, easily gulled Theodore Blake, of course. It seems your father's announcement to any and all who would attend him is premature, if not stillborn. How can you hope to marry Blake when it has been clear to the rest of us these last five years that he barely tolerates you?"

Lady Inglewood's lovely face was frozen. "Lord Blake holds me in the highest affection and esteem."

"He won't when he hears the rumors the earl has started about your betrothal. It is even said," Falkhurst continued with an unpleasant smile, "that he favors the doubtful charms of that little hoyden, Katharine Glyn. How very amusing to see the daughter of an earl bested by a backward country hoyden."

"Theo is entertained by her, that is all."

"That is far more than you have accomplished."

Lady Inglewood glared up at Lord Falkhurst, but her reply was cut short by a shriek that silenced the room.

All eyes turned to observe Miss Fairfax rise from the loveseat where she had been sitting with Sir William, her blue eyes huge in her pale face.

"Jeremy!" she cried, and then ran across the

room to hurtle herself into the outstretched arms of a tall young gentleman with black hair and blue eyes, handsomely outfitted in a scarlet coat.

The room burst into conversation as the guests recognized the newest arrival as the male half of the Fairfax family. Miss Fairfax, meanwhile, was feverishly kissing her brother, laughing and crying and babbling nonstop. Nor did Mr. Fairfax see any reason to temper this fond greeting. He was, in fact, enjoying himself immensely.

"You were clearly meant for the stage, Jeremy," Miss Glyn said with a smile as she advanced on Mr. Fairfax. "Never have I seen a better entrance."

"Rather splendid, wasn't it?" Mr. Fairfax said with a sheepish smile. "Hello, Kate," he said, giving her a hug. "How the hell are you?"

"Speechless for the first time in my life," Miss Glyn said, laughing.

"That alone is worth the most abysmal Channel crossing," Mr. Fairfax replied.

"I can scarcely believe this is real," Miss Fairfax said as she gazed lovingly at her brother.

"Nor can I," Miss Glyn said. "What *are* you doing here, Jeremy? You are supposed to be putting the French to the sword."

"I got an early leave and followed Wainwright's directions to this little shack. I am very impressed by your rise in the world, Georgina, and trust that you will not forget your doting brother in your lucrative whirl of social obligations. Just toss the odd heiress or two my way, and I'll be happy."

"Barbarian," Miss Fairfax said, chuckling as she hugged her brother once again.

"Warfare has done little to improve his character, I see," Miss Glyn commented.

"*You* haven't changed," Mr. Fairfax said with a fond smile.

"On the contrary," Miss Glyn retorted. "I am older and wiser, as I should be."

"Lord, I've missed you, Kate," Mr. Fairfax declared as he hugged her once again. "As has my entire regiment. You made quite an impression on them when you and Georgina came to camp to see me off last time. They all send their loving regards."

"How sweet of them," Miss Glyn said with a smile.

"Enough of all this civility," Mr. Fairfax said. "Where is this Atherton fellow that Wainwright was bending my ear about?"

"William?" Miss Fairfax gasped. "Oh, how could I have forgotten him?! You must come meet him at once, Jeremy. You will adore him, I am certain."

"Consider that an order," Miss Glyn advised Mr. Fairfax before his sister took his hand and quickly led him away.

Lord Blake, who had eavesdropped shamelessly on the entire conversation, drew beside Miss Glyn.

"The camp sweetheart!" he exclaimed. "What a lovely picture that calls to mind."

"You always overhear the most inopportune comments," Miss Glyn said with a sigh.

"From what I have been able to gather from our brief but rich acquaintance, your *life* is one inopportune comment."

"Snipe!"

"Flirt."

"I'm not!"

"Tell that to the cavalry."

"I ignore you," Miss Glyn declared, pointedly turning from Lord Blake.

His lordship burst into laughter. "By God, I like you, Miss Glyn."

With a surprised smile, Miss Glyn turned back. "But is it wise to like me, my lord? The Inglewoods, social decorum, ties of loyalty, and good sense are all against it."

Lord Blake smiled down at her. "You make me harken back to my giddy youth, Miss Glyn. None of the rest matters. Come, let us be friends."

"It seems an extreme step, particularly when I take such delight in abusing you."

"You would not let such a paltry excuse as friendship keep you from that, I am sure."

Miss Glyn laughed. "How astute of you, my lord. Very well, I shall confess in kind that I have a liking for you, though I know I should not. Still, I will be civil enough to call you friend."

"In that case," said his lordship, "since we have met in friendly combat and now swell with warm feelings of good fellowship, I am Theo."

"And I," Miss Glyn said, looking up into his face with a smile, "am Katharine, or Kate, as you will."

"We are friends then?"

"There is much to tell against us on both sides."

"And yet, we are friends."

"Yes," Miss Glyn said slowly, "I believe we are."

Startled to find her heart pounding with unnecessary energy in her breast, Miss Glyn grew increasingly frightened as Lord Blake smiled down at her. He had the most marvelous smile! Friendship seemed suddenly a dangerous proposition.

Had she seen the murderous look Lady Inglewood directed toward them, she would have stated this as fact.

✳

Chapter 12

"OH NO, MY lord, not again!"

Lord Blake grinned at his valet as he pulled off his gloves. "I didn't mean to destroy all your hard work, Max, really I didn't. But Miss Glyn rides a devilish fast race. I was hard put to it to beat her."

"I am pleased that your lordship was victorious," Maxwell said as he grimly surveyed his master's tousled hair, flushed cheeks, and mud-spattered coat, riding breeches, and boots. The cravat made him shudder. The hat made him wince. He could not bear to look at the gloves.

"Do not, I implore you, Max, look so stricken. They're only riding clothes, after all."

Maxwell stared at Lord Blake.

A muscle twitched suspiciously at the corner of his lordship's mouth. "What I meant to say is that no one who signifies saw me in this reprehensible state. Your sterling reputation is intact."

"I am relieved, my lord," Maxwell said, helping Lord Blake from his coat.

Lord Blake hid his smile. He could not remember ever feeling this alive and happy as he had in this fortnight since his parents' garden party. Kate Glyn's acerbic tongue and startling wit had kept him on the ropes from beginning to end. He was no longer a "gloomy goose," as his cousin Peter termed it. He felt downright cheerful—morning, noon, and night. He had shed Hamlet's mantle without remorse to reveal ... Puck? Lord Blake burst out laughing.

"Good God, I've been translated by the Hampshire Hoyden!"

"I beg your pardon, my lord?" Maxwell said, setting out a change of clothes.

But his lordship only smiled and shook his head. How to explain this growing transformation of his life? How to explain Katharine Glyn when she was careful to explain so little of herself? How to explain the depth of need within him to make her smile ... at him? He could not even explain it to himself.

He remembered watching Nigel Braxton dance with her at the Jersey ball a se'ennight before. She had moved with such grace, and made Braxton laugh with every step, that he had envied Braxton that dance and that laughter, wishing to claim them for himself. When Tommy Carrington had led her away to the next dance, Braxton had partnered Priscilla Inglewood ... without laughter, and then strolled to his friend's side.

"I've a castigation for you from Priscilla Inglewood," he said languidly. "She has taken umbrage at your partnering Miss Glyn yesterday in the Montclair card room."

"Priscilla would take umbrage at my inhabiting the same county as Miss Glyn. They are at war, you see."

"Indeed? Well, if it's war between your future fiancée and my charming rogue, then I'll warrant it was Priscilla who fired the first shot and for more than good cause. Our Priscilla is a well-educated, intelligent little puss. She knows the value of a preemptive strike when faced with a superior female. Priscilla never could tolerate being cast in the shade by anyone. Because she has captured my heart with her glib tongue and charming smile, I shall place my money on Miss Glyn, so you really ought to make a wager on Priscilla in the best interests of keen competition, good sportsmanship . . . and future matrimonial harmony."

"*Nigel—*"

"But I digress. We were speaking far more happily of the far more wondrous Kate Glyn."

"She *has* turned your head, hasn't she?" Lord Blake said with a smile.

"She is second only to my tailor in my heart."

Lord Blake laughed at this.

"Do you know, that is the second time I've heard you laugh since Oliver died. And both within the last week. Are you actually returning to the land of the living?"

"I wasn't aware that I had left it."

"You had vanished without a trace." Lord Braxton took a pinch of snuff. "Was it Miss Glyn who found you?"

Lord Blake began to think so that night as he claimed Kate for a dance, their first. She moved so easily into his arms. They danced together as if they had always danced together. She was grace and lightness, and he could not remember ever feeling so happy as she teased him throughout the dance, alternately complimenting his wardrobe and laughing at his sad lot in life. How dreadful to be heir to a dukedom!

Then she had taken his breath away, not altogether pleasantly.

"Very well, sir, you have quizzed me on my arch mask. Let me comment on yours for it is much more formidable than mine."

"How so, Kate?"

"It is well suited to fending people off, I grant you, but it has the unhappy effect of preventing *you* from drawing near to the few deserving others in

127

your world. Must you deny the love of your friends and family?"

The front door bell began desperately pealing. Maxwell, seeing his master properly clothed and coiffed, bowed and went to see who summoned his lordship.

The marquess studied himself in the mirror. No, he did not want to deny love any longer.

Mr. Peter Robbins stormed into his dressing room.

"You're in the soup, Cousin, make no mistake," said Mr. Robbins without preamble.

Lord Blake turned to survey Mr. Robbins through his quizzing glass, noting with much surprise the superb style of his coat, waistcoat, and breeches. His Hessians gleamed in the mid-morning light. His cravat was a very respectable Oriental.

"Bless thee, Bottom! bless thee! thou art translated."

"Theo, are you daft?" demanded Mr. Robbins.

"No, merely knocked off my feet. Why are you rigged out in so stunning a manner? *Are you in love?*"

Mr. Robbins roared with laughter. "God save me from such a fate," he said. "No, I've been dancing attendance on Aunt Aurelia. I'm her heir, you know. Can't let her change her will because she objects to buckskins at the breakfast table."

"Very wise."

"But I didn't come here to discuss my expectations. I came here to warn you of imminent disaster."

"I am agog, Peter. I hang on your every word."

"Dash it, Theo, this is serious! Aunt Aurelia is buying you a wedding present."

Lord Blake stared at his cousin. "You're mad," he managed.

"I begin to think it. Aunt Aurelia informs me that all of London is bent on the same task."

"And who, pray tell, am I to marry?"

"Who do you think? Priscilla Inglewood! Her father's been boasting of the coming nuptials these last three weeks, and she's been playing coy and saying stuff like 'Oh I couldn't possibly tell you of Lord Blake's plans.' I tell you straight, Theo, if you don't act and act now, you're going to find yourself shackled to that witch for life!"

"I am not so meek as to fall into plans that interest me not at all."

Mr. Robbins considered his cousin a moment. "You would have a year ago. Your stupid sense of duty would have had you at the altar with Priscilla by your side."

"I am older and wiser now," Lord Blake said with a smile, thinking of Kate Glyn, "as I should be."

"I'll believe it when I see you put an end to these rotten rumors."

Lord Blake twirled his quizzing glass and stared at the tip of one shoe. "Truth to tell, Cousin, I had heard murmurings of these noxious aspirations and had assumed that Priscilla would stop her father from making fools of us both. And yet you say she has aided and abetted this mad scheme?"

"Perhaps *because* she doesn't know that you're older and wiser."

"Or perhaps because she has her heart set on being a duchess."

"It's very likely both, and in the end, what does it matter? She's put you in the soup, and you've got to get yourself out of it now, before DeBries starts making your wedding clothes."

"Very well, Peter, I shall call on Priscilla this very morning. Lord, what a mess!"

"Ain't it, though?" Mr. Robbins said with a grin.

129

"I'm the one who's got to tell Aunt Aurelia to put your wedding gift in a back closet."

"Well, perhaps a front cupboard. I'm grateful to you, Peter. You're a good friend."

Lord Blake stood in front of the gate leading to the imposing front door of the even more imposing Inglewood town residence in Grosvenor Square considering what he must soon say and how different it was from what he had intended three weeks ago. Then, he had understood his duty and had been grateful that in Priscilla he could fulfill his matrimonial obligations and not threaten his heart. But now he was no longer resigned to such a fate.

Something had changed in him. There was a warmth in his heart instead of the ice that had cloaked it these last five years since Oliver's death. And the warmth, when presented with Priscilla Inglewood, drew back, for it wanted to encounter no more chill, and glaciers flowed in Priscilla Inglewood's veins.

Lord Blake opened the gate and walked up the steps to rap soundly upon the imposing Inglewood door. It was opened a moment later by a liveried footman who bowed and admitted his lordship, taking his card and leading him into a morning parlor decorated in ice blues, before going to fetch Lady Inglewood.

The room felt cold to Lord Blake, despite the fires burning in the grates on opposite ends of the room. He considered sitting down, but the chairs looked uncomfortable, and so he went to a fire and warmed himself. He looked around thinking how different this was from his call yesterday on Kate Glyn and Miss Fairfax in company, of course with William Atherton. That room had been warm, friendly, embracing. Miss Fairfax's sweet smile and very becoming blushes had charmed such a jaded observer as he, while Miss Glyn's absurd conversation had kept him laughing for the whole of the visit.

"Ah Theo, so good of you to call," Lady Inglewood said as she walked gracefully into the room.

Lord Blake went to meet her, taking her outstretched hand, but not raising it to his lips.

"Priscilla, you are looking lovely as always. How are you?"

"Quite fine, thank you, Theo. Won't you sit down? Would you like tea?"

Lord Blake accepted the former, declined the latter, and sat beside Lady Inglewood on the blue settee. Before he could state the purpose of his visit, she began to talk of the Jersey ball and how appalling had been Katharine Glyn's behavior: dancing with some of the acknowledged rakes of the *ton*, laughing uproariously with no feminine decorum whatsoever when conversing with her friends. She recalled the same lack of sensibility in Miss Glyn as a girl. The country drab, accustomed to associating with farmers, had conversed openly about the breeding problems the Glyns were having with one of their prize bulls. All had been appalled by such conversation. And at her debut, Miss Glyn had been no better, waltzing at Almack's before receiving the approbation of its stern patronesses; conversing in an open and offensive manner with anyone and everyone, no matter how censured by the *ton* they might be; driving a phaeton as if she were a man; walking the streets of London without a maid; riding through Hyde Park without a groom.

Lady Inglewood then spoke of this last Wednesday at Almack's when she and Lord Blake had danced together and what pleasure she felt in having a partner endowed with such grace and experience. She spoke of the call she and her father had made on the Duke and Duchess of Insley only the other day and what a lovely time they had had talking together. Wasn't it good to know that old family friends could be depended upon?

In response, Lord Blake rose, walked to the other side of the room, and returned to stand before Lady Inglewood.

"Priscilla," said he, "I must speak to you on a grave and difficult matter. Being blunt when discussing a delicate subject is anathema to me, but I fear that I must speak plainly to you now. Are you expecting an offer of marriage from me?"

Lady Inglewood blushed and coyly looked at her folded hands in her lap. "Why Theo, I could not be so presumptuous."

"Your father, however, can and is, and so has embarrassed us before the whole town. Incorrigible gossips and levelheaded matrons alike are saying that you and I are engaged and will be married before the year is out." The marquess spoke gently. "I cannot countenance such rumors, Priscilla. While I value our friendship and am tied to you by bonds of affection and esteem and family friendship that no one else can rival, I will not fulfill your father's expectations."

Lady Inglewood's face was flushed, not with maidenly modesty, but with growing anger.

"You intend to marry someone else, then?"

"I must needs marry, Priscilla, you know that."

"And who is better qualified than I to be wife to a duke?"

Lord Blake took her hand in his. "You would make an admirable wife to a prince if you cared to reach that high, Priscilla. I should have stated at the outset that the fault lies not in you, but in me."

"You cannot be thinking of marrying that Glyn woman?!"

Lord Blake dropped her hand and stepped back. "We are not discussing Miss Glyn. We are discussing an uncomfortable situation that must be rectified at once. I would speak to your father myself if I did not know the greater unkindness that would work on you. I'll not let you hear secondhand, Priscilla, that which most intimately concerns you."

"You are the soul of consideration, Theo."

"I am a monster, Priscilla, for not doing what you deserve. I acknowledge it freely. But I'll not be gossiped into any marriage, however estimable."

Rigid, Lady Inglewood rose to stand before Lord Blake. "If my father's incautious hopes and words have brought you any embarrassment, I am sorry, and will see to it that he stops putting you to the blush. If you will excuse me, Theo, I must dress for a luncheon appointment with Lady Montclair."

She did not offer him her hand. She turned and swept from the room like a queen, and Lord Blake was glad to see her go. That she would take his words badly, he had known. That she would feel betrayed by her natural hopes, he had assumed. But that her hands should clench into claws, and her eyes speak warfare to him despite her polite words, he had not anticipated. It occurred to him that Priscilla Inglewood would make a formidable enemy. He hoped she had not become one to him.

Chapter 13

IN THE AFTERNOON, after her morning gallop with Lord Blake, Miss Glyn shooed Sir William and Miss Fairfax out into the back gardens, then selected a volume of poetry from the library shelves, and sat down in her favorite chair fully prepared to spend an enjoyable hour in the adjoining lands of history and poetry. She opened to Dryden's *Absalom and Achitophel* and read a mere two dozen lines before coming to "Whate'er he did was done with so much ease, In him alone, 'twas natural to please." She was struck by it—she could not say why—and so read it again, and once again. With a smile she realized that it reminded her of Theo Blake. Finally discovering the silly grin on her face, Miss Glyn resolutely returned to the poem, but had read only a few more lines when memory of the preceding fortnight returned to her.

Wherever she had turned, she had found Theo Blake: at the theater, the Vauxhall Gardens, and at the various parties, routs, and balls that were a compendium of the season. They had talked together, and danced, and laughed the hours away. Her tales of youthful misadventure in Hampshire seemed to inspire the greatest laughter in his lordship, whether it was the recounting of a tumble into a spring bog while chasing a raccoon, and thus being presented to the Duke of Lancaster while covered in mud; or the time at fourteen when she had pinned her father to the wall of his study with her rapier to demand a latin tutor. Theo's rich, warm laughter had poured over her, and she had been glad for she loved to make him laugh, loved to hear him laugh.

Friends. How wonderful to have someone to laugh with at all of the silliness and foibles of town life, to delight in a mad romp on horseback through Hyde Park, to debate Locke and Montesquieu and Plato and Shakespeare for hours on end. She and Theo were friends.

"And in spite of Priscilla Inglewood, too," Miss Glyn murmured, and then frowned.

Having started more rumors than she could name solely for her own amusement, she knew not to heed whatever gossip was caught by the winds and spread through town. But word of Theo's forthcoming marriage to Lady Perfection had been so persistent, and Lady Perfection's smile one of such satisfaction, that Miss Glyn could not help but count as true what all seemed to acknowledge as fact. Well, what of that? If Theo was her friend during so obnoxious an engagement, he would be her friend during so abhorrent a marriage.

It came to Miss Glyn that with Miss Fairfax and Sir William cavorting in the back gardens, she should be weeping the coming loss of her friend and her growing loneliness. But she had never felt less like weeping. She had never felt so little loneliness in her life. Warmth flowed within her. She had met a kindred soul after five-and-twenty years of searching . . . even if he did insist on liking Priscilla Inglewood. Kate and Theo Blake shared the same nonsensical notions, the same love of authors, books, and plays, the same delight in horses, country life, and dancing.

Dancing.

It had been a se'ennight, but she still remembered

the tremor that had passed through her when she had moved into Theo's arms for the first time at the Jersey ball. It was as if two halves of an apple were joining again. It had felt so natural to be held by him, talk with him, tease him into laughter. As if she had done it all her life. The memory struck Miss Glyn so forcefully that her breath caught and her heart began to pound thunderously. Her hands flew to her flaming cheeks.

"Good God, I'm blushing!"

Sensing that things had gotten out of hand, she jumped to her feet, shoved the book of poetry back on its shelf, and then began to pace agitatedly around the room ... which perturbed her even more.

"I am no schoolgirl," she muttered. "What is wrong with me today?"

Miss Fairfax flew into the room in the next instant, colliding with her friend.

"Kate!" she cried and then grabbed Miss Glyn by both shoulders and began to shake her. "Kate, he proposed. William proposed! He asked me to marry him not five minutes ago!"

She pulled Miss Glyn to her and hugged her fiercely.

"And what was your answer?" Miss Glyn managed to gasp.

"Kate, you idiot," Miss Fairfax said, laughing as she released her. "William and I are to be married!"

"Huzzah!" Miss Glyn shouted as she threw her arms into the air, which set Miss Fairfax to laughing uncontrollably for her nerves were not at all steady. "May all the gods bless your union," cried Miss Glyn, "and keep you happy and in good health, but *not* attend your wedding, for they drink a ruinous amount of wine. Oh Georgie," she said as she ecstatically hugged her friend, "I am so happy for you!"

"And I am so happy for me, too!" Miss Fairfax said.

"What took him so long?" Miss Glyn demanded, which set Miss Fairfax to laughing even harder. Miss Glyn, who dearly loved to laugh when justly provoked, quickly joined her.

The resulting hullabaloo brought Jeremy Fairfax and the ever vigilant Wainwright into the library on the run.

"What the devil is going on?" Mr. Fairfax demanded.

"Oh Jeremy," Miss Fairfax said as she threw herself into his arms, "I am betrothed! William asked me to marry him!"

"Dearest Georgina," cried her brother as he kissed her again and again, "my heartiest congratulations. By God, this is wonderful! I thought I'd never get you off my hands."

"May I wish you well on so happy an occasion, Miss Fairfax?" Wainwright intoned, thus skillfully preventing Miss Fairfax from pinching her brother's nose.

"You may do better than that, Wainwright," she declared as she turned to the butler. "Champagne! I want bottles and bottles of champagne. We are going to celebrate!"

"Very good, miss," Wainwright replied with a bow, allowing himself to smile only after he had left the room.

"I say," Mr. Fairfax said, "where's the bridegoom? Loped off already, has he?"

"William has gone to pay his addresses to our uncle," Miss Fairfax said, and then paled. "Oh Jeremy, do you think Uncle Rupert will say yes?"

"He had better," Mr. Fairfax replied with a smile, "or he'll live to rue the day."

It was Sir William Atherton, however, who had already begun to rue the day, the month, and the year as he stood trembling before Lord and Lady Egerton and tried desperately to make his tongue and lips cooperate to produce one coherent sentence. Any coherent sentence. At this point, Sir William could not be particular. He was not, however, having very much success.

Lord Egerton, looking on, had nothing but sympathy for the poor fellow. Recollecting a similar scene some thirty years earlier, he thought he had been much the same, if not worse. He glanced now at his wife, her severest mask firmly in place as she listened to Sir William recite all the reasons why he was not worthy of so great an honor as the winning of Miss Fairfax's hand.

A slight smile touched Lord Egerton's lips as Lady Egerton's eyes met his for a fleeting moment. So she remembered that scene of so long ago, too, did she? And still as great an imp now as she was then, making this poor boy quake in his boots with her frowns when she had been saying only last week that she thought it time Atherton come up to scratch so they could marry Georgina off and return once more to a calm and peaceful existence.

Lord Egerton turned an attentive ear to Sir William once again as the poor boy began his concluding remarks. Deciding that the winning of one's bride should be a cherished memory fifty years after the event—and recollecting that terror did wonderful things to one's faculty for recall—Lord Egerton decided to toy with the fellow a few more minutes before giving his consent. Sir William would thank him for it in the years to come, Lord Egerton was certain of it.

Half an hour after he had left the Fairfax residence, Sir William, having forgotten to collect his horse from the Egerton groom, ran from Berkeley

Square back to Russell Court. He burst through the front door of his beloved's home, running past one startled footman, a parlor maid, and a thoroughly aghast Wainwright, bellowing his beloved's name at the top of his voice as he threw open one door after another.

He came to the library door at last, threw it open, spied his love immediately (indeed, he saw no one else), ran into the room, and pulled Miss Fairfax into his arms.

"He said yes!" he cried, before kissing her. "Georgina, they both said yes!"

He pulled her into a passionate, and extensive, embrace.

"It appears," Mr. Fairfax observed, "that they are engaged."

"So it would seem," Miss Glyn murmured, taking a sip of champagne. "How *can* they breathe like that?"

※

Chapter 14

ON THE FOLLOWING evening at Almack's, news of Miss Fairfax's betrothal to Sir William Atherton was on everyone's lips. A great heiress, an unrivaled beauty, who might have married any one of a dozen men of the highest rank, had selected instead a mere knight! Many a young woman heaved a sigh of relief, and began to plan anew how best to snare an eligible husband.

The happy couple stood along the left wall of the room surrounded by friends, admirers, and gossips, all eager to hear everything that had occurred to bring about so wonderful an event. Across the room, Miss Glyn was entertaining her own circle of friends: Theo Blake, Elizabeth and Tommy Carrington, and Jeremy Fairfax. They, too, were discussing the season's most startling betrothal, despite all of Miss Glyn's protests that if she heard one more glowing comment about the forthcoming union, she would bloody well scream. She was ignored.

"Turncoats," said Miss Glyn. "I am surrounded by unfeeling turncoats. Here I am forced to endure the wallowing en masse in romantical nonsense by all about me, and no one has the simple kindness to offer me the least bit of sympathy."

"Poor, deprived dear," Miss Carrington clucked, which drove Miss Glyn to the verge of a chuckle.

"What's all this I hear about a celebratory party

for the affianced pair?" Mr. Carrington asked with an amazing lack of charity for Miss Glyn's sorely tried temper.

"More of a ball, really, from the size of the guest list," Mr. Fairfax replied. "Our aunt and uncle have decided that the engagement must be announced and celebrated in a properly public and entertaining fashion. Anyone who is anyone will be in the Egerton ballroom a fortnight hence."

"That lets me out," Miss Glyn said. "I am only the friend and confidante of the bride. I simply helped Atherton in his pursuit of Georgina and she in her pursuit of him. I am of no consequence whatsoever."

"Ignore her," Miss Carrington advised the amused group. "She becomes insupportable if encouraged in this mood."

"If you are going to forestall all of my amusements, I shall take myself off," Miss Glyn declared.

"Take me with you," Lord Blake said, catching her arm. "I feel in need of exercise. Ask me to dance."

"Ask? I shall *permit* you to dance with me," Miss Glyn retorted, and thus they made their way to the dance floor.

"Tell me, my dear misanthrope," Lord Blake said to his partner as they made each other their bows, "however did you become the Hampshire Hoyden?"

A raging fever burst into Miss Glyn's veins as Lord Blake drew her into his arms and led them into the waltz. It took a moment for her to find her voice. "I-I-I couldn't say. It happened so long ago, you know, and my memory is not what it once was."

Lord Blake sobered, capturing her gaze with his own. "Kate."

"It is an exceedingly tedious story. It wouldn't interest you in the least."

"Kate."

"Oh, very well," Miss Glyn said crossly. She concentrated on studying his lordship's exceedingly broad shoulder. "My mother died when I was quite young, and Papa could not bring himself to remarry, even though this meant that he would have no son to carry on the line. Being a trifle eccentric, and noting my adventurous spirit, he chose to raise me as the son he would never have: hiring tutors far beyond the feminine level of education, teaching me to ride, to drive, even to fence. Though disdainful of my scholarship, he took a peculiar pride in my masculine accomplishments, gleefully telling one and all that his daughter had a better pair of hands than any young buck in the county. I had no notion this was a fault in me.

"When I was sixteen, Papa died suddenly and, although he denied me Tryon Hall, my home since infancy, he very kindly made me the ward of the Fairfaxes. Mrs. Fairfax was a dear woman and, seeing the neglect of my feminine education, did what she could to improve it. Sewing, dancing, flirting, how to appear interested in the dullest of conversations were all skills that she taught me, trying to prepare me for my debut. She did what she could to warn me of my bluntness, of my giddiness, of my disregard for the opinions of others. But I, in my great wisdom, thought this mere nonsense and paid little heed.

"Soon after my debut, however, I learned that what she had tried to teach me was not at all nonsense, but indeed, the greatest arts of survival. In short, I was a disaster. I heaped untold amounts of humiliation upon myself with every word that I uttered, every step that I took. I was universally reviled. Certainly, there were some in the *ton* who took great delight in furthering my humiliation, but in all truth I must lay the blame squarely at my own door.

142

"When six weeks of disaster after disaster had passed, I sat myself down to look sternly at my situation and decide what was to be done. Should I flee to my first love, the country, and rusticate for the rest of my life, thus admitting defeat; or should I take myself in hand and become the demure young female that all of London idolized; or could there, perhaps, be a third option? I chose to hope so.

"I came to believe that if I studied the ways of the *ton*, the quirks and personalities of its arbiters of fashion and status, if I schooled myself in conversation and in proper behavior, and yet presented myself with some audacity, that I might become not so much an eccentric, but an individual, and one not to be scorned. And so I set about transforming what the world derided into something stronger and more reputable then they or I could ever have imagined.

"By the time I proposed becoming Georgina's chaperone, people might raise their eyebrows, but they all agreed that nothing could be more sensible than the knowledgeable, talented, and witty Miss Glyn overseeing the protection of the lovely Miss Fairfax, for who better than the Hampshire Hoyden knew the ways and dangers of the *ton*? Now, I suppose the tale must have a moral for an ending, so let me see what I can provide. Ah, I have it! Don't be stupid, and respect your elders. The end."

"I think you have it wrong, Kate." Lord Blake said quietly. "There's a good deal to be learned from the tale."

"Yes, what a great ninny I can be. But you were discussing earlier the far more entertaining prospect of Georgina's marriage to your friend. You are pleased with the result of all your moral support, I trust?"

"I am pleased he is so happy, though I will miss his bachelor freedom. What are your plans now that

143

Miss Fairfax is to be married?" Lord Blake inquired as he guided them around the ballroom.

"I think I shall rusticate," Miss Glyn replied. "I have always preferred the country to town life. This is my chance to escape. I find I've grown weary of town life, and long for all the commotion of the country. But first, I shall build a bonfire 'round the Atherton bridal bed."

"Are you so very jealous, then?" Lord Blake said, chuckling.

"Envious, really."

Lord Blake smiled down into her brown eyes. "And what do you envy Miss Fairfax? Her beauty? Her money? Her fiancé?"

"Her happiness," Miss Glyn replied.

"You cannot be serious."

"But I am, very."

"Yet you seem a very happy woman."

"Oh, I am, as a rule. But look at Georgina," Miss Glyn said, nodding toward her friend and Sir William, who were lost in a transport of bliss as they danced together. "She is glowing with a happiness I am certain never to know. I realize such emotion will not last, the fires will turn to embers. But I should like just once to know what Georgina is experiencing at this moment."

"Is such a goal so unattainable?" Lord Blake asked quietly.

"But of course. How can you ask it?" Miss Glyn said, thrown into sudden confusion by the way his lordship studied her. She tried to rally. "I am five-and-twenty, an acknowledged antidote. I lack any sort of an impressive dowry, and I have a tongue that could curdle milk."

Lord Blake smiled at this.

"I inspire friendship in the manly beast, nothing more. And I'm glad of it, for mine is not a marrying nature. I am too independent by half. There are few men in this world who could tolerate such a creature as me, fewer still whom I could tolerate. Besides, if I were to marry, it would not be for position or wealth, for I am happy as a nonentity and I've enough money of my own. That leaves marrying for love and could anything be worse? I'm a sensible woman, and I want no part of love. I don't trust it."

Miss Glyn was unable to interpret the startled expression on Lord Blake's face.

"And since we must needs speak of marriage," she continued, "why haven't you married before this? You're heir to a dukedom, handsome, well spoken, always well dressed. Surely your parents have been clamoring to marry you off?"

"I haven't been around much to give them the opportunity."

"Ah yes, the reclusive Lord Blake, touring the country, acquiring lightskirts left and right, prattling to your sheep. Shall you always run away from your fate?"

Lord Blake's gray eyes narrowed. "Who would not find it untenable stepping into his brother's shoes? It was not my fate to succeed my father. I never wanted to be duke. Oliver was heir. He was suited to the role."

"Your brother is dead," Miss Glyn said quietly.

"I know it. I'm as responsible for his death as if I had fired the gun that killed him."

"It is at just such times as these that I long to kick you."

Startled, Lord Blake burst into laughter.

"My dear friend," Miss Glyn continued, "you have as much right to be duke as I have to be Katharine Glyn. Neither of us planned these destinies, yet here we are living them, and they're not such bad lives on the whole. While I have been denied the beloved home of my youth, I quite enjoy reading good books and charging a fence on a strong horse;

and, while you have been denied the company of a beloved brother, you've told me you enjoy the elegancies of life that your position entails. From what your father has told me, Oliver would not begrudge you your Moroccan bed jacket or your wine cellar. How did the duke describe your brother to me? He called him 'a wonderful boy in every sense. One of those paragons who manage to do everything well.' I thought the description very apt . . . of you."

Lord Blake stared at her. "You are quite mad."

" 'I am but mad north-northwest: when the wind is southerly, I know a hawk from a handsaw.' "

"Not at all apt, Katharine. I've forsaken Hamlet for Puck."

"Much more suitable," Miss Glyn said approvingly, "though the costume is a trifle scandalous. And you will not detour me. You must own yourself a paragon, my friend. Only the other day, the duke was raving about all of the improvements you've been making on the Insley estates. I myself have seen your prowess on a horse or driving a carriage, on the dance floor, doing the niceties to a dragonly matron. Tommy Carrington has raved to me about your skill with your pair of fives, Lord Braxton has mentioned your deadly abilities with a sword, and I have yet to see you spill a cup of punch. You must accept your destiny, Theo. You are a nonesuch, or at least a nonpareil. I amaze myself by staying on good terms with you, for I do not, on the whole, like perfect people. Either I have forsaken my renowned good sense, or your perfection is but a mask cloaking a country boor more in love with his sheep than humanity."

Lord Blake sighed. "Have you never lowered yourself to toad-eating?"

"My dear Theo, you hear so many compliments all day long from fawning females that I would think myself the greatest villain if I condescended to compliment your manly grace or skill on a dance floor . . . even if you are the best partner I've curtsied to."

"I knew there was a reason I've stayed in London so long."

Lord Blake's smile felt like a caress.

"What is that?" Miss Glyn managed.

"I've finally found a woman who knows how to waltz with the grace and intimacy the dance requires, but without the familiarity it so often inspires."

"Your praise would be more circumspect if you had seen my first waltz at Almack's. I tried to lead."

Lord Blake choked back a laugh. "The problem most people have is that they tend to reduce the waltz to a struggle for dominance. I, on the other hand, have always felt it should be danced by two skilled equals intent on complementing each other. I daresay, that is why we deal so well together."

Lord Blake was startled and pleased beyond measure to see a blush steal into Miss Glyn's cheeks. The two concluded their dance in great harmony with one another, which did not go unobserved by Miss Carrington and Mr. Fairfax as they stood together at the foot of the room.

"My, my, my, aren't they chummy?" Miss Carrington said, nodding towards Miss Glyn and Lord Blake, who had captured two chairs along the far wall and were enjoying a quiet tête-à-tête.

"Everyone is remarking on Blake's lengthy stay in London," said Mr. Fairfax, "and his pleasure in Kate's company. I'd wager his delight puts Lady Inglewood back on the mart. Do you think anyone will want her?"

"Undoubtedly, though she's passed over the cream of the crop in her bid for the dukedom," Miss Carrington replied. "She'll have to settle for a fortune hunter."

To say that Lady Inglewood's ears were burning would be to understate the matter. She had endured a miserable fortnight in which all of London had remarked the number of times Lord Blake had stood up with Miss Glyn at Almack's or a ball; the frequency and mirth of their conversations; the pleasure the marquess clearly took in the hoyden's company; and his seeming lack of interest in any other female in town.

Lady Inglewood knew a slap when she encountered one.

In the same fortnight, Lord Blake had been conspicuous by his absence from the Inglewood home. He had not called on her once; and, while she still received invitations from the Duke and Duchess of Insley, Lord Blake on these occasions bestirred himself only so far as to greet her politely, inquire about her activities and the health of her father, and then fob her off with some excuse to go and laugh with Kate Glyn in some private corner.

His name had appeared on none of Lady Inglewood's dance cards.

It was also noted and avidly discussed over every tea tray in town that Lord Inglewood no longer spoke of a forthcoming marriage between his daughter and Lord Blake.

The humiliation was far worse than Lady Inglewood had expected.

To not only lose Theo Blake and her future as a duchess, but to lose her dream to Kate Glyn...! And then to be openly gossiped about, laughed at, pitied ... All because of an uncouth guttersnipe!

Murder burned in her soul. Lady Inglewood stalked across the room, removing herself to a corner. Lord Falkhurst, who had enjoyed one dance with her that evening, quickly joined her.

"Careful, Priscilla," he said, "your petulance is showing."

"That snake!" hissed Lady Inglewood, indicating Miss Glyn still seated with Lord Blake and joined by Lord Braxton, the Carringtons, and Mr. Fairfax. "If I had claws, I'd rip the smile from her smug face. She has deliberately humiliated me."

"The termagant's been far too busy of late," Lord Falkhurst grimly agreed. "It is she who turned Georgina Fairfax against me, I am convinced of it. That female viper was *gloating* when Miss Fairfax told me of this absurd betrothal to that country clod. She undoubtedly played matchmaker to the whole affair."

"I've no doubt. Our Miss Glyn enjoys sticking her nose in where it does not belong. I daresay, she has poisoned Lord Blake's mind against me."

"To be beaten out by a country bumpkin," seethed Lord Falkhurst. "Damn him! Damn them all!"

Lady Inglewood silently echoed these sentiments. She stared at the laughing group across the room, and felt her rage grow. Bested by Fairfax and shamed by a mere chaperone!

"It occurs to me," said she, "that we both have suffered greatly at the hands of that little enclave."

Lord Falkhurst paused and then smiled down at his companion. "Do you think, perhaps, that something should be done?"

"What do you propose?" Lady Inglewood boldly demanded.

"I overheard an interesting piece of information earlier this evening concerning a ball to celebrate Miss Fairfax's betrothal to her knight-errant."

"Of what importance is that?"

"It is everything, my dear Priscilla, if you want to see the engagement shattered and that little enclave, as you called it, utterly routed within a fortnight."

"And Katharine Glyn?"

"Knowing the strength of her ties to Miss Fairfax, she will be served a deathblow I doubt she will survive."

"I find you utterly fascinating, Falkhurst. Pray continue, you have my undivided attention."

※

Chapter 15

ON THE SECOND morning following her betrothal to Sir William, Miss Fairfax and Miss Glyn were seated in their front parlor sorting through the morning's post. Since congratulatory notes had begun streaming in, Miss Fairfax's pile far exceeded that of her friend, a bounty that Miss Glyn regarded with a jaundiced eye. Her mood was not improved by Miss Fairfax's constant chirrups of delight at one note after another and her insistence upon reading one charming passage after another.

"Oh look!" exclaimed Miss Fairfax. "Mrs. Foote has written to me."

"Be still my heart," Miss Glyn said, picking up a magazine from the table beside her and beginning to flip through the pages.

"Kate! She says that she has the opportunity to make a gown for me! An original design!"

"That is odd," Miss Glyn commented idly, glancing up but briefly from her magazine.

"This is above all else marvelous! She can make the gown for my betrothal ball."

"I wonder how she freed herself from Lady Perfection's shackles?"

"I don't care in the least," Miss Fairfax declared. "I am to have a gown designed by the best modiste in London!"

And that very afternoon she made her way to

Mrs. Foote's shop to be measured for her betrothal gown.

A se'ennight after this pleasant undertaking, Sir William Atherton received a note in his fiancée's hand desiring him to meet her at Mrs. Foote's fashionable shop and from there take her to lunch. Sir William sheepishly cried off from a previously planned luncheon with Lord Blake, and went to Mrs. Foote's shop at the time specified in the note. Upon entering the shop, however, Sir William discovered to his dismay that his beloved was not there. A plump, middle-aged woman who announced herself as the owner of the dress shop then addressed the crestfallen lover.

"Miss Fairfax asked that I extend to you her sincerest regrets, Sir William, but her aunt and uncle—the Egertons, you know—called her away, and she will be unable to keep her appointment with you."

Sir William's expression was a mixture of melancholy and chagrin, for how could he explain this sudden turn of events to Lord Blake? He would be roasted soundly for this, he knew.

"I would not have this be a fruitless journey, Sir William," said Mrs. Foote. "You may not know it, but I have designed the very gown Miss Fairfax will wear to your betrothal ball. Would you . . . care to see it? It is beautiful beyond compare, if I do say so myself."

Since anything having to do with his beloved was of interest to Sir William, he replied eagerly in the affirmative, and Mrs. Foote disappeared into the back rooms of the shop to emerge, a moment later, with the gown in her arms.

Sir William stared at it with astonishment and pleasure. He knew little of women's fashions, but he knew what he liked. The dress consisted of a silver silk sheath with spider netting festooned with pearls and diamonds. The sleeves were nonexistent, the bodice nearly so.

"It is magnificent!" he declared.

"Notice the delicacy of the workmanship," Mrs. Foote said, holding the gown up for closer scrutiny, "and the lightness of the train. Ah! She will be a princess in this gown. There is not another like it in all of England."

"It is very beautiful," Sir William murmured, his eyes riveted upon the gown, his mind filling it with the lovely figure of Miss Fairfax. Finally, after a few more minutes conversation, Sir William took his leave and went in search of Lord Blake, who laughed at his acquiring a ring through his nose so soon after his engagement and thereupon bought him lunch.

The two men separated some hours later, and Sir William then made his way to White's and was hailed instantly by three of his friends from school days. They spent the next several hours fondly recalling past escapades and drinking a good deal of White's excellent claret into the bargain. Finally, they went their separate ways. Sir William had just determined to return home for a good night's sleep—the claret he had consumed was beginning to insist upon it—when he found himself addressed.

"Sir William! Sir William! I say, is that you? What a piece of luck running into you here."

Puzzled, Sir William turned to find Lord Falkhurst advancing upon him with every aspect of pleasure. Sir William became positively befuddled as Falkhurst made him his bow, took his arm, and began to pull him toward one of the private lounges.

"I must congratulate you," Falkhurst was saying. "To snare the beautiful Miss Fairfax is an accomplishment," he said, pushing Sir William into a chair and then signaling a waiter, "that must be celebrated with champagne."

"That's decent of you, my lord," Sir William managed to reply, although his head was swimming with confusion. Lord Falkhurst was treating him like a long lost friend and, for the life of him, Sir William could not recall when they had become so fond of each other. Seeing, however, a bottle of champagne brought to their table, and his glass liberally filled, Sir William could not think of insulting his host by asking what the devil had got into him. So he raised his glass in salute and polished off its contents with a quick toss of his hand. The glass was instantly refilled.

"You're a lucky man, Atherton," Lord Falkhurst said, sitting opposite him. "A most fortunate man. I tried like the very devil to make Georgina accept my suit, but once she gets her mind set on something, there's no hope of changing it."

"I . . . don't quite follow."

"*You*, old man!" Falkhurst said with a laugh. "Georgina told me on the very evening you met that she intended to marry you. Ruined my evening's plans, I can tell you."

"Did she, by God?" Sir William said, rather pleased by so flattering and determined a pursuit.

"Mind you, I pleaded with her every day, even went down on my knees. But she's a stubborn little chit. Decided she wanted fair looks rather than fair fortune, after all. Mind you, with her dowry, she could afford to marry a chimney sweep if she'd a mind to it. Bottom's up, old fellow."

Sir William complied. Perhaps the champagne would help him make sense of all that Lord Falkhurst was saying.

"I did not know you and Georgina were on such . . . friendly terms," Sir William said and, to his amazement, Falkhurst burst into a roar of laughter.

"F-f-*friendly*?" he cried. "Oh, that *is* rich!"

154

"Have I said something amusing?" Sir William inquired a bit crossly.

"You mean you really don't know?"

"Know what?"

"Oh, come man," Lord Falkhurst said impatiently. "Don't play the innocent with me. The whole of London knows about Georgina."

"Knows what?" demanded Sir William with mounting fury.

Falkhurst paused and studied him a moment. "Georgina told me at lunch today that you had blinders on, but I never dreamed—"

"Lunch?" ejaculated Sir William. "*Today?* Georgina had lunch with *you*?"

"Yes, of course. At the White Hart."

"I don't believe you."

"There are two waiters to verify my story."

"She lunched with the Egertons!" Sir William cried in growing desperation.

"If you believe that, you are a bigger gaby than even I had imagined," Lord Falkhurst said with a sneer.

"Georgina would not lie to me."

"No? Then where was your precious fiancée last Thursday night?"

"She went to bed early with a headache."

"Oh, she went to bed, certainly, but I would not say with a headache."

Sir William threw the contents of his glass into Falkhurst's face and then, his head reeling, stormed from the club leaving a damp, but satisfied, Lord Falkhurst behind.

On Monday morning, Sir William left his lodgings to attend his daily session at Jackson's. The day was fair, the air warm and fresh, but Sir William, his thoughts still mired in all that Lord Falkhurst had said on Saturday night, took none of this in. Lady Inglewood was compelled to utter his name thrice before Sir William's head came up, his eyes focused, and he found his path blocked.

"Good morning, Sir William," she said a fourth time.

"Oh! Lady Inglewood, I beg your pardon. My mind . . . was not attending."

"Thinking of your forthcoming nuptials, no doubt," Lady Inglewood said with a smile. "I must take leave to tell you, Sir William, that all of London is buzzing about your betrothal. It was always assumed that Georgina would marry Lord Falkhurst."

"Falkhurst?"

"Their passion for each other seemed so ardent and enduring," Lady Inglewood blithely continued, "and naturally when a relationship becomes as . . . intimate . . . as theirs, one does tend to make assumptions about such matters as marriage. But you fooled us all, Sir William. I congratulate you."

"Lady Inglewood," Sir William seethed, catching her slender wrist in his hand, "are you telling me that Georgina has been having an affair with Lord Falkhurst?!"

"Certainly," cried Lady Inglewood. "Oh, surely you knew? All of London has known of it these last six months."

"I don't believe you!" Sir William cried hotly, flinging her arm away.

"I am not accustomed to being called a liar," Lady Inglewood coldly retorted. "If I were a man, I would call you out for such an offense. I tell you only what is common knowledge. It has even been said that Falkhurst and she rendezvous at night when Katharine Glyn is away. Certainly there have been occasions when Miss Glyn has attended a social function and Georgina has remained at home . . . alone. I should not be surprised if Miss Glyn helped them arrange these things, she is so very clever about schemes and plots, as you know. Georgina has often remarked that had she not had Miss Glyn's help, she might never have brought you to your knee. But that is, of course, ridiculous. Everyone knows of your deep love for Georgina. Why else would you ignore her past, and marry her despite all the protests of civil society?"

"Georgina's past is spotless. Spotless!"

"Have it as you will," Lady Inglewood said with a shrug.

"I'll not have you slandering my fiancée in public or private, Lady Inglewood!"

"My dear Sir William, I have said only what I have heard from many others. I naturally assumed that you knew of it as well. I beg your pardon if I have offended you in any way."

"Offended?" cried the distraught Sir William. "*Offended?* When you have called the woman I love, the woman to whom I am betrothed, a common *slut*, you ask if I am offended?!"

"I do apologize. I—"

"I'll not stand here and listen to any of these atrocious lies! Good day, Lady Inglewood," Sir William said, and then stalked off in the opposite direction, forgetting utterly his scheduled session at Jackson's.

How dare she, he seethed inwardly, how *dare* she insinuate such base behavior on Georgina's part? How could anyone think Georgina a common trollop? Her purity and innocence were openly displayed on her face for all to see.

And yet—here Sir William stopped in his tracks— if the whole of the *ton* spoke of these things, how could they not be true?

No! It was impossible! He knew Georgina's soul as he knew his own. She came to him chaste, untouched. Her virtue was real, not some painted facade.

And yet—Sir William slowly continued his journey homeward—Falkhurst had often danced attendance on Georgina, and she seemed to enjoy his company. And there had been rumors, weeks before, that Falkhurst had gone so far as to elope with her to Gretna Green. Georgina had laughed off such tales, but was there not a modicum of truth to every rumor?

And yet . . .

Sir William continued home in this way: plagued by doubts and a burgeoning fear he dared not explore.

He paced the floor of his parlor for a good three hours, unable to dispel the growing anger and doubts within him. If only he could turn to his friends for advice! But how could he utter such black thoughts aloud? At last, sick to death of the closed air of his lodgings, he decided that a walk might clear his head and settle his nerves. So, without bothering with a hat or stick, he stalked out the front door to come almost immediately upon Lord Falkhurst.

"Out of my way," Sir William demanded through clenched teeth.

"Atherton, please, I must speak to you a moment," Lord Falkhurst said, putting a hand on his shoulder, which Sir William murderously removed.

"I have nothing to say to you. I will have nothing to *do* with you!" he declared as he attempted to step around Falkhurst, but the earl once again blocked his path.

"Yes, but I have something of import to say to you. I want to apologize, and humbly beg your pardon for anything I may have said Saturday night to upset you. I . . . was in my cups and yes, I confess it, bitterly jealous of you for winning the one

158

woman I love above all others. Surely, loving Georgina as you do, you can understand what I have endured this last week?"

"I . . . suppose so," Sir William said slowly, unable to look Falkhurst full in the face.

"I have been raking myself over the coals ever since Saturday. Please, Atherton, be the gentleman that I was not that night and accept my apology."

Sir William studied Lord Falkhurst's earnest expression and felt his anger seep out of him. "Very well," he said with a sigh, "I accept your apology."

"Good man! Can I have your hand on it?" Falkhurst asked hopefully, his hand extended.

With another sigh, and a smile, Sir William consented and found his hand firmly clasped.

"Bless you, Atherton," Falkhurst cried. "I cannot tell you what a load this is off my mind. I have not slept in two nights, it's plagued me so. What I said to you was unforgivable."

"That's all right, Falkhurst," Sir William said with the utmost patience. "I understand. I gave you my hand, after all."

"But let me truly make amends. Come, have you eaten? Let me take you to lunch."

"It really is not necessary—"

"But I insist!"

"I am not really very hungry—"

"You are still angry with me, I can see it. Ah well," Lord Falkhurst said with a melancholy sigh, "I should have expected as much."

"No, it is not that at all," Sir William said in exasperation. "It is only that I . . . Well . . . I should be delighted to lunch with you, my lord," he said at last.

Lord Falkhurst led him arm in arm to a fashionable restaurant that he had often visited with his particular friends, and soon Sir William found himself seated at a large table opposite the earl. The

159

restaurant consisted of two levels of seating, the higher level where he and his host had been placed afforded a view of the whole of the room, save for those few tables on the level directly below them. A string quartet played Haydn in a corner while the restaurant hummed with a life only the most prosperous of establishments enjoy.

Lord Falkhurst expressed surprise that this was Sir William's first visit. "Odd," said he. "I should have thought that Georgina . . . Still, you are here now. The food is excellent, the service is superb, and the wine cellar surprisingly good."

"Ah, Lord Falkhurst," their portly waiter said as he swept the menus from their hands, "so good to see you again. Mademoiselle is not with you to-day?"

"Um . . . no, Perkins," Lord Falkhurst said as Sir William shot him a swift, hard glance. "We'll start with the asparagus soup, I think, then continue . . ."

Lord Falkhurst ordered their meal while Sir William sat in a stew of suspicion and malcontent. Mademoiselle? Had that fool of a waiter meant Georgina? From all that Falkhurst had said Saturday night and today, the waiter could have meant no other. Yet Falkhurst *was* considered quite a hand with the ladies. Perhaps it was some other female: an actress, a dancer, a paphian? But looking at Falkhurst's cold, aristocratic face, Sir William doubted this.

He had taken only a sip of his wine when he heard a familiar ring of laughter. Burgundy sloshed onto his hand as he numbly lowered the wineglass to the table and strained to detect the source of the laughter. It came again. From directly below him!

Lord Falkhurst, seeing the strained expression on his companion's face, leaned back in his chair, a slight smile hovering on his lips.

"It is true, I swear it! I love him very much, for all his failings."

Georgina!

Sir William's heart began to pound painfully in his chest.

"You've a forgiving nature, there's no doubt," her companion replied.

"I am no saint, Priscilla," Miss Fairfax replied. "We all have our faults, even my darling fiancé has a few."

"No!" gasped Lady Inglewood, which set Miss Fairfax to giggling. "Not Sir William!"

"Even he."

"*I* see it now. You are swayed by a handsome face. Fair looks or the dark hair and sparkling eyes of your luncheon companion Saturday are all the same to you."

"Not *quite* the same," Miss Fairfax replied, which set both women to laughing.

"I do apologize," Lord Falkhurst murmured. "I did not think Georgina would come here three days in succession. Look, Atherton, even though we *are* rivals, can we not be gentlemen about this?"

"Damn you, Falkhurst," Sir William seethed as he shoved his chair back, lunged to his feet, and threw his napkin to the table like a gauntlet. "Damn you to an everlasting hell!"

He stormed from the restaurant, thrusting waiters and customers aside in his hurry to flee. The uproar he caused brought all eyes to turn upon him, including those of Miss Fairfax.

"William!" she cried, rising from her seat. "William!" But her call went unheeded.

By nine o'clock that evening, Sir William had thrown a boot at his housekeeper, churlishly hurled Peter Robbins out of his lodgings with a great deal of heat and no explanation whatsoever, and had consumed one and one-third bottles of brandy when his housekeeper tentatively reentered the parlor.

"Sir William? I've just had this letter delivered."

"Throw the blasted thing in the fire," Sir William muttered from his prone position on a blue brocade sofa.

"But sir, the footman who brought this said that it was urgent and that I must give it to you at once."

"Footman?"

"From the Inglewood residence."

"What the devil are they writing me about?" Sir William demanded as he struggled into a sitting position.

"I have the letter here, sir," the housekeeper said.

"Well bring it to me, woman! I can't read it from here."

Privately believing that her employer was going to have the devil's own time reading the missive when it was placed under his nose, the housekeeper nonetheless delivered the letter into his hands and quickly withdrew from the room.

Sir William tore open the envelope with unsteady hands, spent the next minute or two trying to focus, and began to read:

Dear Sir William:

I would not normally take a hand in such a matter as this, but when my honor has been impugned, I feel I must defend myself.

If you wish proof of all that I said concerning Georgina Fairfax, position yourself outside of the Fairfax residence in Russell Court no later than eleven o'clock this evening. Georgina has informed me that she has planned a rendezvous with Lord Falkhurst, that they habitually meet outside the southwest entrance of her home before adjourning to her rooms for a private tête-à-tête.

If you doubt my information, you have only to go to your fiancée's home tonight and you will be convinced of the veracity of my words. I shall expect an apology from you in the morning.

Lady Priscilla Inglewood

Sir William crumpled the paper into a tight ball and held it clenched in his fist.

"Damn her," he muttered, and then lurched to his feet. "Damn her!"

The letter was hurled into the grate.

He searched for and found a new bottle of brandy, poured himself a large glass full, and began to pace the room, plagued by anger and doubts, and a growing dread that his life would be destroyed on this night.

As the clock on the mantelpiece above the room's fireplace began to chime ten-thirty, Sir William threw his glass against the wall with sudden fury, grabbed his coat, and stormed from his flat, ignoring his housekeeper's pleas not to go out in such a state.

Sir William, having stalked to within thirty yards of the southwest side entrance to the Fairfax home in Russell Court, suddenly caught sight of a couple wrapped in an impassioned embrace near the doorway. Heart thudding in his breast, he stopped dead in his tracks. The man was clearly Falkhurst and the woman ... Her black hair spilled across her shoulders and part way down her back; her sleeveless gown of silver spider netting festooned with pearls and diamonds molded itself to her lovely frame.

Georgina!

It could be no other. Georgina, wearing the gown meant for the ball to celebrate their betrothal, was kissing Lord Falkhurst with a passion Sir William had once believed she felt only for him. Nausea welled in his stomach and throat as the couple drew apart, Georgina moving into the shadows.

"Shall we go in, my love?" Falkhurst murmured, his index finger tracing a trail along his companion's slender shoulder. She replied by wrapping her arms around his neck and embracing him once again. Finally they parted and, arms about each other's waists, they stepped into the house.

Sir William could fight back the nausea no longer. It overwhelmed him for several minutes and, when at last his retching had ceased, he raked a trembling hand through his hair. Staring at the doorway through which the adulterous couple had entered, he tried to understand what had happened.

The woman that he loved beyond life itself was unfaithful to him, had betrayed and ridiculed him, and all of London had known of it! They had been laughing at him for weeks, and Sir William had not known it. Humiliation flamed his cheeks. Even his friends had kept the secret from him. Not even Theo Blake had tried to rescue him from such a barbaric trap. Had it not been for Lady Inglewood, he might have married Georgina and then have been openly laughed at as the biggest cuckhold in England.

Suddenly a light went on in a second-floor window of the Fairfax house. Falkhurst stepped into view, pulling Georgina once again into an embrace. He freed his right arm and, after groping around, slowly closed the drapes until Sir William's view was blocked.

But he saw all too clearly now.

Early the following morning, Sir William appeared on the doorstep of Falkhurst's home: sleepless, disheveled, a sword clasped in his right hand while his left hand pounded upon the door. It was opened at last by a gaunt, aging butler whom Sir William roughly shoved aside as he stormed into the house, bellowing for Lord Falkhurst at the top of his lungs and slandering his lordship's name with every epithet he had thought of during the night.

Lord Falkhurst, clothed in a black silk dressing gown, appeared at the head of the staircase.

"What is the meaning of this intrusion, Atherton?" he calmly inquired as he slowly descended the stairs.

"I tried to keep him out, my lord," the old butler quavered from behind Sir William, "but he—"

"It's all right, Langton," Falkhurst said as he reached the bottom of the staircase and advanced toward the haggard Sir William, "I will handle this. You may return below stairs."

The old retainer gratefully tottered off.

"Well, Atherton," Falkhurst said, "what do you want?"

In response, Sir William struck him sharply across the face. His lordship was barely able to control his fury.

"You cannot be serious," he said with a good imitation of amused surprise.

"Deadly serious," Sir William replied.

"You are actually calling me out?"

"I am," Sir William replied through clenched teeth.

"But why?"

"You know why!" Sir William cried. "For debasing a good woman and openly humiliating me in the *ton*. Find yourself a sword, for I'll not kill an unarmed man."

"What? You would fight me without seconds?"

"I will kill you like the dog you are!"

"Very well," Falkhurst said with a sigh, "if you insist."

He led Sir William into his study, took down a sword from its mounting on a wall, removed his dressing gown, shoved some chairs aside, and then stood in the middle of the room.

"On guard," said his lordship.

They made the merest pretense of a salute, and their blades clashed together. Sir William lunged in quarte, Lord Falkhurst easily disengaged. Sir William lunged and thrust again and again, his lordship parried with bored dexterity.

"Damn you, Falkhurst! I'll kill you. I'll kill you!" Sir William shouted, leaping at his enemy.

Lord Falkhurst drove him easily to the ground.

"Not like that you won't," he said pleasantly. "Sir William, you are in no condition to fight me. You have played the fool in the past, I grant you. I beg you do not continue to play the fool now. I no more ruined Georgina Fairfax than I put the sun up in the sky. You cannot seriously believe that I am her *first* lover?"

Sir William, breathing heavily, stared up at him. "What are you saying?"

"Good God, man, Georgina began her illustrious career of bed hopping at the tender age of seventeen. Since then she has been mistress to an army colonel, a baron, two viscounts, and a duke that I know of. I no more ruined your precious Georgina than I did the Empress of France. Instead of wreaking your vengeance on me, you should turn your anger on the real instigator of your ... humiliation. Do you really think I could have seduced Georgina if she had not been willing? Do you really imagine I would have continued our affair after your engagement was announced if she had not insisted upon it? I told you once I was too weak to resist her lure. Georgina can be very persuasive when she wants something."

"And she wants you," Sir William said, struggling to his feet.

"Only for as long as I amuse her. I have no illusions. She will soon discard me as she has all the others."

"How could I have been so utterly deceived?" moaned Sir William as he slumped into a chair, his sword dangling from his hand.

"The only comfort I can offer you," Falkhurst said quietly, "is that you are not the first. You are fortunate that you discovered the truth in time."

"Why would no one tell me of her base behavior?" Sir William cried.

"Would you have believed it if someone had told you of it?"

"No," Sir William murmured through dry lips.

There was silence for several minutes. Lord Falkhurst, more than satisfied with his handiwork, was content to let Sir William lead them down the path his lordship had chosen.

"How does she dare hold her head up in society?" Sir William demanded at last.

"She's a clever girl, our Georgina. She has acquired many powerful friends in her career. When someone with the title of prince, shall we say, decrees that she is to move unmolested through society, Georgina freely makes her rounds of the *ton*. With such powerful conquests supporting her, no one dares to challenge her."

"I shall dare," Sir William declared, rising slowly, his eyes glinting with a fierce determination. "I will have my revenge. I shall bring her down, I swear it!"

＊

Chapter 16

GEORGINA FAIRFAX'S ENTRANCE at her betrothal ball created an immediate sensation. Never had she been in greater beauty; never had the women seen such a glorious gown. To her amusement, Miss Glyn found herself shunted to one side and ignored once again.

"I will undoubtedly be locked into a closet at the wedding!" she thought with a smile.

She had just advanced to greet Lord and Lady Egerton when she suddenly spied Lady Inglewood and Lord Falkhurst in conversation at the far end of the room.

"What are they doing here?" she demanded of Lord Egerton.

"Now, now, Katharine, we couldn't exclude such prominent members of the *haut ton*," Lord Egerton replied. "Besides, Sir William insisted and, since he is the bridegroom, Charlotte and I thought it best to heed his wishes, to maintain goodwill in the family and all that."

"I see," said Miss Glyn, and slowly moved away from her host. But she did not see. She did not see at all. How odd that Atherton . . . Miss Glyn experienced a sudden feeling of dread.

"Is something the matter?"

Miss Glyn looked up to see Lord Blake, his handsome face etched with concern, standing before her.

"Have Sir William and Lord Falkhurst become fast friends?" she asked without preamble.

Lord Blake stared at her.

"I see not," said Miss Glyn.

"Certainly not to my knowledge," Lord Blake said. "But then, I haven't seen Will in a few days."

"Then why should he insist upon inviting Falkhurst to tonight's ball?"

"Don't be absurd!"

"It is true. I had it from Lord Egerton himself, and I don't mind telling you it worries me. Falkhurst is poison, a leech that feeds on and infects others. If one remains in his company too long, one acquires his stench." Miss Glyn paused and then began to chuckle. "Would you listen to me?" she said. "I sound worse than the most melodramatic Cheltenham tragedy. Pay me no mind, Theo. I have let my imagination get the better of me for once."

"Yes, but—"

"Excuse me, my lord."

Lord Blake's valet, Maxwell, stood before them.

"Max, what on earth are you doing here?" Lord Blake exclaimed.

"Your pardon, my lord," Maxwell gravely replied, "but this letter arrived from Danforth with urgent exhortations from the carrier that you read it immediately."

Sir William, meanwhile, had joined Lady Inglewood and Lord Falkhurst in conversation.

"I have not yet been able to thank you, Lady Inglewood," he said, "for your kind services on my behalf. You have saved me from what would have been a most degrading marriage. I owe you a great deal."

"I was only too glad to help," Lady Inglewood replied.

"When do you strike?" Lord Falkhurst inquired.

"Tonight, as you suggested," Sir William said.

169

"You are determined on this course?" Falkhurst asked.

"My decision is irrevocable," Sir William grimly replied.

"Sir William!" Lady Egerton cried as she bustled to his side. "I have been looking all over for you. Lord Egerton is about to make his toast. Come along, you naughty boy. This is your ball, after all."

She caught hold of his arm and dragged him to the middle of the ballroom where Lord Egerton and Miss Fairfax stood waiting.

Lord Egerton raised his glass of champagne in the air and called for the attention of his three hundred guests. The ballroom was quickly hushed, all eyes turned to the center of the room.

"My friends," he said, "we are here tonight to celebrate the betrothal of my niece, Georgina Fairfax, to Sir William Atherton, a most fortunate young man I am sure you will all agree. Come, let us toast their health and future happiness."

Glasses were raised, all hearts swelled with joy for the young couple . . . and then Sir William Atherton dashed his glass to the floor.

"Stop!" he shouted with mounting fury. "Stop this obscene charade at once!"

The ballroom buzzed with shock.

"William, what on earth—" Lord Egerton began.

"This ball is a farce, a mockery," Sir William cried, "but I'll not play the fool any longer. The engagement, ladies and gentlemen, is off."

"William!" gasped Miss Fairfax with horror.

"I wouldn't marry this trollop," Sir William shouted as he pointed an accusing finger at his trembling fiancée, "this *whore*, for all the riches in the world."

"William, what are you saying?" cried Miss Fairfax.

"Do you not take my meaning, sweetheart?" sneered Sir William. "Well, if no one else has the courage to denounce your base actions, then I shall do it. Did you really think that your mask of innocence would blind me to the true blackness of your soul? Tell me, Georgina, after our wedding, did you plan to cuckold me with Falkhurst or did you intend to find a new stud horse for your bed?"

Lord Blake, who had advanced on the stunned group at the center of the ballroom, now took hold of Sir William's arm.

"Are you mad or just drunk?" he hissed. "Make your apologies while you have the chance and get out of here!"

"Apologize?" cried Sir William as he jerked his arm free. "To *her*? To someone fit only to grace a *dung heap*? Not I! Find someone else to make your pretty speeches, Theo. I say your precious Miss Fairfax is a damned harlot, and I'll have none of her!"

Sir William turned on his heel and stalked off, the ballroom erupting into pandemonium as Miss Fairfax slipped to the floor in a dead faint.

"Georgina!" Miss Glyn cried as she pushed her way through the crowd and fell to her knees beside her stricken friend.

Lord Blake, Maxwell at his side, quickly joined her.

"We should carry her into the study," he said.

"Yes, yes, anything," Miss Glyn said, numb with horror.

"Satisfied?" Lord Falkhurst inquired of Lady Inglewood.

"Completely," she said with a smile.

Lord Blake gently lifted Miss Fairfax into his arms and, with Maxwell and Miss Glyn on either side of him, strode quickly out of the ballroom and to the Egerton study.

Miss Glyn closed and locked the door behind her as Lord Blake set the still unconscious Miss Fairfax down on a settee. He stepped aside to grant Miss Glyn access to her friend, joining Maxwell for a hushed conversation. Miss Glyn knelt beside Miss Fairfax, feeling for her pulse, the palm of her right hand resting against Miss Fairfax's cold white forehead.

"Maxwell, if you please," said Miss Glyn without looking from Miss Fairfax, "I know there are smelling salts in the house. And then go to the kitchen and prepare a tonic that is at least half brandy. I daresay, you will know what other ingredients to supply."

Maxwell glanced at his master, who nodded slightly, and then quietly left the room.

Lord Blake joined Miss Glyn at the settee.

"How is she?"

"Her pulse is terribly weak."

"Max will return quickly."

There was a moment's silence.

"What in God's name can your sweet, kind, *gentle* William have been thinking of?" Miss Glyn suddenly cried out.

"I know not," Lord Blake replied grimly. "But I shall discover his purpose, I assure you. He cannot have gotten far."

He left the room, closing the door securely behind him.

Hearing loud voices raised in anger near a side entrance to the ballroom, Lord Blake quickly pushed his way through the hundred or so guests who still remained. Nearing his goal, he saw Jeremy Fairfax, Tommy Carrington, and Elizabeth Carrington surrounding Sir William, his back to the wall. Drawing nearer, Lord Blake was able to distinguish the invectives hurled at Sir William by Mr. Fairfax, the demands for satisfaction from Mr. Carrington, and the earnest pleas of Miss Carrington to her brother to come away and not risk his life on such vermin. Sir William was silent and pale with anger. The rest of the ballroom remained in bedlam.

Lord Blake placed a hand on Mr. Carrington's shoulder and pulled him from the pack, dragging Miss Carrington with him for she clung to her young brother's arm with fierce determination.

"What the devil do you think you're doing?" Mr. Carrington demanded as he struggled to free himself.

"Give it up, Carrington," Lord Blake advised. "Will won't meet you on the field of honor, and if he did you would only be arrested and tossed in jail."

"I'll not let that scoundrel live a minute longer on this earth!" cried Mr. Carrington.

Lord Blake blocked his access to Sir William. "Your life is worth much more than his. Do not, I pray you, throw it away on a hangman's noose. Justice will be served, I swear."

"But I can't just stand idly by and let that scoundrel slander the honor of the sweetest girl ever to grace London!"

"He will be brought to account, Carrington, I assure you. And I am a man of my word. Let it *be* for now. You can do no good."

"It's so damned unfair," moaned Mr. Carrington, "for Georgina, of all people, to suffer such a barbarous attack."

"I admire your loyalty, Carrington, but I implore you to leave. Take your sister home. Can you not see how pale she is? She can scarcely stand."

Miss Carrington wrinkled her nose at Lord Blake upon hearing this cue, but nonetheless adopted the mien of a wilting violet.

Mr. Carrington was instantly contrite. "Sorry, Beth. I wasn't thinking."

"You were upset, Tommy. We all were. I understand," Miss Carrington replied with a suitably wan smile. "But please, I *would* like to go home now."

"No sooner said than done," Mr. Carrington replied, gallantly offering his arm.

Miss Carrington took it gladly, flashed a grateful smile at Lord Blake, and then allowed her brother to escort her from the ballroom.

Lord Blake was left to contend with a murderous Jeremy Fairfax and, truth to tell, was more than halfway willing to let him have his head. He would have enjoyed planting a few facers to Sir William himself. But bloodshed, at least at present, must be avoided at all costs.

"Very well," he said harshly, coming up behind Mr. Fairfax, "that's enough. Back off, give him some air."

"I'll give him a taste of the horsewhip before I let him breathe in the stench he's created," Mr. Fairfax hissed, his hand catching hold of Sir William's neck cloth with a deadly, suffocating grip.

"I said," growled Lord Blake, ripping Mr. Fairfax's hand away, "that that is enough! If you've no consideration for your sister, at least think of your hosts and the scandal a fresh corpse would create."

"I'm damned if I'll stand idly by and allow my sister to be abused by this disgusting monster!"

"Did I ask you to?" Lord Blake demanded. "All I'm saying is that this is neither the time nor the place for revenge."

"What would you have me do?" Mr. Fairfax asked, beginning to think on Lord Blake's words.

"Go home. Get drunk. Leave William to me."

"I'm Georgina's brother, damn it!"

"Do you think she would appreciate bloodshed, perhaps of *your* blood?" Lord Blake demanded. "It seems to me that you are thinking more of yourself than of your sister. Let William go for now. I will

174

see to it he doesn't leave town. If you find that you still want to blow his head off tomorrow morning, I'll let you have him with my blessings."

Mr. Fairfax paused. "Very well," he said slowly. "I daresay, I *can* come up with a more fitting end for this swine if given some time. If he is not in town on the morrow, however, Blake, I shall hold you accountable."

Mr. Fairfax stormed off.

Sir William let out a sigh of relief. "I am indebted to you, Theo," he said. "I was beginning to fear for my life."

In response, Lord Blake placed his forearm against Sir William's jugular and thrust him back against the wall.

"Have you lost your mind?" he demanded. "Slandering that sweet girl with the most vile lies ever to blacken man's tongue?"

"Lies?" cried Sir William, unable to force Lord Blake's arm away. "I wish to God they were lies. But every word I said was true. True, do you hear me? I've been made to look like the greatest buffoon since Falstaff. I swallowed it whole, Theo: the innocence, the sweetness, the beauty, all of it." Sir William's voice broke on a sob, but with his next breath he had recovered. "Well, now I've got a little of my own back."

The marquess removed his arm from his friend's throat. "I know not how you came to believe these atrocious lies, William, but you are wrong. So very, very wrong."

"Am I, Theo? Falkhurst told me fascinating tales of Georgina's progress through the better bedrooms of the *ton*. He has even admitted his own sordid and continuing affair with Georgina."

"And you believed that blackguard?"

"Oh no," Sir William replied with a shaky laugh, "I believed my own eyes."

"What?"

"I saw them, Theo, three nights ago. The moon was high, the lamps were lit. I saw them together locked in the most passionate embrace man and woman can accomplish outside of bed. Georgina was wearing the very dress she wore tonight. There was no mistaking, it was she. She was very beautiful in the moonlight, Theo. I don't doubt that Falkhurst found it impossible to resist her allure."

"Will," said Lord Blake, "my God, don't—"

"Then they went upstairs. I saw them embracing in her bedroom. They were a little slow in drawing the drapes. Lies, Theo? Oh no. Not when I have seen and heard all that has gone on between them."

"Will," Lord Blake began, but Sir William pushed away his outstretched hand and ran from the room.

Stunned, the marquess walked slowly back to the Egerton study.

Chapter 17

LORD BLAKE REENTERED the Egerton study to find Miss Glyn seated on the settee, a weeping Miss Fairfax in her arms, as she rocked her and crooned to her in a soft, melodious voice while Maxwell stood impassively to one side. Apparently Miss Glyn had been applying these ministrations for some time, for even as Lord Blake watched, Miss Fairfax pulled herself more and more under control. Miss Glyn looked up, her eyes meeting those of Lord Blake. Neither looked away until the door was suddenly thrust open and Lady Egerton bustled into the room.

"My poor child," she cried as she swept Miss Fairfax up and into her arms. "What a nightmare this must be for you. I have had a room made up. Eugenia has lent you some nightclothes, and I have a nice cup of tea waiting for you upstairs. You come along with me, and I'll tuck you into bed. Tomorrow I am convinced that things will look brighter."

"Thank you, Aunt Charlotte," Miss Fairfax murmured.

Lady Egerton commanded Maxwell's support in helping Miss Fairfax upstairs, and the three slowly left the room.

Miss Glyn, meanwhile, had risen with a jerk from the settee and now stood facing the desk on the far side of the study, her back to the room, her hands clenched in fists beside her.

Silence reigned between Lord Blake and she for several minutes. It was an agony for him to see her hold herself so rigidly, with such pain. He longed to comfort her and knew he could not. He wished that he did not have to repeat what William had said. He had never thought he would be in a position to hurt Kate.

"Well?" she demanded, her voice hard and cold.

"I spoke with William," he said quietly. Miss Glyn did not move. "He is convinced of the truth of his accusations. I know not how or why, but he has been made to believe that Miss Fairfax is . . . not what she seems."

"If I were a man," Miss Glyn said, her back still to the room, "I would kill Atherton with my bare hands, and go gladly to the gallows knowing that I had rid the world of so vile a monster."

"You would have to stand in line for the pleasure."

Miss Glyn turned to face him. The arch mask had shattered. The unshed tears shining in her brown eyes shook Lord Blake far more than anything that had happened that night.

"This is a nightmare, it must be," she said, wrapping her arms tightly around herself. "How could I have been so careless as to have let this happen?"

"You?"

"My God, Theo, I promoted his suit! I gave him every opportunity to be alone with her. Don't you see that I am to blame for this horror? I should have protected Georgina and instead have led her into disaster. I have far more experience than she of the harsh realities of our world. I should have known that Sir William would . . . abuse her love."

"Kate, you could not, for the words he spoke tonight were not his own, I'm convinced of it. Someone has poisoned his mind. I think it must have been Falkhurst."

178

Miss Glyn started at this.

"But how or why," Lord Blake continued, "I cannot guess."

"Falkhurst?" Miss Glyn cried. "*Falkhurst?* Oh dear God, no!"

The tears began to slip unheeded down her stricken face.

"Kate, what is wrong?" Lord Blake said softly, drawing near her.

"It's the most awful thing, Theo," she whispered. "History has repeated itself, and I was not vigilant enough to stop it. I am the most wretched woman. To let Falkhurst dance attendance on her when I knew . . ." She took a breath, but it failed to steady her. "When I was a girl, the Glyn estate adjoined Monticle Park, the Falkhurst estate in Hampshire. It had been agreed between our families from my birth that it would be best if our lands were joined through marriage of me to Bertram. But it was also seen that I was of an independent nature and would not bow meekly to such a decree. Thus, I was kept from society and Falkhurst, who was six years my senior, set about wooing me while I was still in the schoolroom. I was fifteen, inexperienced, impressionable, flattered by the attention of an acknowledged Corinthian, and I fell in love.

"He played his part well, I had no reason to doubt him. But a week after my father's funeral, he came to me and told me what he thought of me. That I was an uncouth, ungraceful, ugly child that no man in his right mind would want for his bed, let alone for his wife. As I was not to inherit the estate, he would no more marry me than he would marry his cow."

Miss Glyn, lost in painful memory, did not see Lord Blake's hands tightening into fists at his sides.

"I remember standing in the drawing room long after he had left," she continued, "and feeling utterly . . . destroyed. I vowed then that no man would have the power to hurt me like that again. And yet, the same man has succeeded twice despite all my fine intentions, only now he has trampled the happiness of my dearest friend."

"And will you not seek the vengeance denied you then and due you now?" Lord Blake asked.

Miss Glyn stared up at him. "What do you mean?"

"You are older and wiser now, certainly stronger, with many powerful friends. If Falkhurst is indeed behind this, you have the opportunity to revenge yourself and Miss Fairfax."

Miss Glyn hastily wiped the tears from her face, accepted the handkerchief proffered her, blew her nose, and stared straight ahead of her.

"I never thought I could behave in so missish a fashion. You are right, Theo. Falkhurst may not have changed, but I have, and this time I shan't let him escape my wrath. But I don't know where to start. How am I to discover what has happened, and how am I to revenge Georgina?"

"*We* shall discover what has happened, and *we* shall revenge Miss Fairfax," Lord Blake corrected.

"But Theo, this is none of your affair."

"You will allow me to decide that for myself. As to how we shall accomplish all this, I have studied Will's every word, every action. His bearing was that of a righteous man terribly abused. He believed all that he said, Kate. He mentioned Falkhurst by name, and it is there that we must start. Is it possible that any part of William's story is true?"

Miss Glyn became rigid. "What do you mean?"

"Could Miss Fairfax in some way be tied to Lord Falkhurst or in some way have committed an indiscretion?"

Miss Glyn struck Lord Blake's face with all the

strength at her command and then turned to run from the room, but Lord Blake caught her arm and spun her around.

"Let me go!" she shouted.

"No," Lord Blake calmly retorted, holding her in place, "not until you've heard me out."

Miss Glyn aimed a brutal kick at his shin, which he only just sidestepped. Then he shook her, hard.

"Hell and damnation, Kate, listen to me! I meant no slander. I know Miss Fairfax is as chaste as you, but there is always a grain of truth in any rumor. That is what makes rumors so damaging. Now you will sit down, Kate. Sit!"

Miss Glyn sat down on the sofa behind her.

"You will listen to me without interruption," said the marquess grimly, "and you will believe me, and then we shall discuss the matter like rational adults."

His lordship repeated all that Sir William had told him in the Egerton ballroom.

Miss Glyn heard him in stunned silence. "I think I must be going mad," she said wonderingly. "To lash out at my friend when the real villain goes free? What is wrong with me?"

"You were right, Kate. This is a nightmare, and no one ever acts properly in a nightmare," Lord Blake rubbed his cheek. "Have you been training at Jackson's Saloon?"

Miss Glyn burst into startled laughter.

"There, that is much better," said his lordship with a smile.

"Oh, Theo, I am so sorry—"

"There is no need. I daresay, anyone would have taken my words in exactly the same manner. I'm surprised you did not shoot me where I stood."

"I would have," Miss Glyn said with a grin, "if I'd had a gun."

"Trust me, you are lethal enough without a

weapon. But come, what have you to say to William's tale? Is Falkhurst behind this horror?"

"Bertie and Georgina engaged in a long-standing affair? Embracing in the moonlight? Oh, the story has Falkhurst's mark on it, there's no doubt. But how did he bring it off? And why? Certainly he is capable of such maliciousness, but only when he feels himself provoked, and Georgina has done him no harm!"

"She refused his suit by becoming engaged to William."

Miss Glyn considered this and agreed to it as a possible motive.

"I think," said Lord Blake, "that we are getting ahead of ourselves. To unravel a knot of such size, we must start at the beginning and work forward slowly, carefully. We know the end, let us find the beginning of the rope on which William has hung himself. I daresay, we shall find Falkhurst holding it for him."

Miss Glyn considered his lordship for a long moment. "And so the mask falls at last," she said quietly.

"We were discussing a course of action, not my wardrobe."

"Very well," said Miss Glyn, taking a deep breath. "Sir William was convinced of the truth of Falkhurst's lies by seeing Falkhurst and Miss Fairfax together."

"Which begs the question: how did Falkhurst arrange such a melodrama?"

"Theo!" Miss Glyn gasped, her hand catching hold of his lordship's arm and pulling him down to sit beside her, "he had to have an accomplice! Falkhurst had to have a female accomplice to play Georgina!"

"An interesting point," said the marquess. "The plot grows more complex . . . of necessity. William would never have believed mere stories. Falkhurst had to show him Miss Fairfax committing the deed."

"Yes, of course!" said Miss Glyn with growing excitement, her tears forgotten. "When did Sir William supposedly see Falkhurst and Georgina together?"

"Three nights ago: Monday."

"The night of the Prince Regent's ball."

"Yes, you're right. Everyone was there—"

"Except Georgina."

Lord Blake stared at Miss Glyn. "Oh no."

"She was home ill. A sudden nausea came on her."

"And she is left without even the shred of a defense. Falkhurst could claim, and undoubtedly did, that she faked the illness to keep her rendezvous with him." Lord Blake glanced at Miss Glyn.

She smiled and shook her head. "No, Georgina was not faking, I assure you. But what troubles me is that the plot hinged on Georgina not being seen in public on that night. Her illness solved that problem, but how could Falkhurst be certain she would fall ill and remain behind in Russell Court? He is not that much of a gambler."

"There are ways of creating at least all the symptoms of illness."

"But he did not come near the house all day."

"Then he would have had to depend upon someone *inside* your house. Perhaps our mysterious accomplice."

"I . . . cannot believe that someone in our household could . . . deliberately harm Georgina in such a fashion," Miss Glyn said shakily.

"Perhaps she did not know Falkhurst's purpose," Lord Blake said soothingly, taking her hand in his. "We need more facts before we can go any further, that is clear enough. As soon as Miss Fairfax is

183

strong enough, I think you should question her. Find out all you can about her Monday illness. She may remember something that will lead us to our mysterious accomplice. Oh, and ask her about her dress."

"Her dress?"

"The one she wore tonight."

"Good God, why?"

"William says that on the night of her rendezvous with Falkhurst, the girl he believes to have been Miss Fairfax was wearing the very gown she wore tonight."

"Impossible."

"Prove it."

"Very well. And what will you be doing, oh seer of all things?"

Lord Blake rose and took a turn around the room. "I am going to grill William. I shall learn everything he knows or thinks he knows, and everything that Falkhurst has told him. Perhaps we will be able to hoist the Black Earl on his own petard."

"If we do, it will be in public," Miss Glyn replied grimly. "Quid pro quo. Falkhurst has publicly ruined Georgina; we can and must do the same by him."

Lord Blake stopped before her. "Agreed. We must also make William see how wrong he has been . . . God, how he will hate himself when he realizes that he has been used. I only hope we can reconcile Georgina and he."

"What?" Miss Glyn gasped. "You cannot be serious! Reconcile that leper to the very woman he has wronged? I'd sooner marry Falkhurst than see that happen."

"That is certainly one way of bringing Falkhurst to justice."

Miss Glyn was startled into a laugh. "Odious, odious man," she chastised Lord Blake.

His lordship bowed. "We are at least agreed," he said, "on revealing Falkhurst's treachery to the world, of locating his accomplice, and of showing William the error of his ways."

"A tall order, indeed," Miss Glyn observed.

"Don't tell me that the indomitable Hampshire Hoyden is balking at the first fence?" Lord Blake said, pulling Miss Glyn to her feet.

"I? Never!"

"Nor I," Lord Blake affirmed. "We are committed, then?"

"Yes," Miss Glyn said quietly. "We are."

Their eyes met and held for a long moment.

"You should go home," Lord Blake said gently. "You must be exhausted, Kate."

"Yes, I will. I . . . I want to thank you, Theo, for helping Georgina, and for pulling me back together, and for your support. To think that I should cuff you!" Her hand reached up and gently touched his cheek. "And such a handsome face, too. It wasn't at all handsome of *me*. I don't know why you should embroil yourself in this nightmare."

"I must act when someone I care for is in need of help," Lord Blake replied quietly.

"But you scarcely know Georgina."

"I was not referring to Miss Fairfax."

The color in Miss Glyn's cheeks turned to chalk. Lord Blake's index finger gently brushed her forehead.

"Go home, Kate," he said softly. "I will call on you tomorrow."

＊

Chapter 18

LORD BLAKE RETURNED home from the Egerton ball
in silence. He handed his many-caped greatcoat,
hat, and gloves to a footman and then, rather than
going upstairs to his bedroom, shut himself up in
his study for nearly two hours. His servants' rampant curiosity at this extraordinary behavior was
then satisfied. His lordship summoned his four footmen; his tiger, Scranton; and Maxwell to his study.

He sat at his desk, six sealed envelopes before
him. His cravat, to Maxwell's eyes, had been mas-
sacred; his coat was off, his waistcoat unbuttoned
as he leaned back in his chair.

"For the near future," he said without preamble,
"you are to undertake new duties. You will undoubtedly hear on the morrow what has occurred
at the Egerton ball tonight. To be brief, Sir William
Atherton has publicly renounced Miss Fairfax in a
brutal fashion. He was manipulated into doing so.
We are to discover how. You, Carroll, and you, Var-
ner, are to follow Sir William day and night. I need
not mention that you are to do so without being
observed. Sir William is not to be permitted to leave
town. I want to know of every call he makes, every
visitor he receives, and the contents of any correspondence entering or leaving his house. You will
find more explicit instructions here," he said, handing the footmen an envelope each.

"Dawson and Merriott," Lord Blake continued,

"you are to do the same, but on behalf of Lord Falk-hurst."

"Lord Falkhurst, sir?" gasped Dawson. "The earl?"

"The same."

"Is he the one that tricked Sir William?" Mer-riott asked.

"I believe so, yes."

"We'll stick to him like ticks to a dog, sir," Mer-riott stated.

"I knew I could trust in you," Lord Blake said with a smile, handing them their envelopes. "Scranton, I want you to frequent every posting house and pub in a twenty-mile circle around Lon-don. Talk to the postillions, the grooms, the serving wenches. Find out if Falkhurst has patronized the establishments, with whom, and when."

"It'll be a pleasure, sir," the grizzled Scranton replied. "I've heard tell some of the post-road tav-erns have a good home brew."

"Drink all you want," Lord Blake said, handing him his instructions, "as long as you keep your wits about you."

"And what would you have me do, my lord?" in-quired Maxwell.

"Sound out Falkhurst's servants," Lord Blake re-plied, "particularly his valet. I want to know of Falkhurst's activities for the last fortnight, down to the last minute."

Maxwell received his envelope without a blink.

Lord Blake leaned back in his chair. "I want a daily report from all of you, hourly if you find any-thing interesting. Any questions?"

His servants quietly regarded Lord Blake.

"Excellent," he said with a smile. "Then start at once."

Scranton and the footmen quickly filed out of the study.

Maxwell hung back, impassively observing his master as Lord Blake wrote down a few hurried notes.

"Yes, Max, did you want something?" his lordship asked without looking up.

"I only wished to say how gratified I am to see your lordship back in fighting form. It is good to see you use your prodigious skills to some good purpose, rather than squandering them over the length and breadth of this chilly island."

Lord Blake regarded his manservant a moment. "What, have you been worrying about me, too, Max?"

"Anyone who cares for you must have worried these last five years, sir. Is Miss Glyn . . . ahem . . . bearing up under the present difficulties?"

"She will fight to the last breath."

"She is a strong woman by all accounts, my lord. But in this circumstance, I think she is fortunate to have you as a friend."

"Thank you, Max. I only hope I may spare her some of the hell our investigations will entail. She will have her hands full with the Fairfaxes as it is . . . and the Carringtons, too, judging by tonight's events."

"Miss Fairfax has many who would wish to defend her."

"Yes," Lord Blake replied, staring into a candle. "It's a pity Kate did not have the same in her girlhood."

"But that has changed now, has it not, my lord?"

Lord Blake looked up and studied his servant a moment. "Yes, Max, it has. Before you go, I've one last favor to ask you. I need your help in maintaining my mask awhile longer. It won't do to make Lord Falkhurst suspicious of my thoughts or actions."

"I will be vigilant in my ministrations, my lord," Maxwell replied before withdrawing.

Lord Blake smiled a moment and then leaned back in his chair, propped his feet up on his desk, and considered the gleaming tips of his shoes for the next hour, his mind very far from his wardrobe.

Late the following afternoon, Wainwright opened the front door of the Fairfax residence to Lord Blake and led his lordship down a passageway to the library, before withdrawing. Quietly, Lord Blake stepped into the room, closing the door behind him.

Miss Glyn was alone and unaware of him. She was simply dressed, standing near the door to the back gardens. Her hair was pulled into a knot at the back of her head, leaving her face open to scrutiny. It was pale and drawn, her brown eyes darkened by the circles beneath them. She had clearly had a wretched night and an unpleasant day, but she was in firm control of both herself and the situation in which she was embroiled.

She turned suddenly, her eyes meeting his and warming instantly.

"Theo, how good of you to come," she said with a smile as she joined Lord Blake.

"I'm sorry I could not come earlier," replied his lordship, taking her hand in his. "How are things?"

"Jeremy stormed out of the house this morning and has not been heard from since, and with Jeremy it is best if one hears nothing at all. Georgina is sleeping in her room."

"She is here?" Lord Blake said in some surprise.

"She insisted on coming home early this morning."

Lord Blake recollected to release Miss Glyn's hand. "How is she?"

"Better than I had hoped. She had herself well in hand. She's got backbone, our Georgina. But it was clear that she had not slept last night, and so I insisted she retire to her bed. Then I placed a few drops of laudanum in her morning chocolate, and she has been sleeping ever since."

"You dosed her chocolate?" Lord Blake said, chuckling.

"What are friends for?"

"I shudder to think." There was a slight pause. "I have much to tell you, Kate."

"And I you. But let us go into the garden. This room seems to me suddenly dark and depressing. Let me give you a tour of our roses."

"I would enjoy touring the Egyptian sands if you were there, Miss Glyn."

Smiling at this memory of his first visit, Miss Glyn placed her hand on Lord Blake's proffered arm, and they stepped outside. The garden, streaked with shadows by the late afternoon sun, was enclosed by a semicircular brick wall. To the left sat a small greenhouse surrounded by fruit trees, which spread along the back of the garden as well. To the right lay flower and vegetable beds. In the center of the garden sat a small white pavilion that held a wooden bench.

"This is lovely," Lord Blake said.

"It is nice, isn't it?" Miss Glyn replied. "It has often served as a place of refuge."

They were silent again for some time as they strolled idly through the yard.

"For two such chatterers as we," Miss Glyn finally said, "this silence is farcical. Since I am playing hostess, I suppose it only right that I begin. Before Georgina began to feel the effects of the laudanum, I had a chance to speak with her, and I learned a great deal. You asked about the gown she wore last night, and thereby hangs an interesting tale." She related Mrs. Foote's sudden ability to design a gown for Miss Fairfax, and the receipt of that gown four days earlier.

"Monday, the day of the Prince Regent's ball," Lord Blake said.

"Precisely. I would swear to you, Theo, that that gown had not been worn prior to last night. If it had sustained those attentions of Falkhurst that Sir William observed Monday night, the dress would have been crumpled and in need of pressing. But such was not the case. No one save Georgina touched that gown from the moment it went into her closet Monday morning until she pulled it out last night. And it was the farthest thing from looking crumpled . . . nor has Georgina any knowledge of or skill with the iron.

"On Tuesday, of course, Georgina noticed that Sir William had altered radically in his behavior toward her. She went so far as to mention it to me, but I foolishly put it down to bridegroom nerves. You see what this means? Sir William did not believe the lies about Georgina until Monday."

"Which means that he was manipulated on a very hurried basis," said Lord Blake. "Falkhurst and his accomplice required a fortnight to have the gown made, but only two or three days to work on Will's mind. Falkhurst undoubtedly feared that if Will was given a chance to think the matter through, he might begin to question the entire fairy tale. That fits very well with what I learned from Will. But more of that anon. What of Miss Fairfax's illness on Monday?"

"Very real and very sudden," Miss Glyn replied. "It came on her just after our late afternoon tea."

"Apparently you are not the only one to dose Miss Fairfax's drinks."

"So I believe."

Lord Blake sighed. "And so Miss Fairfax is effectively removed."

"Worse still, her maid checked on Georgina several times that night, but by nine o'clock Georgina had fallen asleep and at ten o'clock her maid took herself off to bed. I have spoken with all of the servants, none of them looked in on Georgina that night."

"Damn," Lord Blake said softly. "Did Miss Fairfax speak of Falkhurst?"

"Oh yes, and was even so good as to inform me that Falkhurst was in the habit of sending her love letters! I bow to your prescience, my lord. She had not told me of them earlier because she was afraid that I would call him out for such effrontery, and so I should have."

"You would have bested him without the slightest difficulty," Lord Blake averred.

"That is what I think, but Georgina has no confidence in me. To think that Falkhurst would be so brazen in his pursuit ... and that she would not tell me of it!"

Lord Blake stared unhappily at the roses. "She discouraged him?"

"As much as her nature allowed, which is to say that she did not reply to the letters and treated him with some formality. But as for giving him a setdown, Georgina is too tenderhearted to be unkind to one who claims she holds possession of his heart."

"So Falkhurst could continue to think of her as he chose," Lord Blake said with a sigh. "What a wretched business this is."

Again silence moved between Lord Blake and Miss Glyn. Feeling his lordship's unease and suspecting that it came from not wanting to upset her, which was sweet of him, but hardly beneficial to the course they were pursuing, Miss Glyn turned upon Lord Blake with a bright smile.

"Well?" she said. "What had Sir William to say to you?"

"A good deal," Lord Blake replied, "and all of it uttered with unbecoming warmth. First there is the matter of the incriminating gown." Lord Blake went over the events of the preceding Saturday on which Sir William had received Miss Fairfax's note, only to appear at Mrs. Foote's establishment to find that Miss Fairfax had deserted him.

Miss Glyn pulled his lordship to a stop and stared up at him.

"Theo, last Saturday, Georgina, Jeremy, and I went on a picnic to Kensington. We left in the morning and did not return until late in the afternoon. Georgina could not have been in Mrs. Foote's shop on Saturday, and she could not have possibly written him to meet her there . . . unless . . ."

"Yes?"

Miss Glyn considered the matter a moment. "A little over a se'ennight ago, they rendezvoused at Mrs. Foote's prior to going to a rout. Being the romantic sort, Sir William would have been bound to save the letter. Perhaps it was stolen and reused for Falkhurst's purpose."

"But surely Will would have recognized the note."

"Not necessarily. Georgina was so madly in love that her correspondence was far from original. Besides, Sir William would have been happy to read any endearments, however similar."

"True."

"But why would Falkhurst want Sir William to go to Mrs. Foote's?"

"The dress," Lord Blake murmured with sudden illumination. He pulled Miss Glyn to a stop. "Kate, the dress! Mrs. Foote insisted on showing it to Will. Don't you see? He had to be familiar with the gown beforehand to help convince him that it was Miss Fairfax in Falkhurst's arms on Monday night. Will even said that he knew it was she that night because she wore the dress he had seen Saturday."

"Of course! Oh Theo, you've hit it! What else did you learn?"

"Well, after the dress shop incident, there followed a series of what I would term provocative conversations." Lord Blake related Sir William's conversation with Falkhurst on Saturday night at White's in which he admitted an affair with Miss Fairfax, and then Sir William's supposedly chance meeting of Falkhurst Monday afternoon followed by their aborted luncheon.

Miss Glyn groaned at the memory. "Georgina told me of it at the time. Priscilla Inglewood took her to lunch, and they were having a perfectly pleasant conversation when Georgina saw Sir William rush from the restaurant. It unsettled her terribly."

"I don't doubt it. William's story is a bit more lurid. He claims that he overheard Georgina praising Falkhurst to the skies and vowing her love for him. *Then* he rushed out."

"Georgina praise Falkhurst?" Miss Glyn said. "Don't be absurd."

"Will swears to it."

"Well, he did not hear Georgina mention Falkhurst by name, then, for Georgina and Lady Perfection were discussing *Jeremy*. That is why Sir William's actions confused Georgina so. She could not understand why a conversation about her brother would upset him. What other twaddle did your sweet Willie tell you?"

Lord Blake then related Sir William's encounter with "a lady of high repute" who had assured him of Miss Fairfax's adultery, then of the letter she had written luring him to Russell Court on Monday night. Miss Glyn said nothing as she stared straight before her.

"After a considerable amount of drinking," Lord Blake continued, "William came to this house and watched Falkhurst and a woman he believed to be Miss Fairfax embrace, go into the house, and then embrace in front of a window at the southwest corner of the second landing."

"Theo," Miss Glyn said quietly, "Georgina's room has two windows. They look out over the garden. You can see them from here."

Lord Blake gazed reflectively at the large, curtained windows.

"Ah."

"The only window that meets your description belongs to a large housekeeping closet.

"An odd place for a tryst," Lord Blake observed.

"Uncomfortable at best." There was a pause before Miss Glyn met Lord Blake's gaze. "Theo, who was the lady of high repute?"

Lord Blake considered her a moment. "Priscilla Inglewood."

The color drained from Miss Glyn's face. "Are you certain it was she?"

"Very."

Miss Glyn felt herself to be in very dangerous waters. She thought how appalled Lord Blake must be to learn that his fiancée, or the woman who would very soon be his fiancée, would commit such an act. He must feel as if he had been betrayed. Horror and fury mingled in her breast. She wanted to rant and rail against the lady, and knew she must not. It would only add to Theo's pain.

"I'm so sorry," she managed instead. "I know how close she is to . . . your family. This must be very hard for you."

"Hard to believe, certainly. I had not known Priscilla could be so cruel."

"You believe Lady Inglewood to be Lord Falkhurst's accomplice, don't you?"

"Yes."

"Oh, monstrous to betray you in such a manner!" Miss Glyn quickly stopped herself. "I beg your pardon, Theo. My nerves still are not quite settled. But why would Lady Inglewood involve herself in this? I know she is jealous of Georgina, but why attack her in this way? She has not harmed Priscilla."

"I have a few half-formed ideas on the subject," Lord Blake said cautiously. "But I would prefer working on them a bit longer before discussing them with you."

"Very well," Miss Glyn said readily. It was clear to her that Lady Inglewood's involvement in the affair had greatly upset Theo. "Where does all this information leave us? Which of the many paths before us shall we follow?"

"I have been cogitating on that very topic," Lord Blake said with a smile, "and believe that we should retain our sexual division of labors, but train our beady eyes on new targets: you must uncover how Priscilla acted Georgina's part that infamous Monday night."

"Yes, that should prove interesting, for the gown is the key . . ." Miss Glyn began to chuckle in a far from friendly manner. "She had a duplicate dress, I'll wager. She is Foote's patroness, it would be an easy thing to arrange."

"You have something there."

"And it occurs to me that Priscilla would have needed one other ally to pull the rendezvous off: a wig maker. Even if Sir William had been drunk as a wheelbarrow—and I gather that he was—he would have thought twice if he had seen his supposed fiancée tossing about golden curls."

"Impressive, most impressive," Lord Blake said admiringly. "Between finding the wig maker and a means of placing Priscilla in Russell Court on Monday night, you shall not be able to call your time your own." And for this Lord Blake was grateful. The busier she was, the less time Kate would have for painful reflections.

"And what will you be doing while I tramp London's golden streets?"

Lord Blake's smile was grim. "I intend to pull Falkhurst's story apart."

"Ah no! I pray you, Theo, let me uncover the evidence that will place Falkhurst's head on a platter."

Lord Blake's smile died. "He must have hurt you very much."

Miss Glyn was silent for a moment. "It was my own fault," she said at last. "I was made to fall in love with a handsome face and a good address, and my native intelligence refused to come to my rescue."

His lordship covered her hand with his. "Do not blame yourself for being manipulated in so abhorrent a manner. No girl of fifteen could have hoped to escape such a snare. Remember, the same blackguard has manipulated the mind and heart of a soldier, a gentleman, a man of the world. If William could not escape the net, how could you?"

Miss Glyn smiled. "In the intervening years, I have entertained the fantasy that I would have come to my senses in time and denied Falkhurst in church. What a wonderful scandal it would have caused!"

"You are incorrigible," Lord Blake said, chuckling.

"I am in earnest!"

"Yes, I know. You are marvelous. To think that you were shocking society for years, and I did not manage to meet you until seven weeks ago. I blame myself bitterly for the opportunities we have missed. Only think of the fun we might have had."

"The mind boggles," Miss Glyn said with a smile.

"But there is hope. We have our entire future before us, after all."

"Yes," replied Miss Glyn above the sudden pounding of her heart, "there is that. Well, our strategy is planned for the morrow; vengeance awaits us."

"And unfortunately, my doting parents await me now. I must go."

Stifling her disappointment, Miss Glyn led Lord Blake back through the house. Reaching the front door, they stopped and turned to face each other.

"I am very . . . grateful, Theo," Miss Glyn said quietly as she held out her hand. "This is one affair I could not have managed on my own, for all my recklessness. Thank you for all your help. You are a good friend to Sir William."

"You are my friend as well," Lord Blake replied as he took her hand. "And to be quite honest, I have scarcely thought of Will at all, or even Miss Fairfax."

Instead of clasping Miss Glyn's hand, as she expected, Lord Blake raised it slowly to his lips. Miss Glyn felt her face flooding with color, her heart thundering in her breast.

"Adieu, Katharine," Lord Blake said, never taking his eyes from hers.

Miss Glyn was incapable of a reply.

The marquess released her hand at last, turned, and walked out the door held open by a stunned Wainwright, who closed the door behind his lordship and then turned to stare at his mistress.

Miss Glyn, who had yet to get her emotions back firmly under control, glared at Wainwright. The butler quickly assumed his most impassive expression.

"Honestly," said Miss Glyn with an irritable sigh as she started up the stairs to her room, "you would think you had never before seen me say good-bye to anyone."

"No, miss," Wainwright murmured when Miss Glyn was safely out of hearing, "I never thought to witness such a sight in my lifetime."

✳

Chapter 19

LORD BLAKE ROSE early the next morning. He spent the first hours of the day at his desk in his study, smoking three slender cigars, and drinking two cups of tea as he studied the copious reports made by his servants. At last he summoned a footman and told him to send for Lord Braxton and Mr. Robbins, requesting their immediate attendance. Both gentlemen arrived at ten o'clock and were shown into the study.

"No race on earth can match the English for punctuality," said Lord Blake from behind his desk. "Sit down, my friends, sit down."

"Where," demanded Mr. Robbins as, arms akimbo, he studied his cousin's tightly fitted coat of blue serpentine, perfect pantaloons, and glimmering Hessians, "are your moroccan bed jacket, cigar, and Chinese teapot?"

"There is a time and place for decadence," Lord Blake replied. "This isn't it. I have summoned you both on a matter of the utmost urgency. I want you to go rumor gathering over the length and breadth of old London town on this fine April morn."

Lord Braxton and Mr. Robbins gaped at their host.

"I think," said Mr. Robbins, "you had better explain yourself . . . in a reasonable manner!"

Lord Blake spent the next half hour doing just that, recounting all that he and Miss Glyn had discovered and undertaken to accomplish. His repeated references to and praise of Miss Glyn did not go unnoticed. When he had concluded his tale, Lord Braxton and Mr. Robbins exchanged covert glances.

"Seems to me," Lord Braxton commented as he studied a ruby ring on his right hand, "that you are getting yourself into rather deep waters, old bean."

"The deepest," Lord Blake replied.

Lord Braxton and Mr. Robbins once again exchanged glances, which drew a smile from Lord Blake.

"Come now, enough of these significant looks," said he. "Cast your minds onto intrigue instead. William specifically named Falkhurst when castigating Miss Fairfax at the Egerton ball. Falkhurst, wanting to protect himself and seeking Miss Fairfax's ruin, would of necessity have had to hint at an affair with her to others in town. Any claim of his that we can disprove is another nail in his coffin. Therefore, let us divide up the city between us and go hunting rumors."

The three friends separated, agreeing to meet back at Lord Blake's home for a late lunch. Each reported astonishing success when they gathered together once again: Lord Falkhurst, it seemed, had been covering his tracks with a vengeance.

Their luncheon consumed, copious notes taken, Lord Falkhurst's schedule for the day confirmed, thanks to Maxwell, their forthcoming roles carefully plotted, the three friends separated once again, agreeing to rendezvous at White's in an hour. Lord Blake went to his room to change into more stylish garb, befitting the role he must play.

Entering White's, he greeted his many acquaintances, all the while covertly searching out Lord Falkhurst. Finally entering a reading salon, he spied the Black Earl in a leather wing chair near a far window, a glass of brandy on the table beside him and the London *Gazette* in his hands. Satisfaction swelled within Lord Blake. Fixing a brilliant smile upon his lips, he advanced upon his unsuspecting prey.

"Falkhurst, by all that's marvelous!" he exclaimed, much to that lord's surprise. "What luck finding you here. I know that you are a member, of course, but I haven't seen you about. A bit stodgy at times, I quite agree, but the place has its own charm, and it's frightfully good *ton*. What are you drinking? Brandy?" Lord Blake signaled a nearby waiter. "Another brandy for Lord Falkhurst, and claret for myself. Well, well, old fellow, how are you getting on?" Lord Blake inquired heartily as he plopped himself down in the chair beside Falkhurst. "Have you recovered from that intolerable dustup at the Egertons? Beastly affair, simply beastly. I think Atherton's quite mad, you know. Known him for years, of course, but I've had to cut the connection. His behavior has been intolerable. Terribly bad *ton*. Ah, thank you," he said as the waiter placed a glass of claret in his hand.

"Fortune smiles upon me," Lord Braxton declared as he strolled up to the two men. "Theo, be my guardian angel and partner me in a game of whist. Peter is mad to trounce me after I emptied his pockets last night."

"Nigel, I couldn't possibly," Lord Blake replied. "I have just found this extraordinarily comfortable chair, and Falkhurst and I were engaged on a cozy tête-à-tête."

"Well, bring him with you, then," Braxton said. "Peter must be partnered, and I've heard Falkhurst is devilish talented with a hand of cards."

"I have known some good luck," Falkhurst conceded, "but really, I cannot play. I had meant to—"

"But you must play!" Braxton cried. "You'll be doing me an enormous favor if you would, Falkhurst. Peter Robbins has been hounding me the whole of this day. The only way to fob him off is to play with the wretched fellow. And on my oath, he's a fine gamesman. The cards weren't running in his favor last night, that's all. It happens to everyone. Be a gentleman, I implore you, and join us at a table."

"Come along, Falkhurst," Lord Blake said, rising, "no one can say nay to Braxton when he's got that winning smile on his lips. Play a few hands with us, I'll supply the brandy, Braxton will supply the style, and Peter will supply the entertainment."

Lord Falkhurst was at last cajoled into playing cards. They found Mr. Robbins holding a table in a far corner of the card room, bottles of brandy, port, and claret awaiting them. The four men sat down, the stakes immediately agreed to, the first hand dealt.

"Falkhurst and I were discussing that dreadful to-do at the Egertons' the other night," Lord Blake said as he discarded. "Bit of a rum go for you, I expect, Falkhurst. Having all those slanderous lies about you tossed around in public like that. Shocking state of affairs, really. Damaging to one's character, I expect."

"Not at all," Lord Falkhurst replied smoothly, taking Lord Blake's discard. "It is rather flattering to be so intimately linked to one of the most desirable women in the *ton*."

"Now there's a knowing man," said Mr. Robbins, refilling Lord Falkhurst's glass. "That Fairfax wench is a marvelous looker, there's no doubt, and ripe for plucking."

"According to Sir William Atherton," said Falkhurst, "she has already been . . . plucked."

The gentlemen burst into ribald laughter.

Lord Falkhurst and Mr. Robbins won the hand, the cards were reshuffled, and dealt again.

"You've a wit, Falkhurst, there's no doubt," Lord Blake declared, and then took a badly needed swallow of claret. "Still," he said, leaning toward Lord Falkhurst, "man to man, just between us and all that, *was* there any truth to Atherton's accusations?"

"But do you not know?" said the Black Earl. "Don't you have Kate Glyn's ear?"

"Heaven protect me!" Lord Blake said with a shudder. "No, the hoyden has barred me from the door. She blames me for Atherton's bad manners. It's all been a blessing, really. The hoyden's conversation had become tedious. But what of Miss Fairfax? Was her conversation more . . . entertaining?"

"As it happens," Falkhurst drawled, a smile on his lips, "Sir William was not entirely wrong in what he said."

"No!" Lord Blake gasped. "You don't mean it! Georgina Fairfax? Why, she's the complete little actress, isn't she?"

"She is that," Falkhurst said after a swallow of brandy. Mr. Robbins again refilled his glass. "She fooled them all. She nearly fooled *me*. But I've a sixth sense about women. I knew she was not what she seemed." Lord Falkhurst's fingers began to stroke his brandy glass. "And she wasn't, gentlemen, I assure you. She was much, much more."

With both Mr. Robbins and Lord Braxton importuning him, with occasional encouragement from Lord Blake, Lord Falkhurst was led to detail in the next half hour several of his illicit rendezvous with Miss Fairfax, which he eagerly related, thanks to the brandy and the increasing size of his winnings.

"You've unplumbed depths, Falkhurst," Lord

Blake said, forcing a leer onto his lips. "If the good ladies of the *ton* only knew your true character, you would have every door closed in your face."

"On the contrary," Lord Falkhurst said with a smile as he took a swallow of brandy, "women find a rake irresistible. My invitations would multiply twofold if the truth ever came out."

"You know," said Lord Braxton, "it's a wonder to me that Miss Glyn never found you out. She seems a most determined watchdog."

"Oh, I daresay she knew the truth of the matter," Falkhurst said dismissingly, "but she's a loyal mongrel, I'll give her that, and wouldn't betray her treasured friend for the world, whatever the provocation. The Egertons charged her with maintaining Miss Fairfax's reputation, and that is what Kate Glyn did."

"She deserves a medal," Lord Blake averred.

"Certainly I've had occasion to be grateful to her . . . discretion," said Lord Falkhurst.

Lord Blake laughed. "Discretion is something I never thought Miss Glyn to be charged with. A regular little harridan with a tongue that could curdle milk."

Lord Falkhurst—well down the road to being happily foxed—roared with laughter at this assessment of Miss Glyn's attributes. "Sums her up beautifully," he declared. "I tell you, gentlemen, it's a lucky thing her father died when he did. I might have been tied to that baggage for life! Can you imagine being *married* to Katharine Glyn?"

"It does give one pause," Lord Blake replied, studying his cards.

"Why, the chit isn't even entertaining in bed."

Observing Lord Blake's clenched jaw and the murderous gleam in his gray eyes, Lord Braxton hurriedly interceded.

"Do you speak from experience?" he asked.

"Just between us," Falkhurst said, leaning forward, his breath reeking with brandy. "I confess to a roll or two in the hay in our youth. It was mediocre at best, but there was no other game to be had at the time."

Lord Blake swallowed the last half of his claret.

"I daresay, you can be forgiven even that transgression," Lord Braxton said with a forced smile. "That's quite an interesting pair, Miss Fairfax and Miss Glyn. How long can they maintain the charade, do you think?"

"Not long," Falkhurst said dismissingly. "After the stink Atherton raised, society will regard the both of them with more than a little suspicion."

"Serves them right," Mr. Robbins stoutly maintained.

"Yes," Lord Falkhurst drawled, "it's good to see Kate Glyn finally getting the set-down she so richly deserves."

"And Miss Fairfax?" Lord Braxton inquired.

"She was always too high in the instep, if you ask me. She's been shown her place in society, I think she'll keep to it."

"Thanks to William Atherton," Lord Blake murmured, his keen gray eyes on the Black Earl.

"Yes, he did a proper job of it," Falkhurst said, beginning to slur his words. "I couldn't have done it better m'self."

Chapter 20

LATE THE FOLLOWING afternoon—her brown hair pinned back and hidden under a green kerchief, her fashionable wardrobe replaced by a dress of rugged gray wool, scratchy black stockings on her legs—Katharine Glyn returned to Russell Court and knocked upon her front door. She was met by Wainwright, who fixed her with an icy gaze.

"The servants entrance is in the—" Then he observed a familiar, whimsical grin spreading across the mouth of this intruder. "Miss Glyn!" he gasped.

"In the flesh," Miss Glyn said jauntily as she stepped into the house. "The interminably itchy flesh. Anyone else about?"

"Lord Blake, miss," Wainwright replied, forcing himself to return to his usual reserve, "called on you not ten minutes ago and is waiting for you now in the front parlor."

"Marvelous. We'll have tea, Wainwright," Miss Glyn instructed as she set off, the butler staring after her.

Miss Glyn reached the parlor, threw open the door, and cried out in French: "That is the man, officer. Arrest him! He saved me from the guillotine only to sell me into a life of infamy! Oh, the shame! For the dear friend of my father to repay the many kindnesses showered upon him with such villainy!"

Lord Blake choked on the sip of Madeira he had just taken and spun around.

"Kate!" he gasped.

"Hello, Theo," Miss Glyn replied as she closed the door behind her, sauntered into the room, and removed the glass from his hand. "I've ordered tea."

Lord Blake roared with laughter. "A French émigré," he said with a hiccup. "What next?"

"Oh, that is nothing. In the last forty-eight hours I have been an Italian contessa and today an Irish laundress."

"Katharine, Katharine, Katharine," said Lord Blake as he leaned back in his chair and studied Miss Glyn with a lopsided grin, "you are, indeed, a wonder."

"Yes, I know. *I* have had a very successful two days. I trust that you can say the same?"

Lord Blake took the cup of tea that Miss Glyn handed him. "I believe that I can," he said. "But you first."

Miss Glyn took a sip of tea and proceeded to relate her adventures at the various London wig emporiums, concluding triumphantly with the information she had cajoled and flattered out of a French émigré—a Monsieur LeBeau—who had confessed to making a black wig for Lady Priscilla Inglewood. She then told Lord Blake all that she had learned from Harriet Pern, a recently hired under parlor maid who had been forced to contend with Lord Falkhurst's severe manipulations. In short, she had been cruelly blackmailed into doing his bidding: dosing Miss Fairfax's tea last Monday night, leaving the southwestern side entrance open for Falkhurst and Lady Inglewood, and telling them of the linen cupboard with the convenient window to suit their grim purpose.

"And whence comes the guise of the Irish laundress seated before me today?" Lord Blake inquired.

Miss Glyn then related all that she had discovered

as she had scrubbed the hours away in the Inglewood laundry room.

She had spent those hours assisted by Bonnie, a Yorkshire lass hired as a chambermaid only recently. Bonnie, who enjoyed a good gossip, had much to tell concerning Lady Inglewood on the night of the Prince Regent's ball for she had entered her ladyship's room before Lady Inglewood had donned her cloak for the evening. Not only was her mistress wearing a black wig, she was wearing a gown of silver with diamonds and pearls that Bonnie had not seen since. More importantly, Lady Inglewood had returned from the ball late that night in a pink empire gown and without the wig. Bonnie did not know what to make of this, but Lord Blake and Miss Glyn did.

"You are a wonder," Lord Blake declared.

"So you insist. I only hope we can convince the rest of the *ton* of it. Now be a good boy and tell me all about your adventures."

"Which do you want first: the part where Falkhurst's henchmen tried to push me off of Tower Bridge, or the part where I was trapped in a room filled with huge, poisonous snakes?" Lord Blake asked and received a grim glare in reply. "Or perhaps," he hastily added, "I could tell you about my conversation with Falkhurst."

"How tedious it must have been."

"It was rather," Lord Blake said with a grin. "He was amazingly indiscreet, for which we must thank White's excellent brandy and Braxton's and my ability to play a bad hand of cards when necessary. Falkhurst went so far as to name dates, times, and places of his supposed rendezvous with Miss Fairfax. He has, in fact, exhibited a remarkably loose tongue of late."

Lord Blake then drew out his notebook and handed it to Miss Glyn, who, after quickly scanning the notations, was able to assure his lordship that there would be little difficulty providing Miss Fairfax with alibis for the supposed appointments of illicit pleasure.

"I have done a bit of checking into Falkhurst's stories," Lord Blake continued, "and some of them contain a grain or two of truth. He has certainly enjoyed a variety of rendezvous at one or two inns on the road out of town, but the innkeepers are prepared to swear in court that none of Falkhurst's amours bear any similarity to Miss Fairfax. I was even able to track down one lovely damsel who, when presented with the certain downfall of her protector, was only too happy to provide whatever evidence we require."

"Why your efforts cast mine into the shade! We have him, Theo. I know it. I feel it!"

"I really think we will be able to pull this thing off. Falkhurst's ego, if nothing else, will be his undoing."

"Did he tell you anything else?"

"What? Falkhurst? He . . . no, nothing else."

"Come on now, be a big boy," Miss Glyn said with a grin, "and tell Aunt Kate all about it."

"I really don't think that—"

He met Miss Glyn's measuring gaze.

"Oh, very well," said Lord Blake with a sigh. "He made some lurid remark about you and he . . . That is to say . . . he claims to have dallied with you in your youth."

Miss Glyn stared at Lord Blake for a moment, and then gave vent to a shriek and fell back against her chair, howling with laughter.

Lord Blake stared at her with a bemused smile.

Miss Glyn kept trying to get herself in hand, but every time she saw Lord Blake's face, she was lost again. "Dallied!" she moaned. "Dallied!" and she was off again. Even the marquess began to chuckle.

When she had regained her composure, the two spent the next quarter hour comparing the schemes each had developed to repay Lord Falkhurst and Lady Inglewood for their villainy and found, somewhat to their surprise, that their minds had followed the same path. It took but a moment to refine the plot to their mutual satisfaction, and then Miss Glyn, fearful of Lord Blake dwelling too much on the fate of Lady Inglewood, tried to make some quip about great minds thinking alike, but Lord Blake would not laugh.

"We have the entire story now, Kate," he said, "and nearly all the evidence. The trap is set, we will act soon. It is time to lay the whole of the affair before Miss Fairfax."

"I know," Miss Glyn said with a sigh, "and I dread it. She will feel so abused, and sickened, and overwhelmed by the enormity of this maelstrom."

"But she has strength and you at her side to help her weather it through. Tell her, Katharine. Today."

"You are right, of course. I will." Miss Glyn paused. "This must be . . . hard for you."

Lord Blake cocked his head. "How so?"

"Learning such harsh things of Priscilla. No man likes to discover that his fiancée is not what she seems."

"Fiancée? What fiancée?"

There was a peculiar flutter in Miss Glyn's heart. "You have broken with her, then?"

"I was never tied to her. I am not now, nor have I ever been, nor will I ever *be* engaged to Priscilla Inglewood."

Miss Glyn's teacup rattled in her hand, and she hastily set it on the tea tray. "But Theo, the whole of London is out buying you wedding presents."

"Then the whole of London has as much wit as hair. I am amazed, Katharine, that you could be-

211

lieve such foolishness, particularly after the way Priscilla has betrayed you and Miss Fairfax."

"Yet you are bound to her by familial ties—"

"There is a great deal I must explain to you, though not all of it today," Lord Blake said, taking her hand and capturing her brown eyes with his gray gaze. "The losses you have suffered in your life will perhaps give you an understanding of what I endured when my brother died. I felt that I was to blame for something I truly could not have prevented, as you have felt toward Miss Fairfax. I castigated myself, punishing myself by withdrawing from association with those I cared for most. I convinced myself of a number of the most absurd lies ever to poison man's brain, chiefly that I no longer wanted love in my life. In a way, I owe Priscilla a debt of thanks, for in contemplating marriage to her, I realized how repugnant such a cold union was to me. Through her determination to become the next Duchess of Insley, whether I wished it or not, she taught me the foolhardiness of my sense of responsibility and obligation toward her. I owe her nothing now save vengeance on behalf of Miss Fairfax and yourself."

"Yes, she was careful to harm me, wasn't she?" said Miss Glyn in a soft voice. She seemed to withdraw without actually moving away.

"Kate," Lord Blake said, his hand clasping hers, "what is it? What is wrong?"

Miss Glyn took a shuddering breath. "It has occurred to me that the malignant actions of Falkhurst and Lady Priscilla are out of all proportion to the supposed provocation. Yes, Priscilla is jealous of Georgina, and Falkhurst of Sir William, and yes, Falkhurst believes himself abused and humiliated by Georgina. But there is some key element missing. A trigger, if you will. And I believe I have found it, Theo. It is me."

"Kate—"

"Do not try to dissuade me!" Miss Glyn cried. "I know the truth. Falkhurst and Priscilla and I have waged war for nearly ten years and . . . I went too far as usual. No one could tolerate the abuse I've meted out to the two of them. I have been going over and over it in my mind, and it is the only answer that satisfies. How best to attack me, how best to extract their pound of flesh, than by destroying Georgina? And how best to destroy Georgina than by turning the man she loved against her? Don't you see, Theo? It fits. The whole, wretched thing fits." Miss Glyn turned quickly away.

Lord Blake grasped her shoulders and turned her back to him, his hands remaining on her shoulders.

"Kate, that is enough. You cannot blame yourself for any of this, you have not the right. If Priscilla and Falkhurst had wanted to harm only you, they could have come up with a hundred different and simpler schemes. They did not. They attacked Miss Fairfax and William directly because they sought to harm *them*. Certainly you have been hurt as well and . . . and I cannot deny that I believe they intended it. But the chosen victims were our friends, the people that Priscilla and Falkhurst hate beyond reason. And you have hardly been destroyed by this, you know. You are a little battered and bruised, perhaps—"

"You are very convincing, Theo," Miss Glyn said with a wan smile as she pulled away. "Well, now you know the worst of me. I can be a great thimblecap at times."

"On no, never *that*!"

A watery chuckle escaped Miss Glyn. "Wretch!"

Lord Blake saw her smile waver and took both her hands in his.

"Kate, I know you are not wholly reassured, that you will never be so. There is some basis for your fears, but that is all. If truth were told, I have some responsibility in this, too, for I . . . said some things to Priscilla that she might have thought unforgivable. If she chose to lash out . . . well, she knew you for my friend. And in the end, what does it matter? There can be no justification for what she and Falkhurst have done. Their actions have harmed not only Miss Fairfax and William and you, they have harmed Jeremy Fairfax, the Egertons, your friends . . . the list is endless . . . and that shall be their downfall."

Wainwright knocked on the door and entered. "When shall I have dinner served, Miss Glyn?"

"Theo, will you stay?" Miss Glyn inquired.

"Thank you, no," said Lord Blake, rising. "I've other calls to make. Another time, perhaps."

"In an hour, then, Wainwright."

The butler withdrew.

"Well," Miss Glyn said, as she, too, stood, "it has been . . . an interesting visit." She held out her hand and had it firmly taken by Lord Blake. She squeezed his hand in turn. "Thank you, Theo," she said softly. "I am grateful for all that you have . . . said . . . and done."

"It has been, I assure you, my very great pleasure," Lord Blake replied as he raised her hand to his lips. "Good night, Katharine."

Miss Glyn watched Wainwright escort the marquess to the front door. Her thoughts and emotions tumbled over each other, like pebbles in the ocean's waves, and she longed for the solitude of her room to gather herself back together. But a grim task awaited her attention first. She walked into the front hall.

"Is Georgina in, Wainwright?" she asked of the butler.

"Yes, miss," Wainwright replied, his expression masked.

"Thank you."

Miss Glyn walked slowly up the stairs to her room, tossed aside her laundress costume, and replaced it with a dressing gown. Then, taking a deep breath and squaring her shoulders, she marched into Miss Fairfax's sitting room.

＊

Chapter 21

THURSDAY MORNING PRODUCED an overcast sky. The spring warmth of the last few weeks had suddenly changed to a grim chill. Colors were muted, people were less eager to stop on the streets to chat, fires were laid and kept burning all day. The Duke and Duchess of Insley and Katharine Glyn sat quietly in one of the Insley drawing rooms awaiting the arrival of Lord Blake and Sir William Atherton.

"I do wish the weather would not match our mood quite so well," Miss Glyn said with a sigh.

"It is rather dreary, isn't it?" the duchess said.

"You need not stay for this, you know," Miss Glyn said. "I daresay, Theo and I can handle Sir William."

"No, no, Miss Glyn, we will see this through," the duke replied. "From what Theo has said of William's current frame of mind, the poor boy might refuse to believe the truth, claiming that you are merely protecting Miss Fairfax. With us two backing your story, however, he will be forced to accept what you tell him."

Lord Blake, with William Atherton in tow, strode into the room in the next moment.

"Ah, you are all here," he said. "Marvelous! Will, you know my parents, of course, and I am certain you recollect Miss Glyn."

Startled, Sir William looked around the room. "What is all this?" he demanded.

"You are unfortunately about to find out. Have a seat, Will," Lord Blake said, indicating a chair opposite the duke and duchess. "I have a story to tell."

"If this is about Georgina—" Sir William began hotly.

"It is, in a roundabout fashion," Lord Blake replied. "But more importantly, it is about Priscilla Inglewood and Bertram Falkhurst. Sit down, Will," Lord Blake said again as he gave his friend a shove, which toppled him into the chair behind him.

"I never knew anyone so intent on having people sit," Miss Glyn commented.

Lord Blake grinned at her.

"Now then," he continued as he advanced to the fireplace and turned, leaning against the mantel, to gaze at his audience, "once upon a time there were a lord and a lady who were jealous of and hated a pair of lovers. Since the lord and lady were very selfish and cruel, they decided to collaborate on a plot to ruin the happiness of this loving pair."

"Look, Theo," Sir William said, "if you expect me to sit here quietly and listen to this tripe—"

"It is rude to interrupt someone in the middle of a story," the duchess remarked in a quelling voice.

Lord Blake continued his tale, with Miss Glyn supplying much of the more dramatic and colorful descriptions of how Sir William had been deceived.

"Do you take me for a gaby?" Sir William exploded at the end of the recitation. "Do you actually expect me to believe such a Banbury story? I know what I heard, I know what I saw! Do you think I can deny my own eyes and ears? Georgina and Falkhurst are lovers, no matter what her loyal friends may think!"

Miss Glyn said quietly: "We have a sworn statement from Mrs. Foote, a renowned modiste whom you have met on one notable occasion, that Lady Inglewood compelled her to make two gowns for your betrothal ball, identical gowns, one to be worn by Lady Inglewood the night of the Prince Regent's ball when she pretended to be Georgina."

"Very pretty," Sir William sneered. "How much did you pay Mrs. Foote for that affidavit, Theo?"

Lord Blake's eyes narrowed. "I am far more your friend, Will, than Georgina Fairfax's. I pray you do not accuse me of bribery and blackmail. I do not accuse you of stupidity."

"William," the duchess said with quiet authority, "I know that you need to deny all that you have heard this morning. To admit the truth would cut the ground right out from under you. But you must be strong for Miss Fairfax's sake and your own. Open your heart and your mind and believe all that you have been told here today for it is the truth."

"Theo has gathered sworn statements," the duke put in, "refuting all of Falkhurst's supposed rendezvous with Miss Fairfax. Where Falkhurst has named days and places, Theo has been able to prove that Miss Fairfax could not possibly have been with him."

"You have been used, Will," Lord Blake said quietly. "Horribly used. It is not an easy thing to accept, I know, but for your own peace of mind, you must believe all that we have told you. Which is worse: to believe in Miss Fairfax's innocence, or in the lies that have poisoned you?"

Sir William looked slowly from one face to another. His own face became ashen, his stomach began to heave. His gaze returned to Lord Blake and held there a long moment.

"Oh *God*," he groaned, and fled the room before his nausea overwhelmed him.

Lord Blake quickly followed.

"That poor boy," said the duchess.

"Falkhurst and Priscilla have much to answer for," the duke said.

"To think that I could know someone all of her life and understand her character so little," the duchess said.

Lord Blake returned a moment later.

"How is he?" the duchess inquired.

"I doubt if he will be able to keep anything on his stomach for the next fortnight," Lord Blake replied as he eased himself into a chair. "Lord, what a mess," he said with a sigh. "Was it this grim when you told Miss Fairfax?"

"Worse," Miss Glyn replied. "She has not left her room since Tuesday night. She refuses to eat and will talk to no one."

"I didn't know."

"I didn't tell you," Miss Glyn said with a shrug. "I'm not worried, really. She'll come around in the end. It is the getting there that is so difficult."

"This must be a very trying time for you, Miss Glyn," the duchess said.

"I've known worse," Miss Glyn said with another shrug.

Sir William Atherton, looking like little more than a ghost, reentered the room.

"I believe," he said weakly, "that I owe you all an apology. I have . . . used you quite badly when you were only trying to help me."

"There is no need, William," the duke replied. "Any young man in your position would have done the same."

"God, I wish I were dead!" Sir William groaned as he slumped into a chair and buried his head in his hands. "How could I have been so blind?"

"Falkhurst and Priscilla planned this very carefully," Lord Blake replied gently. "It was done quickly to catch you off guard and keep you off balance."

"But why?" Sir William cried as his head came up. "Why would they do this to me? To us?"

"Apparently, Lord Falkhurst believed that it was he Miss Fairfax favored," the duchess replied. "When your engagement was announced, his jealousy and rage became ungovernable. And it seems that Priscilla took this opportunity to harm her greatest rival. Jealousy, William, is a formidable foe."

"I must see her," Sir William said as he turned an imploring gaze upon Miss Glyn. "I must speak to Georgina."

"Not just yet," Miss Glyn said quietly. "She now knows all that you have just learned, and I think it has upset her far more than your accusations. She needs time to marshal her resources. I, or perhaps even she, will write you when she is able to speak to you."

"When . . . if ever," Sir William moaned, and buried his face in his hands once again.

Miss Glyn returned to Russell Court in a somber mood, walked up the stairs to the first landing in a desultory manner, and then stood staring at her friend's bedroom door. With a resolute breath, she rapped firmly upon the door.

"Yes?" replied a dull voice.

"It is Kate, Georgina. Let me in."

"I don't want to see anyone," Miss Fairfax replied.

"Nonsense," Miss Glyn replied as she opened the door and marched into the room, closing the door behind her.

Miss Fairfax, still clad in her peach dressing gown, her black hair lying in a tumble on her shoulders, was standing at a window, staring without seeing at the gray day outside.

"You're a pretty sight," Miss Glyn commented.

"Go away, Kate," Miss Fairfax said with a sigh. "I am not in the mood for company."

"Poor dear. You will just have to be strong, because company is what you have got."

"Honestly, Kate," Miss Fairfax said with another sigh as she shuffled to her bed, crawled onto it, and curled herself into a ball, "haven't you got any sense of privacy?"

"Not when I see you like this," Miss Glyn replied as she sat down beside her friend. "What I fail to understand is why you are not up and dressed for battle. This is not at all like you. Why are you not fighting back, Georgina?"

"What would you have me do?" Miss Fairfax demanded, snatching her hand from Miss Glyn's grasp. "Scratch Priscilla's eyes out? Slap Falkhurst's face? Take out an advertisement in the *Gazette*?"

"Any or all of them," Miss Glyn replied earnestly. "Only *do* something, Georgina."

"Why should I? What would I gain?" Miss Fairfax challenged. "Will it erase the hell I have known these last few days? Will it erase all those horrible things William said of me? Will it give me back the happiness I once had?"

"No, but it will make you feel better."

"*How?*"

"Georgina, you and Sir William have been manipulated from start to finish, there is no denying that. You undoubtedly feel powerless, helpless, something you have never experienced before and must certainly loathe. But if you do something about this whole terrible affair, you will feel more in control of your life again. And I think you will regard yourself with more kindness than you now display."

"What would it matter?" Miss Fairfax said bitterly. "I won't be married in June. I won't have William's friendship and love. I won't have William."

"Do you want him?" Miss Glyn asked in some surprise.

"I don't know!" Miss Fairfax shouted as she slammed a fist into the mattress. "It is ridiculous to love a man after all the things that William has said to me, done to me. And I *hate* him for being so manipulated, for hurting me, for not trusting me."

"The cards were stacked against him, Georgie."

"That shouldn't have mattered!"

"You are being irrational."

"I know! If he can act irrationally, why cannot I?" There was a long pause. "I am filled," Miss Fairfax said quietly, "with such rage, such pain, such terror, Kate, that I cannot bear it. I have never felt like this before. Oh Kate, I am so scared!" Miss Fairfax cried.

Miss Glyn quickly drew her into her arms, and began to gently rock her friend back and forth.

"If only I did not still care for him," Miss Fairfax sobbed. "I am so ashamed of myself."

"And why do you think Sir William has acted so brutally toward you?" Miss Glyn demanded. "Despite everything he was told and thought that he heard and witnessed, Sir William still loved you. He still loved the woman he believed had betrayed him, and he hated himself for it."

"Does he really still love me?" Miss Fairfax asked, pulling far enough away to study Miss Glyn's face. "In spite of all the things he thought of me?"

"I believe so, yes."

"How . . . strange."

"No more strange than you loving him in spite of everything."

"But that is different."

"How?"

"All right," Miss Fairfax said with some heat, "perhaps it is not different. But at least I did not

222

believe lies about *him*. Yet he believed every scathing accusation he hurled at me, Kate! How can I love him, how can I *forgive* him, knowing that?"

"Why do you feel you have to?" Miss Glyn inquired. "You have been wronged, Georgina. No one would blame you if you walked right up to Sir William and spit in his eye."

"Don't be absurd," Miss Fairfax said, chuckling in spite of herself.

"But Georgina, I do absurdity so well!"

"Goose," Miss Fairfax said with a fond smile. "You've not had much chance for absurdity of late, I think. They committed a crime against nature when Lord Falkhurst and Lady Inglewood replaced your wit with grim purpose. How go *your* plans for revenge?"

"The prince is planning a small ball to honor the new English ambassador to Spain. I have not yet heard of a date being set. The Duke and Duchess of Insley will ask His Highness if we can use that ball as the setting for our little melodrama. Nothing is certain as yet."

"You've written a part for me, I suppose?"

"My dear Georgina, you lead off the whole of the third act!"

Silence reigned.

"And will William . . . play a part?" Miss Fairfax asked at last.

"I don't know. I hope so. He is unable at this point to think of anything save the horror he has wrought. He does not believe that you will ever forgive him, you see. Facing all that he has done to you has . . . shattered him." Miss Glyn took a breath. "He wants to see you."

Miss Fairfax's pale face turned ashen. "Oh God, Kate, what am I to do?"

"I don't know, Georgie," Miss Glyn said softly. "I wish that I did. Theo, and I think even the duke and duchess, want to see you and Sir William reconciled, while Jeremy and Tommy Carrington want him tarred, feathered, and decapitated. Part of me wants to see Sir William hanging from the highest yardarm, and the other part . . . pities him. And Sir William himself lost all hope of any happiness on the night he saw Priscilla and Bertie play their scene. I would give anything to be able to advise you, Georgina, but I cannot. This is something you will have to work out for yourself."

The next morning, Miss Fairfax wandered into the breakfast room where Miss Glyn and Mr. Fairfax were just sitting down to their morning meal.

"Georgina!" gasped Miss Glyn.

"Morning all," Miss Fairfax replied as she poured herself some coffee at the sideboard, took a piece of toast, and joined them at the table. The circles under her eyes attested to a night without sleep.

"It's good to see you out and about," Mr. Fairfax said warmly. "We've missed you."

"I have written to William," Miss Fairfax announced. "I have asked him to call on me this afternoon."

"Good God, why?" said her brother in disgust.

"Because I have to talk to him," Miss Fairfax calmly replied.

"Salute!" Miss Glyn said from the other side of the table, and raised her teacup in toast. "Luck to you, Georgina."

That afternoon, as Miss Fairfax paced nervously back and forth across the day parlor floor, she felt that she needed all the luck she could get. Had she been utterly mad to write to William as she had done? Indecision and uncertainty seemed so much safer just at present.

There was a knock at the door, and Wainwright

showed her former fiancé into the room, then quietly backed out and closed the door behind him.

Miss Fairfax was left face-to-face with William Atherton, horrified by the transformation he had undergone. He was pale and haggard, and looked as if he had lost twenty pounds.

"Thank you for seeing me," he said into the stillness of the room.

"You do not look at all well," she replied softly.

"I've . . . had a rather difficult week."

"Please, sit down," Miss Fairfax said, indicating the chair opposite the settee where she now seated herself. Sir William did as he was bid. "Would you like tea?"

"No. Thank you, no."

An uncomfortable silence moved between them. Sir William's eyes never left her face while Miss Fairfax's gaze never left her lap.

"You wrote . . ." Sir William said at last. "Your letter said that you . . . wanted to talk to me."

"Yes."

Again there was silence.

"Look, if you'd rather not—" Sir William began.

"On no, I do," Miss Fairfax said hurriedly, looking up. "It is just rather difficult. I . . . know not where to begin or even what it is I want to say to you."

"I know what I wish I could say to you," Sir William said intently.

"Yes?"

Sir William jumped up and began to pace nervously on the carpet before Miss Fairfax.

"Look," he said at last as he came to a stop before her, "I know that I have killed any love or friendship you might once have felt for me. I have hurt you beyond bearing both by public accusation and by . . . betraying the love and trust you once had in me. I . . . I know that we can never return to the

225

way things were between us, but our love is a memory I shall cherish the rest of my life. I know that you can never forgive me for what I have done to you. But ... but Georgina, I do ask that you not hate me. You have every reason in the world to do so, I know. No one on earth has a better right to hate than you. It is just that ..." Sir William said as he raked a trembling hand through his already disheveled blond hair, "it is just that I couldn't bear it, Georgina. Please tell me that someday you will not hate me. Just *someday*, Georgina. I beg you, give me that one hope."

"William," Miss Fairfax said quietly, "you have caused me to feel such pain and such anger as I never thought humanly possible. I feel violated."

"Dear God, Georgina," Sir William cried as he fell to his knees before Miss Fairfax, "only say that someday you will not hate me, I beg you."

"Sweet William," Miss Fairfax said tenderly as her fingers slipped through his soft hair. She suddenly felt calm and peace settle within her. "I do not hate you. I love you. I have loved you from the moment we met, and I have not stopped loving you for even a second since that time."

Sir William gazed up into her face as if he were a man near death in a desert, suddenly coming upon an oasis.

"And because I love you," Miss Fairfax continued, "and because I know you too have been cruelly used, it is very easy for me to forgive you."

"Bless you, Georgina," Sir William said on a sob, tears sliding down his white face.

Miss Fairfax pulled his head to her breast and held him gently.

"Oh my love," she said, "we have been to hell, and it was far worse than either of us could imagine, for we were alone. If there be a next time, let us go together."

"Together?" gasped Sir William, looking up into Miss Fairfax's face.

"You did once ask me to marry you, did you not? I trust you are not planning to abandon me at the altar?"

"You . . . still want to marry me? After what I have done?"

"After what has been done *to us*," Miss Fairfax corrected, "and yes, I do."

Sir William stared at her as if he had gone mad, and then abruptly pulled her into his arms and a crushing embrace that she eagerly returned.

"Oh, that is much better," Miss Fairfax said with a happy sigh some time later. Sir William now sat on the settee with her. Her arms were twined around his neck, her cheek rested against his chest.

"I will make you happy, Georgina, I swear it!" Sir William fiercely declared. "I will make you forget that we ever lived through this horror."

"Oh no, Will, do not do that," Miss Fairfax said quietly. "I don't want to forget. I have seen your worst and best sides, and you have seen me when I am most vulnerable. We have both been changed by this, we cannot deny it. We are better for it, I think. Most couples do not know how they will react in a storm until well into their marriage. But we are lucky: we do know, and I do not think we have anything of which to be ashamed. We have loved each other when most others would have broken the bonds, and gladly. We were tried and not found wanting."

Chapter 22

"HAVE YOU ACTED in a play before?" Lord Blake inquired as he and Miss Glyn adjusted their costumes on the night of the Prince Regent's ball for the new ambassador to Spain.

"Once," Miss Glyn replied as she studied herself in a mirror, "in my girlhood."

"And did it have a torrid love scene?"

"I would hardly call it torrid," Miss Glyn replied, patting her wig. "I was ten and played Beatrice to the eleven-year-old son of the local vicar's Benedict. I was not, as I recall, terribly moved at the time."

"Insensible creature. I trust you will react differently tonight."

"I do not recall a torrid love scene being dropped into our script," Miss Glyn commented sternly.

"We may get as far in the plot as Falkhurst and Priscilla did on the fateful night . . . and the best actors always improvise."

"Not tonight, thank you. I do not want to be discomposed."

Lord Blake regarded Miss Glyn with a wholly disconcerting smile. "And would you be discomposed?"

"With all the *haut ton* as an audience? I should bloody well think so!"

"Very well," said Lord Blake with a sigh, "we shall leave the experiment to another day. But you

228

had best be on your guard, Kate. My curiosity requires satisfaction."

"Curiosity, as the saying goes, killed the cat."

"A little death is a more desirable end."

"Your love scene grows more complex by the minute."

"Improvisation, as I have said, is the key," Lord Blake murmured.

"Is that carved in stone?"

"Oh no, in a much more supple medium."

Refusing to allow Lord Blake to discompose her (despite the rising beat of her heart), Miss Glyn looked his lordship in the eye and retorted: "You have had ample opportunity to test the veracity of such a claim, I trust?"

"Not so often as some would have you think."

"Flummery! By all accounts you have out-paramoured the Turk."

"You have a wicked tongue, Miss Glyn."

"It is useful . . . in improvisational situations."

A delighted smile lit Lord Blake's face, but his reply was forestalled by a hurried knock upon the anteroom door.

Mr. Jeremy Fairfax stuck his head in the room and announced that his sister had just arrived in her betrothal gown, causing the expected sensation.

"Everyone is in place," he said. "It shouldn't be much longer now."

And he departed as quickly as he had come.

"I don't mind telling you," Miss Glyn remarked, "the sooner this is over, the happier I shall be. If only I did not have to wear this odious wig!"

"I do sympathize," Lord Blake replied as he moved before Miss Glyn. "I confess to greatly missing those brown locks of yours."

Lord Blake's right fingers brushed one of the blond ringlets of the detested wig, and then—by a

229

path of which Miss Glyn was burningly sensible—
they trailed caressingly across her bare shoulder,
eliciting a sudden tremor throughout her entire
body as she caught her breath. His lordship's fingers then moved to the back of her head while a
thumb moved under her chin, tilting her head up.

"Katharine, you have the power—" Lord Blake
began, but was interrupted by three abrupt raps
upon the door.

"The prince!" gasped Miss Glyn. "They are
ready."

Frustration glinted in Lord Blake's eyes as he
slowly released her and moved to the door.

Miss Glyn was exceedingly grateful for this brief
respite so that she might get her breath back, her
heart calmed, and her wits collected.

"Are you ready?" Lord Blake inquired.

Miss Glyn studied his lordship for a moment. "I
believe that I am," she murmured, and almost
jumped as his gray gaze turned to lightning and he
strode to her. For one wild moment, she thought he
was going to pull her into his arms. But he stopped
only a breath away and offered her his arm, which
she took, her heart pounding with something other
than stage fright. Without another word, they left
the anteroom.

With but a week's preparation, the Prince Regent's staff had created a sumptuous ball with
which to honor the newest English ambassador.
Only the *haut ton* had been invited to share in this
honor, favor going to the weightier titles, the pret-
tier women, the more entertaining of the young
men. By all rights, Sir William Atherton, the Fairfaxes, the Carringtons, and Peter Robbins should
not have been in attendance, but they had received
special dispensation from the prince. The Egertons,
Lord Braxton, and the Duke and Duchess of Insley
had been invited as a matter of course.

The Prince Regent's corpulent form moved slowly up the stairs that led to a small landing on the far side of the ballroom. There, as the last bell tolled midnight, he raised his arms for silence.

"My dear friends," said the prince, smiling genially upon one and all, "I have a rare treat for you tonight. A little divertissement, if you will. A tableau, a play, a mystery in which you are to guess the characters portrayed. I ask only that you remain silent until the actors have finished the particular scene chosen for you tonight. *Mesdames et Messieurs*, I present 'The Plot,' authors soon to be revealed."

There was a great round of applause as the prince bowed happily several times and then walked back down the stairs. All eyes returned to the landing as a door opened and an elegantly attired couple emerged.

"Is that not Priscilla Inglewood?" Lady Jersey whispered into Lady Montclair's ear.

"I believe so, but who is the man?"

"I cannot be sure, but it looks like Lord Falkhurst. Certainly I saw him come dressed in such a coat."

"Why are they playing at being actors?" Lady Montclair queried, but was roundly shushed by those around them and so received no reply.

The divertissement began.

"The gown is ready?" the actor demanded of his blond companion.

"Yes," the actress replied, "and the wig. What of that fool, Adonis?"

"My tales of adultery have worked him to a fever pitch. Your letter telling him of my supposed rendezvous with Glorianna will drive him over the edge. When you and I enact our scene tonight, we cannot fail to convince him that Glorianna and I are lovers, and that all of the *ton* is laughing at him because of it."

"The maid will dose Glorianna's tea and leave the side door unlocked?"

"I have brought sufficient weight to bear upon her, Lady Perfection. She will not fail us. Remember when you are playing at being Glorianna not to speak. Inflamed as Adonis is, he might question your north country accents."

"I am no fool, Lord Fiend. Just *you* be certain that we stand in the light so that he can see the dress. It and the wig will convince him that I am his precious fiancée. Play your part well, and we shall ruin your pretty rival."

"And yours as well. And no one will know that any mischief has been done."

"The perfect crime," said the actress, chuckling.

"And our reward shall be the look on Glorianna's face when Adonis accuses her of cuckolding him. Every injury I have suffered will be forgotten on that night."

"And the humiliation I have endured at that hussy's hands will be avenged."

"That is enough!" Lord Falkhurst shouted as he began to storm toward the landing on which this scene had been enacted. "I will not stand here and allow myself to be slandered by these frauds a moment longer! Let me pass, I say! I'll see you in jail. I'll see you both in jail!"

"I believe," the Prince Regent said as he stepped before the raging Lord Falkhurst, who had advanced to the middle of the room, "that it is you who will be in jail, my lord, not Miss Glyn and Lord Blake, if you continue in this manner."

A buzz filled the room as the mystified but wholly intrigued audience realized the identity of the two actors.

"Your Highness," Lady Inglewood cried as she

ran to the prince, "you cannot think these lies to be true?"

"But I do," the prince replied mildly.

The buzz grew in intensity.

"And how clever of you both to recognize yourselves in the play," the prince continued, "when you were not even named."

"It is a plot!" Lord Falkhurst bellowed. "A damned dirty plot to defame me." He continued raging at those nearby. They quickly withdrew before his onslaught. Even the prince stepped back.

"My lord," he called, and Falkhurst turned to glare at his future monarch, " 'methinks you doth protest too much.' "

The room erupted into sycophantic laughter.

Miss Fairfax then advanced defiantly upon the instigators of her downfall.

"I charge you both with base slander," she cried. "You have invaded my home, blackmailed my servants, poisoned me, and nearly destroyed a pure love. You have called me whore. I say you are no better than jackals attempting to feed yourselves on the carcass of my honor and happiness."

"I attest before God," Sir William Atherton shouted as he strode to Miss Fairfax's side, "that Lord Falkhurst and Lady Inglewood poisoned my mind with lies so vile it sickens me to think on them. They used me as a pawn in my own destruction and in the dishonoring of the woman I love. To look on you," said he to the shocked pair, "disgusts me."

He threw his champagne into Falkhurst's face, dropped his glass at his lordship's feet, and then pulled Miss Fairfax back to their places.

"My lords and ladies," Jeremy Fairfax shouted as he raised a glass of champagne into the air, "I wish to propose a toast to Lord Falkhurst and Lady Inglewood, who had nothing to work with but their own hatred and jealousy, yet nearly succeeded in ruining an innocent woman's reputation and destroying the good name of an old and honorable family."

He downed his champagne with a single swallow and then dashed the fragile goblet to the floor at Falkhurst's feet, a bit of improvisation that pleased him no end and won a shocked gasp from the assembled guests.

"To the pair who defiled my home with their treachery!" Lord Egerton said, and he threw his glass of champagne at Lady Inglewood's feet.

She cried out in terror.

"I'll not stand here and listen to this absurd melodrama a moment longer!" Lord Falkhurst exploded.

He went to push his way from the room, but suddenly found himself thrown back. He tried another direction, and then a third, but each time he was rudely thrust back. He and Lady Inglewood stood alone in a circle, a circle formed by Georgina Fairfax's allies. Panic began to steal through Lord Falkhurst's veins.

One by one, from Lord Braxton to Elizabeth Carrington, those who formed the circle called out their accusations and their reproofs to the lies that Lord Falkhurst and Lady Inglewood had spread in the preceding three weeks.

"This . . . this is an outrage!" Lady Inglewood sputtered, finding her voice at last. "How dare you . . . How dare any of you say such things of *me*?"

"How dared *you* pour such vile lies into Sir William's ear?" Miss Glyn countered from the landing.

"I am the daughter of an earl!" Lady Inglewood declared with mounting anger as she rounded upon Miss Glyn. "I will not stand here and be challenged by the common offspring of a drunkard!"

"What, running away, Priscilla?" Lord Blake inquired. "Do you fear a trial by a jury of your peers?"

"You see, you are quite found out," said the prince as he stepped into the center of the circle. "Denials and protestations of innocence will do you no good. I have here sworn statements by over twenty people of honor," he said, holding up a tied package of documents, "refuting every lie, every innuendo, that you two have spread in this matter, and I pronounce you both guilty of the most insidious plot I have ever been unfortunate enough to encounter. I assure you both that you are quite, quite ruined.

"Lady Inglewood, you shall be a pariah in your own class," said the prince. "All of society's doors shall be closed to you. I forbid any man of good family and character to marry you. And you, Lord Falkhurst, whose deeds in this affair are more heinous than those of Lady Inglewood, shall be stripped of your title and your estates. I plan to make your Hampshire estate my wedding gift to Sir William and Miss Fairfax."

Lady Inglewood slumped to the floor in a dead faint as the ballroom became bedlam.

"Happy?" Lord Blake inquired of Miss Glyn.

"No," she replied. "How could anyone be happy looking on such miserable creatures. But I am . . . grateful. Thank you, Theo."

*

Chapter 23

EIGHT DAYS AFTER the extraordinary events at the Prince Regent's ball, Wainwright stepped into the library to inquire if Miss Glyn wished to see the Duchess of Insley, who had called.

"Good God, Wainwright, are you mad to keep Her Grace cooling her heels in the hall? Show her in, man!" Miss Glyn cried, rising from her chair and hurriedly smoothing her gown.

"But Miss Glyn, you left express orders that you wished to see no one."

"Wainwright, don't go soft-brained on me now when I need you most. Show the duchess in!"

Wainwright showed the duchess in.

"I am so glad I found you at home," said the duchess with a smile as she took Miss Glyn's hand.

"Rather than raising scandal throughout the *haut ton*?" Miss Glyn archly inquired.

"If you had been, I would not be here now. I am looking for Theo."

Miss Glyn's heart stopped for a moment.. "Good God, ma'am, why are you looking for him here?"

"Because people have seen as little of you this last se'ennight as they have seen of him. The duke fears you two are plotting an overthrow of the *haut ton* so that Theo will not have to succeed to the dukedom."

Miss Glyn smiled. "Nothing so interesting. I have had my nose in a variety of books, and have seen

236

neither hide nor hair of your erstwhile son. I understand it is his habit to leave town without a word to anyone and disappear for months at a time. He has undoubtedly done so now, for what is there to hold him in London? Have you contacted any of his favorite correspondents? Perhaps he is dueling with Percy for the fair hand of Phoebe Lovejoy."

"I would much rather he fight for *your* hand, Miss Glyn."

"Me?" ejaculated Miss Glyn, thoroughly nonplussed. "Begging your pardon, Your Grace, but are you mad? I have neither looks, fortune, nor title to recommend me. Don't look to me for a daughter-in-law. The Insleys always marry well, everyone knows that."

"It is my opinion that I could ask for no better daughter-in-law than the Hampshire Hoyden."

Miss Glyn stared at the duchess. "Have you been nipping at the sherry of late?"

"I *have* missed your whimsy," the duchess said, chuckling. "How are you, Miss Glyn?"

"Very well, thank you, Duchess."

"Really? I should not have thought it. You are pale, and there are circles under your eyes."

"You could never be accused of flattery, Duchess," Miss Glyn said with a smile.

"I do not hold with insipid conversation and empty praise. Is something troubling you?"

"Me? Good heavens, no. Why should there be?"

"Perhaps because you have not seen Theodore in the last se'ennight."

The color drained from Miss Glyn's face. "What? That? Oh, I own to being a trifle miffed. After all that we shared together on behalf of Georgina and William to just suddenly disappear without so much as a word. . . ."

"It was most unfeeling of him."

"One might almost think he was avoiding me.

Certainly I wouldn't blame him if he were. I have this habit of doing the most bizarre things, as Georgina calls them, and—"

"Katharine, are you in love with my son?" the duchess asked quietly.

Miss Glyn was startled into a sob. She pressed her hand against her mouth to stifle the growing storm, but it was of little help. Tears streamed down her face.

"Now, now my dear," the duchess said, pulling her into her arms, "there is really no need."

"I am being very silly, I know," Miss Glyn said as she gulped for air, pulled herself free, and hastily wiped the tears from her cheeks. "Please forgive me. My nerves are a bit unsteady today."

"Don't be absurd," the duchess retorted, "there is nothing to forgive. And I am quite certain that Theo adores every bizarre thought or action you have undertaken. He is too direct to ever be misleading on matters of such importance."

"Be that as it may," Miss Glyn said as she drew in a deep breath and fixed a smile on her lips, "you may assure the duke that the *haut ton* is safe from overthrow. You have come looking for Lord Blake, and I think I am safe in saying this is the last place he will be found. So good of you to call," she said, taking the duchess by the arm and leading her from the room, "it's been a lovely tête-à-tête. We really must do this again sometime."

"Miss Glyn, are you throwing me out?"

"Oh dear, was I being obvious?"

The duchess studied Miss Glyn a moment, and then smiled and kissed her cheek.

"I think you're wrong, you know. I have a feeling this is exactly the place Theo will resurface when he deigns to remind us of his existence. Adieu, Katharine."

The Duchess of Insley sailed out the front door.

Wainwright, closing the door, could not recall ever seeing his young mistress so wan and spiritless. She merely nodded when he announced that the Fairfaxes and Sir William had gone to the Carringtons' rout and hoped to see her there, informed him that she was going to her room and did not want dinner, then slowly made her way up the stairs. Wainwright stared at her, and wondered if he should risk Miss Glyn's wrath by sending for Dr. Lindley.

A doctor, however, would have been of little use to Miss Glyn. Moving with leaden slowness, she removed her day gown, pulled on her nightdress, and then sat in her rocking chair feeling castaway, tiresome, and out of charity with herself. She had no one to blame but herself for this miserable state. It was she, after all, who had been so foolish as to fall in love with Theo Blake. His lordship could hardly be faulted for not returning the honor. Clearly his glib tongue and natural ability to attract any and all marriageable females had headed him down a path he had not meant to follow, and he had taken the first opportunity to distance himself from all future suppositions as to his intentions. After what he had suffered from Lady Inglewood's ambitions, Miss Glyn could not blame him in the least.

Eight days. She was pleased that she had survived them with such outward good form. This afternoon's missish performance before the duchess was an aberration that must not be repeated. To think that she could be so transparent! Miss Glyn spent several minutes taking herself most severely to task. She was the Hampshire Hoyden. She had an impressive reputation to uphold. Sobbing on a duchess's shoulder and wondering every waking minute of the day what Theo Blake was doing with himself were not conducive to maintaining her character in the *ton*.

Miss Glyn thereupon damned her hard-earned

reputation and the *haut ton* with every epithet she knew, and then wondered once again what the devil Lord Blake *had* been doing with himself these last eight days. She did not deign to notice the tears slipping down her cheeks.

On the eighth night after the Prince Regent's ball, Lord Blake drew his team of grays to a stop before his London home, wearily tossed the ribbons to his tiger, Scranton, and stepped down to the pavement, every bone aching from his journey. To travel nearly two hundred miles in one day, no matter how well sprung the phaeton, was a torture he thought must have been devised by the Spanish Inquisition.

He entered his house, allowed the footman to take in hand his coat, hat, and gloves, and then climbed slowly upstairs to his bedroom. Maxwell awaited him, forbearing to comment on the filthy clothes he helped his lordship to remove, saying only that a bath was being readied and dinner awaited him. Unhappily discovering that his clothes were not the only thing which stank, Lord Blake chose the bath first, relishing the hot water that scorched every inch of his skin and returned him to a semblance of human form.

He dined in his room, approved the purchases of furniture Maxwell had made at his request during his absence, and allowed that the improvements he had been supervising at Rosebriar this last se'en-night were well in hand. He then ordered his man-servant to his own dinner, refused to peruse the correspondence Maxwell offered him, agreed to a glass of brandy, and bid Maxwell good night.

Seated before the fire, the glass of brandy in one hand, a slim cigar in the other, Lord Blake allowed his exhaustion to consume him. Anyone seeing the pace he had set himself these last eight days could only have assumed that he was bent on suicide. Lord Blake laughed softly. Suicide had been the furthest thing from his thoughts, although a little death was a most desirable end.

He drained the glass of brandy, tossed the cigar into the fire, blew out the lamp, and gratefully sprawled onto his new bed. He had slept but little since the Prince Regent's ball, he had been too busy, and too lonely, to indulge in sleep for more than a few hours each night. His thoughts then, as now, were consumed with one image, one desire.

"All shall be realized on the morrow," he muttered, plumping his pillow, "if I can but sleep tonight."

This was unfortunately not to be. His lordship counted with the clock each hour that crept by. After what seemed an eternity of near manic tossing and turning, he was no closer to sleep than when he had climbed into bed. With a resigned sigh, he relit the lamp on his bedside table, propped himself up, and spent several minutes in this position, glowering at his feet. He had survived eight lonely days, surely he could survive one more night.

Lord Blake spent several more minutes fuming in bed before finally getting up in disgust and dragging on his dressing gown. He then began to pace the length of his bedroom, his mind working at a feverish pitch. It was madness to act now. All was arranged for the morrow.

As his clock chimed three o'clock, Lord Blake decided that anything after midnight *was* the morrow. He threw off his dressing gown; dragged on a pair of buckskins, his boots, and a white shirt; and ran a comb once through his hair. He then pulled open his door and marched from the room. A drowsy Maxwell, awakened by the at times violent pacing in his lordship's bedchamber, met him in the hall.

"Is there anything wrong, my lord?" he inquired

as he observed his employer draw on a cape over a costume that could only be considered horrific.

"I am going out, Max," Lord Blake announced as he pulled on his gloves.

"Might I be so bold as to point out the lateness of the hour, my lord?"

"Better late than never, Max. My wife and I should return by dawn. Have things in order, will you?" Lord Blake said before running down the stairs.

"Very good, sir . . . *Wife*, sir?"

A few minutes later, Miss Glyn's manservant was as near to a nervous spasm as was Maxwell.

"Miss Glyn, Miss Glyn!" Wainwright whispered despairingly as he agonized over whether or not to shake his mistress awake. "Please wake up, Miss Glyn, I implore you."

With a groan, Miss Glyn rolled over in bed and managed to prop one bleary eyelid open.

"What is it, Wainwright?" she mumbled.

"It is Lord Blake, miss. He is downstairs and demands to see you. He *refuses* to leave, Miss Glyn."

"Theo?" Miss Glyn cried, sitting bolt upright. "Here? *Now?*"

"Yes, miss. Shall I summon Ross to throw him out?"

"Don't you dare!" Miss Glyn said furiously as she jumped from her bed.

She dragged her dressing gown on and, mindless of her tousled hair or her bare feet, ran from the room and flew down the stairs, her heart pounding as she came to a breathless stop before Lord Blake. He stood in the light of a single lamp and was dressed almost as casually as she.

"Hello, stranger," she said, attempting without success to quell the hammering of her heart.

"It has not been *that* long," Lord Blake replied with a smile. "It is good to see you, Kate."

"I fail to understand how the pleasure could have been any less at any other time in the last eight days," Miss Glyn remarked, forcing herself to appear calm in the face of Lord Blake's devastating smile.

"You are peeved."

"I am not peeved. No woman of good breeding is ever peeved. I am merely put out."

"Oh, how I have missed you," Lord Blake said in an odd voice that sent tremors through Miss Glyn's body. "I must speak to you. Alone."

Her gaze caught by the intensity of Lord Blake's gray eyes, her skin blazing with warmth, Miss Glyn ordered Wainwright back to bed.

"But Miss Glyn!" the butler protested from behind her. "This is most unseemly."

Miss Glyn's gaze never wavered from Lord Blake's face. "Go to bed, Wainwright. I shall attend to his lordship."

"But—"

"Wainwright."

"Mr. Fairfax would not approve," the butler sniffed.

"Go!" Miss Glyn and Lord Blake said as one.

With a heavy sigh and several backward glances, Wainwright reluctantly left the hall.

It was several moments before Miss Glyn realized that she was still gazing raptly at Lord Blake. A blush flooded her cheeks, which brought her to seek rescue in speech.

"Has something happened, Theo? Is there anything wrong?"

"Yes," Lord Blake replied, "as a matter of fact, there *is* something wrong. I am tired of the loneliness of my life. I am tired of being alone in my home, and I am tired of being alone in my bed. I should think you have the same problem as well, and so I have decided that we should be married."

Miss Glyn blinked and considered this statement for a moment.

"To whom?" she retorted.

Lord Blake's lips twitched. "To each other, you odious woman. Tonight, in fact. Now."

"In my nightshift?" Miss Glyn queried.

"It will save time later," Lord Blake replied with a smile.

"Are you foxed?"

"Oh no," Lord Blake replied as his fingers moved through the thick brown locks that rested on Miss Glyn's shoulder. "I wanted every sense to be clear and alive." He drew closer to Miss Glyn.

"You . . . you have not done one thing to show me you love me," Miss Glyn protested, albeit weakly. "You have not spoken one word of love."

"Every word, every act, has been from love for you," Lord Blake murmured as he pulled Miss Glyn into his arms, "and you know it."

"You take a lot for granted," Miss Glyn stammered, mesmerized by the sensual shape of Lord Blake's mouth. "You have not asked me of my feelings for you."

"There is no need. You love me. Don't you?"

"Yes, of course I do," Miss Glyn replied reasonably. "But I would rather I told you of it than you tell me."

"Well?" said Lord Blake, his mouth a scant inch from her own.

"I love you, Theo," Miss Glyn murmured an instant before his lordship abandoned the last bastions of self-control and kissed her with all the fierceness that the strength of his regard required. Miss Glyn, in turn, wrapped her arms around Lord Blake and returned his embrace with all the passion in her soul.

"Oh God, Kate," Lord Blake said as he pressed kisses to his beloved's brow, ear, cheek, "I had meant to come to you in the morning, marry you at noon, and carry you immediately off to Rosebriar where we could celebrate our marriage in complete privacy. But I couldn't wait."

"I'm so glad," Miss Glyn gasped, breathless and shaken as she returned his caresses. "Who is Rosebriar?"

Lord Blake chuckled. "*It* is a charming country estate that is even now being rendered fit for a honeymooning couple. I have seen to it personally."

"Is that where you were?"

"Yow!" exclaimed Lord Blake. Miss Glyn had brought her heel down upon his foot.

"What the devil do you mean by riding off without a word, staying away from me for over a se'ennight, and making me miserable?" she demanded.

Lord Blake was torn between laughter and wanting to crush Miss Glyn in his arms. "It's a little difficult to explain," he said instead. "I don't fully understand it myself. I only knew that I needed you so much that if I saw you, spoke to you, I would have carried you off without benefit of clergy, and I couldn't do that."

"Why ever not?"

Lord Blake stared at Miss Glyn. "To quote your trusty Wainwright, it would have been unseemly."

"As if I should care for that!"

"Kate—"

"Theo, did you hear me? I have been miserable! If you had come to me and offered carte blanche until the wedding could be properly arranged, I would have accepted gladly. Anything would have been preferable to this last se'ennight. Besides, living with you in sin would not have been a hardship."

Lord Blake gave way to his laughter. "No, no, it would not do, you must see that," he said chuckling. "I will not mind idiotic gossip swirling around your head when we are married, but malicious gossip I could not tolerate. No, it's best we follow social decorum . . . at least a little."

Miss Glyn sighed heavily. "He offers carte blanche to half the cyprians in England, and with me he must needs be noble."

"I'm sorry, my love," Lord Blake replied before capturing his beloved's lips with his own. "It's been misery with me as well. I tried distraction, it didn't work. But still, the work at Rosebriar is out of the way, and your wedding present secured. We should be able to move into Tryon Hall next month. You will like living next door to the Athertons, won't you?"

The color drained from Miss Glyn's face. "What?" she whispered.

"It took several days of hard bargaining, your cousin is a parsimonious wretch, but Tryon Hall is yours once again."

Lord Blake got no further, for Miss Glyn was covering him with kisses and apologizing for every churlish thought she had ever harbored against him.

With a smile, the marquess tilted up her head. "My toes and I forgive you."

Miss Glyn nestled against his shoulder. "You are a dear, sweet, wonderful man, and I adore you."

"You'll marry me then?"

Miss Glyn kissed him. "Yes, for I shall be miserable if I don't, Tryon Hall or no. But 'tis madness, Theo. I'll make a wretched duchess, you know I will. And the Insleys always marry well."

"You will make a superb duchess, and I could not marry any better than you, my darling Kate."

Miss Glyn smiled up at her beloved. "You always say the nicest things."

"I . . . have a special license in my pocket," Lord Blake murmured, trembling as Miss Glyn's fingers caressed his cheek and the nape of his neck, "and the bishop of London lives only two blocks away."

"Clever, clever Theo. You have thought of everything."

"Not entirely everything," Miss Fairfax called to the pair as she leaned over the first landing railing. "You will need a maid of honor, you know."

"And a best man," Mr. Fairfax added at his sister's side.

"We have had an audience," said Miss Glyn to Lord Blake.

"So it would seem," he replied.

Miss Glyn's lips gently caressed his lordship's mouth. "We will deal with them later."

"An excellent plan."

"When do we fetch the bishop?" Mr. Fairfax called down.

With a sigh, Lord Blake pulled slightly away from his fiancée. "We will have to take them with us, I suppose."

"Very well," Miss Glyn replied, "but if they come, I insist that your parents attend us as well."

"Oh come now, Kate, be reasonable."

"I am always reasonable," Miss Glyn retorted. "If I am going to become a member of your family, I want the full approbation of the duke and duchess. There will be no nasty little surprises for them like an unexpected and unwanted half-mad daughter-in-law greeting them on the morrow. They must understand what we are getting them into."

"Oh, very well," said his lordship with a resigned sigh. "This will, however, necessitate a slight change in the wedding arrangements. Katharine and I," Lord Blake called up to their highly entertained audience of two, "will go roust out the bishop while you get yourselves ready. We will rendezvous at my parents' house in Grosvenor Square. And be sure to bring some slippers for my blushing bride-to-be," he said, swinging Miss Glyn up into his arms. "I'll not have her catching her death of cold on her wedding night."

Thirty minutes later—as a sleepy (and rather confused) bishop of London, Miss Glyn, and Mr. and Miss Fairfax waited in the Insley drawing room— Lord Blake ran upstairs to fetch his loving parents. Merrily whistling a rather ribald tune, his lordship walked into their bedchamber without even the courtesy of knocking and began to shake the duke awake.

"I say, *Pater*, it is time to arise," his lordship cheerfully proclaimed. "Come along, *Maman*, you too."

Lord Blake sat himself atop the footboard on his parents' bed, his booted feet resting upon their bedclothes, as the duke and duchess sleepily pulled themselves into sitting positions.

"Theo, what on earth is going on?" the duchess demanded with discernible ill-humor.

"Do you know what time it is?" the duke sputtered. "How could even you be so inconsiderate?"

"*Mon cher Papa*, I am the very soul of consideration," Lord Blake replied. "I knew without a doubt that you would wish to attend your son and heir's wedding, so I have come to fetch you down."

"*Wedding?*" the duke and duchess gasped as one.

"The Hampshire Hoyden and I," Lord Blake said with a grin as he slid off the footboard and began to shamble toward the door. "She thought you would like to know beforehand. Damned decent of her, don't you think? Don't dawdle now. It would be most uncivil to keep the bishop waiting."

Just before four o'clock on a May morning, the bishop of London authorized the placement of Lord Blake's ring upon Miss Glyn's fourth finger and pronounced the pair husband and wife. Lord Blake took this opportunity to pull his bride into his arms.

"Come on and kiss me, Kate!"

"Oh honestly, Theo," Lady Blake said with a sigh denoting great weariness, "could you not have thought of something a trifle more original?"

Titters were heard from the wedding attendants.

"Sweet Kate," Lord Blake replied, his voice trembling, "make me immortal with a kiss."

"That will have to do, I suppose," said his lady, and then threw her arms around her husband and kissed him until both were insensible.

This shocking behavior elicited a round of raucous cheers and applause from their wedding party.

"You know," murmured Lady Blake into her husband's ear, "I think I'm going to like married life after all."

"I shall see to it personally," he replied.